SON

By LOIS LOWRY

HOUGHTON MIFFLIN HARCOURT

Boston | New York

Other novels in the Giver Quartet

The Giver

Gathering Blue

Messenger

www.hmhco.com

The text of this book is set in Centaur.

The Library of Congress has cataloged the hardcover edition as follows:
Lowry, Lois.
Son / by Lois Lowry.
p. cm.
Companion book to: *The Giver, Gathering Blue,* and *Messenger.*
Summary: Unlike the other Birthmothers in her utopian community, teenaged Claire forms
an attachment to her baby, feeling a great loss when he is taken from their community.
[1. Science fiction. 2. Mother and child—Fiction. 3. Separation (Psychology)—Fiction.]
I. Title.
PZ7.L9673So 2012
[Fic]—dc23
2012014034

ISBN: 978-0-547-88720-3 hardcover
ISBN: 978-0-544-33625-4 paperback

Manufactured in the United States of America
DOC 10 9 8 7 6 5 4 3 2 1
4500465311

In memory of Martin

BOOK I

BEFORE

ONE

T HE YOUNG GIRL cringed when they buckled the eyeless leather mask around the upper half of her face and blinded her. It felt grotesque and unnecessary, but she didn't object. It was the procedure. She knew that. One of the other Vessels had described it to her at lunch a month before.

"Mask?" she had asked in surprise, almost chuckling at the strange image. "What's the mask for?"

"Well, it's not really a mask," the young woman seated on her left corrected herself, and took another bite of the crisp salad. "It's a blindfold, actually." She was whispering. They were not supposed to discuss this among themselves.

"Blindfold?" she had asked in astonishment, then laughed apologetically. "I don't seem to be able to converse, do I? I keep repeating what you say. But: blindfold? Why?"

"They don't want you to see the Product when it comes out of you. When you birth it." The girl pointed to her bulging belly.

"You've produced already, right?" she asked her.

The girl nodded. "Twice."

"What's it like?" Even asking it, she knew it was a somewhat foolish question. They had had classes, seen diagrams, been given instructions. Still, none of that was the same as hearing it from someone who had already gone through the process. And now that they were already disobeying the restriction about discussing it — well, why not ask?

"Easier the second time. Didn't hurt as much."

When she didn't respond, the girl looked at her quizzically. "Hasn't anyone told you it hurts?"

"They said 'discomfort.'"

The other girl gave a sarcastic snort. "Discomfort, then. If that's what they want to call it. Not as much discomfort the second time. And it doesn't take as long."

"Vessels? VESSELS!" The voice of the matron, through the speaker, was stern. "Monitor your conversations, please! You know the rules!"

The girl and her companion obediently fell silent then, realizing they had been heard through the microphones embedded in the walls of the dining room. Some of the other girls giggled. They were probably also guilty. There was so little else to talk about. The process—their job, their mission—was the thing they had in common. But the conversation shifted after the stern warning.

She had taken another spoonful of soup. Food in the Birthmothers' Dormitory was always plentiful and delicious. The Vessels were all being meticulously nourished. Of course, growing up in the community, she had always been adequately fed. Food had been delivered to her family's dwelling each day.

But when she had been selected Birthmother at twelve, the course of her life had changed. It had been gradual. The academic courses—math, science, law—at school became less demanding for her group. Fewer tests, less reading required. The teachers paid little attention to her.

Courses in nutrition and health had been added to her curriculum, and more time was spent on exercise in the outdoor air. Special vitamins had been added to her diet. Her body had been examined, tested, and prepared for her time here. After that year had passed, and part of another, she was deemed ready. She was instructed to leave her family dwelling and move to the Birthmothers' Dormitory.

Relocating from one place to another within the community was not difficult. She owned nothing. Her clothing was distributed and laundered by the central clothing supply. Her schoolbooks were requisitioned by the school and would be used for another student the following year. The bicycle she had ridden to school throughout her earlier years was taken to be refurbished and given to a different, younger child.

There was a celebratory dinner her last evening in the dwelling. Her brother, older by six years, had already gone on to his own training in the Department of Law and Justice. They saw him only at public meetings; he had become a stranger. So the last dinner was just the three of them, she and the parental unit who had raised her. They reminisced a bit; they recalled some funny incidents from her early childhood (a time she had thrown her shoes into the bushes and come home from the Childcare Center barefoot). There was laughter, and she thanked them for the years of her upbringing.

"Were you embarrassed when I was selected for Birthmother?" she asked them. She had, herself, secretly hoped for something more prestigious. At her brother's selection, when she had been just six, they had all been very proud. Law and Justice was reserved for those of especially keen intelligence. But she had not been a top student.

"No," her father said. "We trust the committee's judgment. They knew what you would do best."

"And Birthmother is very important," Mother added. "Without Birthmothers, none of us would be here!"

Then they wished her well in the future. Their lives were changing too; parents no longer, they would move now into the place where Childless Adults lived.

The next day, she walked alone to the dormitory attached to the Birthing Unit and moved into the small bedroom she was assigned. From its window she could see the school she had attended, and the recreation field beyond. In the distance, there was a glimpse of the river that bordered the community.

Finally, several weeks later, after she was settled in and beginning to make friends among the other girls, she was called in for insemination.

Not knowing what to expect, she had been nervous. But when the procedure was complete, she felt relieved; it had been quick and painless.

"It that all?" she had asked in surprise, rising from the table when the technician gestured that she should.

"That's all. Come back next week to be tested and certified."

She had laughed nervously. She wished they had explained everything more clearly in the instruction folder they had given her when she was selected. "What does 'certified' mean?" she asked.

The worker, putting away the insemination equipment, seemed a little rushed. There were probably others waiting.

"Once they're sure it implanted," he explained impatiently, "then you're a certified Vessel.

"Anything else?" he asked her as he turned to leave. "No? You're free to go, then."

* * *

That all seemed such a short time ago. Now here she was, nine months later, with the blindfold strapped around her eyes. The discomfort had started some hours before, intermittently; now it was nonstop. She breathed deeply as they had instructed. It was difficult, blinded like this; her skin was hot inside the mask. She tried to relax. To breathe in and out. To ignore the discom — *No*, she thought. *It is pain. It really is pain.* Gathering her strength for the job, she groaned slightly, arched her back, and gave herself up to the darkness.

Her name was Claire. She was fourteen years old.

TWO

THEY CLUSTERED AROUND her. She could hear them, when her mind was able to focus through the surging intermittent pain. They were talking urgently to each other. Something was wrong.

Again and again they checked her with their instruments, metallic and cold. A cuff on her arm was inflated, and someone pressed a metal disk there, at her elbow. Then a different device against her stretched and shaking belly. She gasped as another convulsive pain ripped through her. Her hands were tied on either side of the bed. She was unable to move.

Was it supposed to be like this? She tried to ask but her voice was too weak—mumbly and scared—and no one heard.

"Help me," she whimpered. But their attention, she sensed, was not on her, not really. They were worried about the Product. Their hands and tools were on her taut middle. It had been hours, now, since all this began, the first twinge, then the rhythmic, hardening pain, and later, the buckling on of the mask.

"Put her out. We'll have to go in for it." It was a commanding voice, clearly someone in charge. "Quickly." There was a startling urgency to it.

"Breathe deeply," they ordered her, shoving something rubbery up under the mask, holding it to her mouth and nose. She did. She had no choice. She would have suffocated otherwise. She inhaled something with an unpleasantly sweet scent, and immediately the pain subsided, her thoughts subsided, her being drifted away. Her last sensation was the awareness, pain-free, of something cutting into her belly. Carving her.

※ ※ ※

She emerged to a new, different pain, no longer the throbbing agony but now a broad, deep ache. She felt freed, and realized that her wrists were unshackled. She was still on the bed, covered with a warm blanket. Metal rails had been lifted with a clanking sound, so she was protected on either side. The room was empty now. No attendants or technicians, no equipment.

Only Claire, alone. She turned tentatively, assessing the emptiness of the room with her eyes, and then tried to lift her head but was forced back by the pain the attempt caused. She couldn't look down at her own body but carefully moved her hands to rest there on what had been her own taut, swollen belly. It was flat now, bandaged, and very sore. The Product was what they had carved out of her.

And she missed it. She was suffused with a desperate feeling of loss.

* * *

"You've been decertified."

Three weeks had passed. She had recuperated in the Birthing Unit for the first week, tended and checked—pampered a bit, actually, she realized. But there was an awkwardness to everything. There with her were other young women, recovering, so there was pleasant conversation, a few jokes about being slender again. Their bodies, hers as well, were massaged each morning, and their gentle exercise was supervised by the staff. Her recuperation was slower, though, than the others', for she had been left with a wound and they had not.

After the first week they were moved to an interim place, where they amused themselves with talk and games before returning two weeks later to the large, familiar group of Vessels. Back they went, to the Dormitory, greeting old friends—many of them larger in size now, their bellies growing as they waited—and taking their places again in the group. They all looked alike, in their shapeless, smocklike dresses, with their identical haircuts; but personalities distinguished them. Nadia was funny, making a joke of everything; Miriam very solemn and shy; Suzanne was organized and efficient.

As Vessels returned following Production, there was surprisingly little talk of the Task. "How did it go?" someone would ask, and the reply would be a nonchalant shrug, and "All right. Fairly easy." Or a wry "Not too bad," with a face indicating that it had not been pleasant.

"Good to have you back."

"Thanks. How were things here while I was gone?"

"The same. Two new Vessels, just arrived. And Nancy's gone."

"What did she get?"

"Farm."

"Good. She wanted that."

It was casual talk, inconsequential. Nancy had delivered her third Product not long before. After the third, the Vessels were reassigned. Farm. Clothing Factory. Food Delivery.

Claire remembered that Nancy had hoped for Farm. She liked the outdoors, and a particular friend of hers had been assigned Farm some months before; she hoped to spend the next part of her working life in the company of someone she enjoyed. Claire felt happy for her.

But she was apprehensive about her own future. Although her memory was hazy, she knew that something had gone wrong at her own Production. It was clear that no one else had ended up with a wound. She had tried, somewhat shyly, to ask the others, those who had produced more than once. But they seemed shocked and confused by her questions.

"Is your belly still sore?" Claire whispered to Miriam, who had been in the recuperation place with her.

"Sore? No," Miriam had replied. They were sitting beside each other at breakfast.

"Mine is, just where the scar is. When I press on it," Claire explained, touching her hand gently to the place.

"Scar?" Miriam made a face. "I don't have a scar." She turned away and joined another conversation.

Claire tried again, carefully asking a few other Vessels. But no one had a scar. No one had a wound. After a while, her own ache subsided, and she tried to ignore the uneasy awareness that something had gone very wrong.

Then she was called in. "Claire," the voice from the speaker announced at midday while the Vessels were eating, "please report to the office immediately after lunch."

Flustered, Claire looked around. Across the table was Elissa, a special friend. They had been selected the same year, both Twelves at the same time, and so she had known Elissa through her school years. But Elissa was newer here; she had not been inseminated as soon as Claire. Now she was in the early stages of her first Production.

"What's that about?" Elissa asked her when they heard the directive.

"I don't know."

"Did you do something wrong?"

Claire frowned. "I don't think so. Maybe I forgot to fold my laundry."

"They wouldn't call you in for that, would they?"

"I don't think so. It's so minor."

"Well," Elissa said, beginning to stack her empty dishes, "you'll find out soon enough. It's probably nothing. See you later!" She left Claire still sitting at the table.

But it was not nothing. Claire stood facing them in dismay as the committee told her of their decision. She had been decertified.

"Gather your things," they told her. "You'll be moved this afternoon."

"Why?" she asked. "Was it because . . . well, I could tell that something went wrong, but I . . ."

They were kind, solicitous. "It wasn't your fault."

"What wasn't my fault?" she asked, aware that she shouldn't press them but unable to stop herself. "If you could just explain . . . ?"

The committee head shrugged. "These things happen. A physical problem. It should have been detected sooner. You should not have been inseminated. Who was your first Examiner?" he asked.

"I don't remember her name."

"Well, we'll find out. Let's hope it was her first error, so that she will have another chance."

They dismissed her then, but she turned at the door because she could not leave without asking.

"My Product?"

He looked at her dismissively, then relented. He turned to another committee member near him at the table and nodded to the papers in front of her, directing her to look up the information.

"What number was it?" the woman asked him, but he

ignored the question. "Well," she said, "I'll check by name. You're—Claire?"

As if they didn't know. They had summoned her here by name. But she nodded.

She moved her finger down a page. "Yes. Here you are. Claire: Product number Thirty-six. Oh yes, I see the notations about the difficulties."

She looked up. Claire touched her own belly, remembering.

The woman returned the paper to the pile and tapped the edges of the stack to make it tidy. "He's fine," she said.

The committee head glared at her.

"It." She corrected herself. "I meant that it's fine. The medical difficulties didn't affect it.

"You'll be fine too, Claire," she added, affably.

"Where am I going?" Claire asked. Suddenly she was frightened. They hadn't yet said she was being reassigned. Just decertified. So she would no longer be a Birthmother. That made sense. Her body had not performed that function well. But what if—? What if decertified people were simply released? The way failures often were?

But their reply was reassuring. "Fish Hatchery," the committee head told her. "You're being moved there. They need help; they're short of workers. Your training will start in the morning. You'll have to catch up. Luckily you have a quick mind."

He dismissed her now with a wave of his hand, and Claire went back to the Dormitory to gather her few things. It was rest time. The other Vessels were all napping, the doors to their cubicle-like rooms closed.

He, she thought as she packed the few personal items that she had. It was a *he*. I produced a baby boy. *I had a son.* The feeling of loss overwhelmed her again.

THREE

Y OU'LL BE ISSUED a bicycle." The man—his name-tag said DIMITRI, HATCHERY SUPERVISOR—gestured toward the area where bicycles were standing in racks. He had met her at the door, unsurprised by her arrival. Obviously he had been notified that she was on her way.

Claire nodded. Confined to the Birthing Unit and its surrounding grounds for over a year now, she had not needed any kind of transportation. And she had walked here, carrying her small case of belongings, from the Birthmothers' area to the northeast. It wasn't far, and she knew the route, but after so many months, everything seemed new and unfamiliar. She had passed the school and saw children at their required exercise in the recreation field. None seemed to recognize her, though they looked curiously at the young woman walking along the path at midday. It was unusual. Most people were at their jobs. Those who needed to be out and about were on bicycles making their way from one building to another. No one walked. A small girl with hair ribbons grinned at Claire from the exercise routine, and waved surreptitiously; Claire smiled back, remembering her own beribboned days, but an instructor called sharply to the child, who made a face and turned back to the assigned calisthenics.

Across the Central Plaza, she caught a glimpse, in the Dwelling area, of the small house where she had grown up. Other people would live there now, couples newly assigned to each other, perhaps waiting for . . .

She averted her eyes from the Nurturing Center. It was, she knew, where the Products were taken after the birthing. Usually in groups. Early morning, most often. Once, sleepless at dawn, she had watched from the window of her cubicle and seen four Products, tucked into baskets, loaded into a two-wheeled cart attached to the back of a bicycle. After checking their security in the cart, the birthing attendant had ridden off toward the Nurturing Center to deliver them there.

She wondered if her own Product, her boy, number Thirty-six, had been taken to the Nurturing Center yet. Claire knew that they waited—sometimes days, occasionally weeks, making certain that everything was going well, that the Products were healthy—to make the transfer.

Well. She sighed. Time to put it out of her mind. She walked on, past the hall of Law and Justice. Peter, whom she had once known as a teasing older brother, would be inside, at work. If he glanced through a window and saw a young woman walking slowly past, would he know it was Claire? Would he care?

Past the House of Elders, the place where the governing committee lived and studied. Past small office buildings; past the bicycle repair shop; and now she could see the river that bordered the community, its dark water moving swiftly, foaming around rocks here and there. Claire had always feared the river. As children they had been warned of its dangers. She had known of a young boy who had drowned. There were rumors, likely untrue, of citizens who had swum across, or even made their way across the high, forbidden bridge and disappeared into the unknown lands beyond. But she was fascinated by it too—its constant murmur and movement, and the mystery of it.

She crossed the bike path, waiting politely until two young women had pedaled by. To her left she could see the shallow fish-holding ponds and remembered how, as younger children, she and her friends had watched the silvery creatures darting about.

Now she would be working here, at the Hatchery. And living here too, she assumed, at least until . . . until when? Citizens were given dwellings when they were assigned spouses. Birthmothers never had spouses, so she had not thought about it until now. Now she wondered. Was she eligible now for a spouse, and eventually for—? Claire sighed. It was troubling, and confusing, to think about such things. She turned away from the holding ponds, made her way to the front door of the main building, and was met there by Dimitri.

* * *

That night, alone in the small bedroom she'd been assigned, Claire looked down from her window to the darkened, surging river below. She yawned. It had been a long and exhausting day. This morning she had awakened in her familiar surroundings, the place where she had lived for so many months, but by midday her entire life had shifted. She had not had a chance to say goodbye to her friends, the other Vessels. They would be wondering where she had gone, but would likely forget her soon. She had taken her place here, been issued a nametag, and been introduced to the other workers. They seemed pleasant enough. Some, older than Claire, had spouses and dwellings, and left at the end of the day's work. Others, like herself, lived here, in rooms along the corridor. One, Heather, had been the same year as Claire; she had been a Twelve at the same ceremony. Surely she would remember Claire's Assignment as Birthmother. Her eyes flickered in recognition when they were introduced, but Heather said nothing. Neither did Claire. There was nothing really to say.

She supposed that she and the younger workers, including Heather, would become friends, of a sort. They would sit together at meals and go in groups to attend community entertainments. After a while they would have shared jokes, probably things about fish, phrases that would make them chuckle. It had been that way with the other Vessels, and Claire found herself missing, already, the easy camaraderie among them. But she would fit in here. Everyone welcomed her cheerfully and said they'd be glad of her help.

The work wouldn't be hard. She had been allowed to watch the lab attendants, in gowns and gloves, strip eggs from what they called the breeder fish, anesthetized females. A little like squeezing toothpaste, she thought, amused at the image. Nearby, other attendants squeezed what they told her was "milt" from the male; then they added the creamy substance to the container that held the fresh eggs. It had to be very precisely timed, they explained. And antiseptic. They worried about contamination, and bacteria. The temperature made a difference as well. Everything was carefully controlled.

In a nearby room lit by dim red lights, she had watched another gloved worker look through trays of stacked fertilized eggs.

"See those spots?" the worker had asked Claire. She pointed to the tray of glistening pink eggs. Claire peered down and saw that most of them had two dark spots. She nodded.

"Eyes," the girl told her.

"Oh," Claire said, amazed that already, so young and tiny that she could hardly think of it as a fish, it had eyes.

"See here?" Using a metal tool, the girl pointed to a discolored, eyeless egg. "This one's dead." Carefully she plucked it from the tray with her forceps and discarded it in the sink. Then she returned the tray to its rack and reached for the next one.

"Why did it die?" Claire asked. She found that she was whispering. The room was so dimly lit, so quiet and cool, that her voice was hushed.

But the worker replied in a normal tone, very matter-of-fact. "I don't know. The insemination went wrong, I guess."

She shrugged and removed another dead egg from the second tray. "We have to take them out so they don't contaminate the good ones. I check them every day."

Claire felt a vague discomfort. *The insemination had gone wrong.* Was that what had happened to her? Had her Product, like the discolored, eyeless egg, been thrown aside someplace? But no. They had told her that number Thirty-six was "fine." She tried to set aside her troubling thoughts and pay attention to the worker's voice and explanations.

"Claire?" The door opened and it was Dimitri, the supervisor, looking for her. "I want to show you the dining room. And they have your schedule almost ready to give you."

So she had continued her tour of the facility, and been instructed in her next day's duties (cleaning, mostly—everything had to be kept spotless), and later she had had supper with a group of the workers who lived, as she would now, at the Hatchery. They talked, mostly, about what they had done during recreation time. There was an hour allotted each day when they could do whatever they liked. Someone mentioned a bike ride and a picnic lunch along the river; apparently the kitchen staff would pack your lunch in a basket if you asked in advance. Two young men had joined a ball game. Someone had watched repairs being done on the bridge. It was aimless, pleasant chat, but it served to remind Claire that she was freer now than she had been in a long time. She could go for a walk after lunch, she thought, or in the evening.

Later, in her room, thinking, she realized what she wanted to do when she had time. Not just an ordinary walk. She wanted to try to find a girl named Sophia, a girl her own age, a girl who had turned twelve when Claire did. They had not been particular friends, just acquaintances and school-mates who had happened to share a birth year. But Sophia had been seated next to Claire at the ceremony when they were given their Assignments.

"Birthmother," the Chief Elder had announced when it was Claire's turn to stand and be acknowledged. She had shaken the Chief Elder's hand, smiled politely at the audience, taken her official Assignment papers, and gone back to her seat. Sophia had stood, next.

"Nurturer," the Chief Elder had named Sophia.

It had meant little to Claire, then. But now it meant that Sophia, an assistant at first, probably by now fully trained, was working in the Nurturing Center, the place where Claire's Product — her child, her baby — was being held, and fed.

✳ ✳ ✳

Days passed. Claire waited for the right time. Usually the workers took their breaks in pairs or groups. People would wonder if she wandered off alone during a break; there would be murmurs about her, and questions. She didn't want that. She needed them to see her as hard-working and responsible, as someone ordinary, someone without secrets.

So she waited, worked, and began to fit in. She made friends. One lunchtime she joined several coworkers in a picnic along the riverbank. They leaned their bikes against nearby trees and sat on some flat rocks in the high grass while they unpacked the prepared food. Nearby, on the path, two young boys rode by on their bikes, laughing at something, and waved to them.

"Hey, look!" One boy was pointing. "Supply boat!"

Eagerly the two youngsters dropped their bikes and scrambled down the sloping riverbank to watch as the barge-like boat passed, its open deck heavy with wooden containers of various sizes.

Rolf, one of the picnickers, looked at his watch and then at the boys. "They're going to be late getting back to school," he commented with a wry smile.

The others all chuckled. Now that they were finished with school, it was easy to be amused by the regulations that they had all lived by as children. "I was late once," Claire told them, "because a groundskeeper sliced his hand when he was pruning the bushes over by the central offices. I stopped and watched while they bandaged him and took him off to the infirmary for stitches.

"I used to hope I'd be assigned Nursing Attendant," she added.

There was an awkward silence for a moment. Claire wasn't certain if they knew her background. Undoubtedly there had been some explanation given for her sudden appearance at the Hatchery, but probably they had been told no details. To have failed at one's Assignment—to be reassigned—had something of a shame to it. No one would ever mention it, if they did know. No one would ask.

"Well, the committee knows best," Edith commented primly as she passed sandwiches around. "Anyway, there's an element of nursing at the Hatchery. All the labs and procedures."

Claire nodded.

"Hatchery wouldn't have been my first choice," a tall young man named Eric said. "I was really hoping for Law and Justice."

"My brother's there," Claire told him.

"Does he like it?" Eric asked with interest.

Claire shrugged. "I guess so. I never see him. He was

older. Once he finished his training, he moved away from our dwelling. He might even have a spouse by now."

"You'd know that," Rolf pointed out. "You see the Spouse Assignments at the Ceremony.

"I've applied for a spouse," he added, grinning. "I had to fill out about a thousand forms."

Claire didn't tell them that she had not attended the last two ceremonies. Birthmothers did not leave their quarters during their years of production. Claire had never seen a Vessel until she became one. She had not known, until she had both experienced and observed it, that human females swelled and grew and reproduced. No one had told her what "birth" meant.

"Look!" Eric said suddenly. "The supply boat's stopping at the Hatchery. Good! I put in an order quite a while ago." He glanced down at the riverbank, where the two youngsters were still watching the boat. "Boys!" he called. When they looked up, he pointed to the watch on his own wrist. "The school bell is going to ring in less than five minutes!"

Reluctantly they climbed back up the bank and went to retrieve their bikes. "Thank you for the reminder," one said politely to Eric.

"You think the supply boat will still be there after school?" the other boy asked eagerly.

But Eric shook his head. "They unload quickly," he told the boy, who looked disappointed.

"I wish I could be a boat worker," they could hear one boy say to the other as they set their bikes upright. "I bet they go lots of places we don't even know about. I bet if I were working on a supply boat, I'd get to see—"

"If we don't get back on time," his friend said nervously, "we're not going to be assigned *anything!* Come on, let's get going!"

The boys rode away toward the school building in the distance.

"I wonder what he thought he'd get to see, as a boat worker," Rolf commented. They began to tidy up the picnic and to pack away the uneaten food.

"Other places. Other communities. The boats must make a lot of stops." Eric folded the napkins and placed them in the basket.

"They'd all be the same. What's so exciting about seeing a different hatchery, a different school, a different nurturing center, a different—"

Edith interrupted them. "It's pointless to speculate," she said in her terse, businesslike tone. "Accomplishes nothing. 'Wondering' is very likely against the rules, though I suppose it isn't a serious infringement."

Eric rolled his eyes and handed Rolf the basket. "Here," he said. "Strap this on your bike and take it back, would you? I have to do an errand. I told the lab chief that I'd pick up some stuff at the Supply Center."

Rolf, attaching the basket to his bike by its transportation straps, commented, "It might be nice to travel on the river, though, just for the trip. Fun to see new things. Even," he added facetiously, "if you haven't wondered about them."

Edith ignored that.

"Could be dangerous," Eric pointed out. "That water's deep." He looked around, making sure they had collected everything. "Ready to go back?" Claire and Edith nodded and moved their bikes to the path. Eric waved and rode off on his errand.

Even if it might be against the rules, some kind of infringement (it would be hard to know without studying the thick book of community regulations, though it was always available on the monitor in the Hatchery lobby, but there were pages and pages of very small print, and no one ever bothered to look at it, as far as Claire could tell), there would be no way for anyone to get caught in the act of wondering, Claire thought. It was an invisible thing, like a secret. She herself spent a great deal of time at it . . . wondering.

Pedaling back, she rehearsed in her mind, silently, how easy it would be to say in a casual voice, "I have to run an errand." How she could slip away — it wouldn't take long — and ride over to the Nurturing Center, to find Sophia and ask some questions.

——

FOUR

THEN THE OCCASION came.

"I just realized that the biology teacher never returned the posters I let him use," Dimitri said irritably at lunch. "And I'll need them tomorrow morning."

"I'll go get them," Claire offered.

"Thanks." The lab director nodded in her direction. "That's a help. There will be a group of volunteers starting indoctrination, and the visual aids make things easier."

They were eating in the Hatchery cafeteria, six of them at the same table. There was no assigned seating, and today Claire, balancing her tray of prepared food, had made her way to an empty chair at this table where the director was already sitting with several technicians. He was talking about a set of demonstration posters that he liked to use when there were visitors being given a tour of the facility. The biology teacher had borrowed them and they had not yet been returned.

"Notify the school. They'll have a student bring them." One of the technicians had finished eating and was tidying his tray. "And they'll chastise the teacher," he added, with a malicious chuckle, as he stood.

"No need," Claire said. "I have another errand over that way. It'll be easy for me to stop by the school." That wasn't really a lie, she told herself. Lying was against the rules. They all knew that, abided by it. And she hadn't made it up, the other errand she had mentioned. She only hoped no one would ask her what it was. But their attention was elsewhere now. They were crumpling their napkins, looking at their watches, preparing to return to work.

It was her chance to look for Sophia.

* * *

Her stop at the school was brief, and the biology teacher didn't recognize her. Claire had never studied biology. At twelve, when the selections were made and the future jobs assigned, the children's education took different paths. Some in her group—she remembered a boy named Marcus, who excelled in school and was assigned a future as an engineer—would continue on and learn various sciences. He had probably completed biology by now, she guessed, and would be studying higher mathematics, or astrophysics, or biochemistry, one of the subjects that was whispered about, when they were young, as incomprehensibly difficult. Marcus wouldn't be in this ordinary school anymore, but in one of the higher education buildings reserved for scholars.

Though she had been young at the time, Claire remembered when Peter, her brother, had moved on to higher education. Maybe Peter had even learned biology in school. But then he had been transferred over to the law buildings, for his clerkship and studies.

The hallways were familiar, and she found the biology classroom without difficulty.

"I had intended to return these," the biology teacher told her, handing Claire the rolled-up posters. "Would you please tell him that I didn't realize he would need them back so soon?" He sounded slightly annoyed.

"Yes, I'll tell him. Thank you." Claire left the teacher there at his desk in the classroom and made her way down the hall toward the front door. She glanced into the empty rooms. School hours had ended and the children had gone to their various volunteer jobs in the community. But she was familiar with some of the rooms, and she recognized a language teacher who leaned over a desk, packing things into a briefcase. Claire nodded uncertainly when the woman looked up and saw her.

"Claire, is it?" The teacher smiled. "What a surprise! What—"

But she didn't continue the question, though the look on her face was curious. Certainly the teacher would have remembered her selection as Birthmother, and clearly a Birthmother had no business in the school, or in fact anywhere in the day-to-day geography of the community. But it would have been extremely rude to ask why Claire was there. So the teacher cut off her own question and simply smiled in greeting.

"I'm just here collecting something," Claire explained, holding up the cylinder of posters. "It's nice to see you again."

She continued down the hall and out through the front entrance of the education building, and took her bicycle from the rack by the steps. Carefully she attached the bundle of papers securely to the holder on the back of the bike. Nearby, a gardener transplanting a bush glanced at her without interest. Two children on bicycles pedaled past quickly, rushing toward something, probably worried about being late for their required volunteer hours.

Everything was familiar, unchanged, but it still felt odd to Claire to be back in the community again. She had not ventured far from the Hatchery before this, just the short excursions with her coworkers. *Over there,* she thought, looking down the path she had ridden to get to the school, *I can almost see the dwelling where I grew up.*

Briefly she wondered about her parents, whether they ever thought of her—or, for that matter, of Peter. They had raised two children successfully, fulfilling the job of Adults with Spouses. Peter had achieved a highly prestigious Assignment. And she, Claire, had not. *Birthmother.* At the ceremony, standing on the stage to receive her Assignment, she had not been able to see her parents' faces in the crowd. But she could imagine how they looked, how disappointed they would have been. They had hoped for more from their female child.

"There's honor in it," she remembered her mother saying reassuringly that night. "Birthmothers provide our future population."

But it felt a little like those times when they had opened the dinner delivery containers to find that the evening meal would be grains prepared with fish oil. "High vitamin D," her mother would say in that same cheerful voice, in an attempt to make the meal seem more appealing than it really was.

Claire biked away from the education buildings and hesitated at the corner, where several paths intersected. She could turn right and ride past the back of Law and Justice, straight along that path, and be back at the Hatchery in a few minutes. But instead, she continued straight, then turned left, so that the House of the Old, surrounded by trees, was just ahead of her. She turned right here and slowed her bicycle near the Childcare Center, steering carefully around a food delivery vehicle being unloaded. Then she made her way straight ahead toward the Nurturing Center.

It was surprising, she thought, as she approached the structure, that she had never spent volunteer hours there as a schoolgirl. She had worked often at the Childcare Center, and had enjoyed the time playing educational games with the toddlers and young children, but infants—they were called newchildren—had never interested her. Some of her friends and age-mates had thought the little ones "cute." But not Claire. From what she had heard described, they were endless work—feeding, rocking, bathing—and they cried too much. She had avoided doing her hours there.

Now, planning how she would present herself at the entrance to the Nurturing Center, Claire realized that she was excited, and a little nervous. She rehearsed what she might say when she went inside. To ask for Sophia would be foolish. Sophia would probably barely remember her; they had not been particular friends. But why else would she be appearing there, asking to enter?

Well, Claire decided abruptly, she would lie once again. Against the rules. She knew that. Once, she would have cared. Now she didn't. As simple as that. And it was just a small lie.

She wheeled her bicycle into the rack where several slots had been left open for visitors. Then she disengaged the rolled posters from the carrier and took them with her to the front door. Inside, a young woman sitting at a desk looked up from her papers and smiled at her. "Good afternoon," she said politely, peering at Claire's nametag. "Can I help you?"

Claire introduced herself. "I'm a worker at the Hatchery," she explained. "We have these extra posters explaining the life cycle of salmon. I was wondering if you could use some to decorate your walls."

If the young woman said yes, she realized, she would have some explaining to do to the Hatchery director, who was at this very moment expecting his posters back. But it was a pretty safe assumption that the answer would be no. Who would care about examining the growth of fish? It wasn't even that interesting to those who worked with them.

And, indeed, the young woman smiled and shook her head. "Thank you," she said, "but we have specially designed equipment to engage the attention of newchildren. We don't deviate from the standard means of helping them to focus their attention span and to exercise their small muscles. Everything's pretty carefully calibrated by the experts in infant development."

Claire nodded. "Interesting," she said. "I'm sorry I never volunteered here. I don't know much about nurturing at all. Do you ever let visitors have a tour?"

The receptionist appeared pleased at her interest. "Never been here at all? My goodness! It's such a fun place! You should certainly take a look, since you're here anyway! Let me see who's on duty." She ran her finger down a list of names.

"Is Sophia here?" Claire asked. "She was with my age group."

"Oh, Sophia! She's such a diligent worker. Let me look. Yes — there's her name. Let's see if she's available."

Summoned through the intercom by the receptionist, Sophia entered the front hallway from a corridor on the side. She hadn't changed much since they had both been twelve almost three years before. She was thin, with her hair pulled back under a cap, which seemed to be part of her uniform. Claire smiled at her. "Hi," she said. "I don't know if you remember me. I was a Twelve when you were. My name's Claire."

Sophia looked at Claire's nametag and nodded with a small smile of recognition, after a moment. "We don't wear nametags," Sophia explained, "because the newchildren would grab at them. But I remember you. I think we were in the same math class."

"I hated math. I was never very good at it." Claire made a face.

Sophia chuckled. "I did pretty well, but it never interested me much. Remember Marcus? He got such high marks in math! He's in engineering studies now."

Claire nodded. "He was always studying," she recalled.

Sophia frowned and peered toward the small print under Claire's name on her nametag. "I forget what your Assignment was," she said. "Your uniform is . . ."

"Fish Hatchery," Claire explained quickly. Good. Sophia didn't remember that she had been assigned Birthmother.

"And so what are you doing here?"

"Hoping to get a tour!" Claire told her. "Somehow I missed out on the whole Nurturing section. And I have a little free time this afternoon."

"Oh. Well, all right. You can follow along and I'll explain things. But I have to work. It's almost feeding time. Come on. Clean your hands first." Sophia pointed to a disinfectant dispenser on the wall of the corridor, and Claire followed her example, rubbing her hands carefully with the clear medicinal liquid.

"The youngest ones are in this first room." Youngest ones. That meant the most recent newchildren. Claire thought back, and remembered which of her sister Vessels had been preparing to give birth when she was dismissed. These would be their Products.

"We can't go in this one without changing to sterile uniforms. But we can look at them." Sophia pointed through a window to a spotlessly clean area filled with small wheeled carts, many empty. Two workers, a young man in a nurturer's uniform and a volunteer, a girl of ten or so, were tidying things. They looked up at the window, saw the two observers, and smiled.

"How many newest?" Sophia called through the glass. The volunteer held up four fingers. Then she moved to one of the carts and pushed it closer to the window so Sophia and Claire could see. A card on the side had a gender symbol indicating Female, and the number 45.

"Forty-five?" Claire asked, looking down at the infant, who was wrapped tightly in a light blanket with only its small face exposed. The eyes were tightly closed. "What's that mean?"

Sophia looked at her in surprise. "Number forty-five. Forty-fifth newchild this year. Just five more to come. Don't you remember? We all had numbers. I was Twenty-seven."

"Oh. Yes, of course. I was one of the earliest ones our year. I was number Eleven."

And she did remember, now that Sophia had reminded her. After age twelve, the numbers didn't matter much, were rarely referred to. But being number Eleven had served her well when she was young. It had meant she was the eleventh newchild her year—older, therefore, than so many others (like Sophia) who had been later to walk and talk, later to shoot up in height. By twelve, of course, most of that evened out. But Claire could remember being a Five, and a Six, and proud that she was a little ahead of so many others.

"What about the other ones in this year's batch?" Claire asked.

Sophia gestured. "The oldest—numbers One to Ten? They're in that room over there. A couple of them can walk already." She rolled her eyes. "It's really a nuisance to chase after them." She started down the hall and turned a corner, Claire following. "Then the next oldest are here." Another large window allowed the two young women to look into a room where a group of infants crawled on the carpeted floor strewn with toys, while their attendants prepared bottles at a counter and sink against the wall.

"So they're arranged in groups of ten?"

Sophia nodded. "Five rooms, and ten in each, when we

have our full fifty. Right now we still have a few newborns due to come in. Then, when we reach fifty, no more till after the next Ceremony." She waved cheerfully at the volunteer putting the bottles into the warming device, and the young girl grinned and waved back.

"Then, of course, after this year's fifty are assigned, we start fresh, after the Ceremony, with new ones coming in gradually. It's like a little vacation!"

"It's a while, still, till the Ceremony. But you almost have the full fifty?"

"It's timed, over at the Birthing Unit, so we don't get a batch of newborns late in the year. Parents being given newchildren don't want brand-new ones."

"Too much work?"

"Not really. You saw, a minute ago—those newest ones? They mostly sleep. But it's a lot of responsibility, keeping everything sterile. Also, you can't *play* with the new ones. Parents like to play with their children when they get them."

Claire was half listening. *Thirty-six*, she thought. Her Product had been number Thirty-six. She had kept the number firmly in her mind.

"So next is the third ten?" she asked. "Let me think. One to Ten. Then this group is Eleven to Twenty. The next group will be Twenty-one to Thirty, right?"

"Yes. Over there, across the hall. I usually work with that group. I'm going to have to go back in, in a minute, to help feed." Claire glanced through the window that displayed Sophia's group of infants, who were dangling in swings suspended from the ceiling, kicking their bare feet against the carpet. A male attendant was changing one on a padded table. He noticed the girls and pointed meaningfully to the large clock on the wall. Sophia opened the door a crack, and Claire could hear the gurgles and giggles as the infants "talked" to one another. She smiled. She had not thought of newchildren as being appealing, not at all. But there was a sweetness to these little ones, she had to admit. She could understand why new parents wanted ones they could play with.

"I'll be right in," Sophia was telling her coworker. "I'm giving a tour. "Or"—she turned to Claire—"we could stop here. There's only one more group, the next to youngest. They're not that interesting. Want to come in and play with these? You could feed one if you want."

Claire hesitated. She didn't want to seem oddly interested in a particular group. "You know," she told Sophia, "I'd really like to peek at the last group, just so I can say I've seen them all. If you don't mind?"

Sophia sighed. "I'll be back in a minute," she told the uniformed man, who had placed the newly changed infant back in a swing and was now taking small bowls of cereal from the warmer.

"Over here," Sophia told Claire, and led her to the last room in the corridor.

"So these would be, let me think, Thirty-one to Forty?"

"Correct." Sophia was clearly eager to get back to her own charges. "Next to newest."

"May I go in?" Claire was looking through the observation window. Each small crib held an infant, and two attendants were propping warmed bottles on padded holders beside their heads so that they could suck.

"I guess." Sophia opened the door and asked. "We have a visitor. Could you use a hand for this feed?"

A uniformed man smiled. "How about *two* hands? We can use all the help we can get!"

"I have to get back to work with my own group. But I'll leave her here with you."

"Thanks, Sophia. It's been good to see you again." Claire smiled. "Maybe we could get together for lunch or something?"

"Yes. Come back anytime. Best is when they're napping, though." Sophia gave a brief goodbye gesture and returned to her own assigned room.

Claire entered timidly and stood watching as the final

bottles were distributed. "There," the attendant said. "Every-one's been served. Now we have to check from time to time and make sure they're all properly placed. Of course they'll yell if they lose hold of the nipple! Won't you?" He glanced down with a smile at one of the infants who was industriously suck-ing at the milk. "And then one by one we pick the little guys up and pat their backs till they burp. Ever done that?"

Claire shook her head. Till they burp? She couldn't even imagine it. "No."

He chuckled. "Well, you can watch. Then, if you want to give it a try—"

He lifted one of the infants from its crib. Claire moved forward and saw the number. Forty. She glanced around to see if the numbers were in order. But the little beds were on wheels, and seemed to have been placed randomly. As she watched, the attendant took Forty to a rocking chair in the corner and sat down with the little one against his shoulder.

The other attendant, a young woman, leaned forward over a crib with a sniff, and said suddenly, "Uh-oh! Thirty-four needs changing!" She wrinkled her nose and pushed the crib over to the changing area. "You'll have to finish your bottle after I clean you up, little girl!" she said with a chuckle, and lifted the infant to the table.

Claire noticed, then, that each small crib here was also

tagged with a gender symbol. She made her way past the little beds, glancing in at the infants, some sucking serenely on their milk, others gulping lustily. Suddenly one in a crib marked *male* let out a shriek, then switched to a loud wail.

"I don't need to ask who *that* is!" the man said, continuing to pat and stroke the back of the infant he held. "I recognize his voice!"

Claire looked at the number on the crib that contained the howling newchild. "It's Thirty-six," she told him.

"Of *course* it's Thirty-six!" the man replied, laughing. "It's *always* Thirty-six! Pick him up, would you? See if you can get him to stop screeching."

Claire took a deep breath. She had never held an infant before. The man, watching her, sensed that. "He won't break. They're quite tough, actually. Just be sure to support his head."

She leaned down. Her hands seemed to know what to do. They slid easily under him, and found the way to hold his neck and head. Gently Claire picked up her son.

———

FIVE

NOTHING CHANGED. CLAIRE'S life didn't change. She woke each day, showered, donned her uniform, and attached her nametag: CLAIRE. HATCHERY ASSISTANT. She went to the cafeteria, greeted her coworkers, ate the morning meal, and began her assigned tasks. The superiors at the Hatchery were pleased with her work.

But at the same time, everything was different. Her every thought now was on the newchild she had met only once, had held for a moment, whose light eyes she had gazed into briefly, whose curly hair had touched her chin for too short a time. Number Thirty-six.

"Have they chosen the name yet?" she had asked the young woman attendant, who was re-propping the bottle for the female one she had changed and returned to her crib.

"For this one? I don't think so. They don't tell us, anyway. We never know their names until they're assigned."

Each newchild was given to his assigned parents at the Ceremony that would take place in December. Their names, chosen by a committee, were announced then.

"I meant this one," Claire explained. She had taken an empty rocking chair, and moved back and forth now with Thirty-six, whose loud crying had subsided. He was looking up at Claire.

"Oh, *that* one. He might not even get a name at the next Ceremony. They're already talking about keeping him here another year. He's not doing well. They call it failure to thrive." The young woman shrugged.

"Actually, he does have a name lined up." The man returned the infant he'd been burping to the crib, re-propped her bottle, came to where Claire was, and looked down at Thirty-six. "Hey there, little guy," he said, in a singsong voice.

"He does? How do you know?" The young woman looked surprised.

The man took Thirty-six from Claire, who relinquished him reluctantly. "I've been concerned about him," he explained. He looked down and made a funny face, as if encouraging the unhappy infant to laugh. "I thought it might make him more responsive if I started using his name. So I sneaked into the office and took a look at the list."

"And?" his assistant asked.

"And what?"

"His name is—?"

The man laughed. "Not telling. I only use it in secret. If it's overheard? Big trouble. So I'm being careful." He jiggled the infant in his lap. "It's a good name, though. Suits him."

The woman sighed. "Well, it had better perk him up before December," she said, "if he wants to get a family. And right now," she added, looking at the wall clock, "it's going to be naptime soon, and we haven't even finished the feeds."

They had forgotten Claire was there. She rose from the rocker. It was true; the time had passed quickly. "I have to get back," she told them. "I wonder: Would it be all right if I visit again?"

They were both silent for a moment. She realized why. It was an odd request. Children volunteered at many different places; it was required. But after the Assignments, after childhood, people worked at their assigned jobs. They didn't visit around, or try out other things. She tried to come up, quickly, with an explanation that seemed logical.

"I have a lot of free time," Claire said. "It's a slow time

of year at the Hatchery. So I wandered over today to visit Sophia. You know Sophia; she works down the hall, with the next older newchildren?"

They nodded. "Twenty-one to Thirty," the man said. "That's Sophia's group."

"Yes. Anyway, she showed me around a bit. And I can see that you can use an extra pair of hands from time to time. So I'm just offering to help out. If you'd like me to, of course." Claire was aware that she was talking very fast. She was nervous. But the pair didn't seem to notice.

"You know," the man said, "if you wanted to do it on a regular basis, make it official, I think you'd have to fill out some forms."

The young woman agreed. "Get permission," she added.

Claire's heart sank. She could never do that, never fill out official forms. They would identify her immediately as the Birthmother who had been reassigned.

Thirty-six wiggled and wailed. The man carried him to his crib and propped his bottle, but the wailing continued. The man patted the thrashing legs in a vain attempt to soothe him. He looked over at Claire with a wry smile.

"But come on over when you have free time," he said. "Just on a casual basis."

"Maybe I will," Claire said, keeping her voice light, as his had been, "if I have a few moments sometime."

She turned and fled. Thirty-six continued to cry. She could still hear him as she left the building.

* * *

Now she thought of nothing else, of no one else.

———

SIX

I T FELT VERY strange, to have this feeling — whatever this feeling was. Claire had never experienced it before, the yearning she had to be with the newchild, remembering his face — how the solemn light eyes had stared at her, the way his hair curved around at the top of his head and lifted into a curl there, the wrinkling of his forehead, and his quivering chin before he began to cry.

Each family unit was allotted two children, one of each gender, and she had been the younger. They had waited several years after receiving Peter before they had applied for their girl. So Claire had never known an infant or a small child well.

She asked her coworkers, trying to make it a casual question, at the evening meal. "Do any of you remember getting your sibling?"

"Sure," Rolf said. "I was eight when we got my sister."

"I was older," Edith said. "My parents waited quite a long time before they applied for my brother. I think I was eleven."

"I was the second child in my family," Eric said. "Anyone want that last piece of bread?"

They all shook their heads, and Eric took the last slice from the serving plate. "My sister was only three when they got me. I think my mother actually liked little children." He made a face, as if the idea mystified him.

"That's what I was wondering about, actually," Claire explained. "Is it, well, *usual* for people to become really fond of newchildren?"

"Depends what you mean by 'fond,'" Dimitri said. The head of the entire Hatchery operation, Dimitri was an upper-level worker; he was older, and had studied science intensively. "But you know, of course, that infants of any species—"

He stopped and looked at the rest of them, at their blank expressions. "Didn't you study this in evolutionary biology?" he asked.

Finally, at the silence, he chuckled. "All right, so you don't know. I'll explain. Infants are born with big wide-spaced eyes, generally, and large heads, because that makes them look appealing to the adults of the species. So it ensures that they will be fed and cared for. Because they look—"

"Cute?" Edith interrupted.

"Right. *Cute.* If they were born ugly, no one would want to pick them up, or smile at them, or talk to them. They wouldn't get fed. They wouldn't learn to smile or talk. They might not survive, if they didn't appeal to the adults."

"What do you mean by 'any species'?" Eric asked.

"Well, we don't have mammals anymore, because a healthy diet didn't include mammal, and they detracted from the efficiency of the community. But in other areas there are wild creatures of all sorts. And even here, people once had things they called pets. Usually small things: dogs, or cats. It was the same in those species. The newborns were—well, cute. Big eyes, usually. Animals don't smile, though. That's a skill unique to humans."

Claire was fascinated. "What did people do with 'pets'?"

Dimitri shrugged. "Played with them, I think. And also, pets provided company for lonely people. We don't have those now, of course."

"Nobody's lonely here," Edith agreed.

Claire was quiet. She didn't say this, but she was thinking: *I am. I am lonely.* Even as she thought it, though, she realized she didn't really know what the term meant.

The first buzzer sounded, meaning time to finish up.

They began to stack their trays. "Rolf? Edith?" Claire asked. "When you got your siblings—and they were infants, with big eyes, and big heads, and so they were *cute* . . ."

Both of her coworkers shrugged.

"I guess," Edith said.

"Did you think about them all the time, and want to hold them and not ever leave them?"

They looked at Claire as if she had said something preposterous, or unintelligible. She hastened to rephrase her question. "Or maybe I meant your mothers. Did your mothers cuddle your siblings and rock them, and, well—"

"My mother *worked*, just like every other mother. She took very competent care of my sister, of course, and she took her to the Childcare Center every day," Rolf said. "She wasn't a cuddler, though. Not my mother."

"Same with my mother and my brother," Edith said. "My father and I helped her to take care of him, but both of my parents had very demanding jobs. And I had school, of course, and then my training. We were all happy to drop him off every day at the Center.

"We took great pride in him, of course. He was a very intelligent infant," she added primly. "He's studying computer science now."

The final buzzer sounded, and they all rose to go back to work.

I must put Thirty-six out of my mind, Claire told herself.

∗ ∗ ∗

But she found it impossible. Each day, at her microscope, examining the embryonic salmon for flaws in their structure, Claire looked at the large dark spots that were their primitive, unformed eyes. She imagined that they were gazing at her. It was clearly impossible. Those murky, glistening orbs were not capable of vision, not yet; and there was no intelligence within the quivering blob, nothing that craved affection or even attention. But she found herself reminded, again and again, of the pale, long-lashed eyes that had looked up at her briefly, and of the small fingers that had encircled her thumb.

She began to dream of Thirty-six. In one dream, she wore the leather mask again, but they handed her something to hold. It moved tentatively in her arms, and she clasped it tightly, knowing it was he, not wanting them to take him away, weeping behind the mask when they did.

In another, recurrent dream, Thirty-six was here with her, in her small room at the Hatchery, but no one knew. She kept him hidden in a drawer, and opened it from time to time. He would look up and smile at her. Secrecy was forbidden in the community, and the dream of the hidden newchild caused her to wake with a feeling of guilt and dread. But a stronger feeling was the one that stayed with her after that dream: the excitement of opening the drawer and seeing that he was still there, that he was safe and smiling.

As children, within the family unit, they had been required to tell their dreams each morning. For single, working members of the community, like those at the Hatchery, the requirement was set aside. Occasionally, at the morning meal, one of the workers would recount an amusing dream. But there was none of the discussion that had been part of the family ritual. And Claire kept her new dreams private.

But she felt restless now, and different, in ways that she didn't understand. In keeping with the demands of her new job and its meticulousness, its constant analyzing, she tried to examine her own feelings. She had never done so before, had never needed to. For Claire's entire life, her feelings had been those of — what? She searched in her mind for the right descriptive word. *Contentment.* Yes, she had always been content. Everyone was, in the community. Their needs were tended to; there was nothing they lacked, nothing they . . . That was it, Claire realized. She had never *yearned* for anything before. But

now, ever since the day of the birth, she felt a yearning constantly, desperately, to fill the emptiness inside her.

She wanted her child.

Time passed. It became mid-November. She was busy
with her work. But finally she found a time to return to the
Nurturing Center.

———

SEVEN

"HELLO AGAIN!" THE man's greeting was cheerful and welcoming. "I thought you'd forgotten us!"

Claire smiled, pleased that he recognized her. "No. But it's a busy time at work. It's been hard to get away."

"Well," he agreed, "it's almost December. Lots going on."

"Especially here, I imagine." Claire gestured to indicate that she meant the entire Nurturing Center, not only this one room, where the lights were dimmed—it was just past the midday mealtime, and the newchildren were all napping. She and the man spoke in lowered voices. In the corner, his female assistant was quietly folding clean laundry that had just been delivered.

"Yes. We're getting them all ready. Apparently the assignments have all been made. I haven't seen the list yet."

A sudden thought struck Claire. "Do you have a spouse? Could you apply for a child, and then—I suppose this would be against the rules, but—could you choose the one that would be assigned to you?"

He laughed. "Too late for that. Yes, I have a spouse—she works over at Law and Justice. But we already have our complete family: boy first, then girl. And it was quite a while ago that we got them. I was just an assistant then. No clout."

"So you didn't even hint at which ones—?"

He shook his head. "Didn't matter. They match them pretty carefully. We've been very satisfied with ours."

A sound from one of the cribs caught his attention, and he turned. It grew louder: the fussy whimper of an infant. Claire could see a small arm flail.

"You want me to get him?" the assistant asked, looking over.

"No, I will. It's Thirty-six again. Of course!" His voice was resigned and affectionate.

"Could I?" Claire asked, surprising herself.

"Be my guest." The man made a joking gesture toward the crib. "He likes being talked to, and sometimes patting his back helps."

"Or not," the woman in the corner interjected wryly, and the man laughed.

Claire lifted the restless newchild from his crib. "Walk him in the hall," the man suggested, "so he doesn't wake up the others."

Holding him carefully, she carried the wriggly, whimpering bundle out of the room and walked back and forth in the long hallway, jiggling him against her shoulder so that he calmed slightly. He held his head up and looked around with wide eyes. She found herself talking to him, nonsense words and phrases, in a singsong voice. She nuzzled his neck and smelled his milky, powdered scent. He relaxed in her arms, finally, and dozed.

I could walk out of here, Claire thought. *I could leave right now. I could take him.*

Even as she had the thought, she could see the impossibility of it. She had no idea how to feed or care for an infant. No place to hide him, despite her tempting dream of the secret drawer in her room.

The man appeared in the doorway, smiled when he saw that the infant was asleep, and beckoned. "Good job," he whispered when she approached.

They stood in the hallway together by a window that looked out across scattered dwellings and the agricultural fields beyond. Two boys rode past on bicycles, and the man waved, but the boys were talking eagerly together and didn't notice.

The man shrugged and chuckled. "My son," he explained. She watched and could see the boys turn left where the path intersected another just past the Childcare Center. They were probably going to the recreation field.

"You've got just the right touch," the man said, and Claire looked at him questioningly. He nodded toward the sleeping infant she was still holding.

"He hardly sleeps. Classic failure to thrive. So they've decided not to assign him to a family at the Ceremony. We're going to keep him here another year, give him a chance to mature a bit. Some newchildren do take longer than others. Thirty-six has been very difficult.

"I take him back to my dwelling at night," he explained. "The night crew here has been complaining about him. He keeps the others awake. So he spends nights with my family."

He reached for the infant and Claire relinquished him reluctantly. As she passed him from her arms into the man's, she felt something. She pushed the blanket aside and looked at a metal bracelet encircling one tiny ankle.

"What's this?"

"Security. It would set off an alarm if he were removed from the building."

Claire took a quick breath, recalling the thought she had had briefly: *I could take him.*

"All the newchildren wear them. I'm not sure why. Who would want one?" The man chuckled. "I'll take his off when I take him with me at the end of the day."

The infant slept on, and the man murmured to him quietly. "Good boy," she could hear him say. "Coming home with me tonight? That's a good, good boy."

He turned away, still murmuring, and took the newchild back to his crib. Watching and listening, Claire thought she heard the nurturer whisper a name. But she couldn't quite make out what it was. Abe? Was that it? It sounded, she thought, like Abe.

EIGHT

CLAIRE DIDN'T ATTEND the Ceremony. Almost everyone in the community did, every year. But each facility needed to leave someone in charge, and Claire had volunteered to stay at the Hatchery. The Birthmothers, the Vessels, were exempt, and so Claire had not attended the two previous years either; and now she found that she didn't have much interest in the two-day event anymore.

The Naming and Placement of Newchildren was always first on the program, so that the infants could be taken away and cared for during the remaining hours, and wouldn't be disruptive. Claire would have wanted desperately to attend the Ceremony if her own child, Abe (she was trying to think of him now by the name she had overheard) were to be given to a parental pair. But it would be another year for him, and she had little interest in watching the placements of the others.

Neither did she care much about the Matching of Spouses. Like Claire, most people found the Matching boring—important, of course, but with few surprises. When an adult member of the community applied for a spouse, the committee pondered for months, sometimes even *years*, making the selection, matching the characteristics—energy level, intelligence, industriousness, other traits—that would make two people compatible. The spouse pairs were announced each year at the Ceremony and shared a dwelling after that. Their pairing was watched and monitored for three years, after which they could apply for a child, if they wished. The Assignment of the Newchild, when they received one, was actually more exciting than the Matching.

Thinking about it as she wandered the halls of the empty lab, so quiet and unoccupied today, Claire found herself wondering, suddenly, if she would be able to apply for a spouse. As Birthmother, she had not been eligible. But now? Rolf, her coworker, had put in an application and was waiting. And so had Dimitri, she'd heard. Could she? She wasn't old enough yet. But when she was? She didn't know. The regulations for ordinary citizens were so clear, so well known, so carefully followed. But Claire's situation was unusual. And she had been given very little information when she was dismissed and transferred to the Hatchery. It was as if they had lost interest in her. *They.* She wasn't even sure who *they* were. The Elders. The committees. The voices that made announcements over the speakers, like the message this morning: PLEASE GATHER AT THE AUDITORIUM FOR THE OPENING OF THE CEREMONY.

She glanced at the time. It was late morning now. The spouses would be paired, the newchildren named and assigned. Soon there would be a lunch break, with tables set up and lunch packets distributed, outside the Auditorium. Then they would reconvene for the beginning of the Advance in Age and the rituals of growing older.

The younger children were presented in groups: all the Sevens, for example, receiving their front-buttoned jackets; the Nines, brought to the stage and given their first bicycles to great applause. Haircuts for all the Tens, with the little girls losing their braids, and then the sweepers coming quickly to the stage to remove the shorn hair. But the Advance in Age Ceremonies usually moved quickly along, to applause — and some laughter as well, because every year someone burst into tears for one reason or another, or felt compelled to show off on the stage and did something foolish.

Claire had participated in those rituals throughout her childhood. She didn't mind missing them now.

The Ceremony of Twelve, which would begin on the second morning, was always the highlight. Here was when the unexpected could happen, as the children received their Life Assignments. It had always been fun, watching the Assignments given out. Until her own, of course.

Well. It was in the past. But she was happy not to be there today, in the audience, watching as other young girls heard that they too had been found fit only to breed.

It seemed odd, the silence with everyone gone for the day. There was not much, really, for her to do; she was simply required to be there, to be certain nothing went awry. But everything—the temperature in the labs, the humidity, even the lighting—was carefully calibrated and controlled. Claire checked the screen of her computer periodically for incoming Hatchery messages, but nothing was urgent.

She glanced through a window at the supply boat that was moored at the dock. It had arrived at a bad time. With the Ceremony taking place, they would have to wait two days before they could unload. Probably, she realized, they'd be happy to have some time free of work. She wondered what the crew was doing on this unexpected vacation. She had watched them previously, and heard them, lifting and stacking and carrying and directing. Their clothes were different;

they didn't wear the loose-fitting tunic of the community. And they spoke with a slight accent, an inflection that was unfamiliar.

Claire had never been curious about those from Elsewhere. It was part of the contentment she had always known. *Here* had always been enough.

Now, through the window, she stared at the heavy-laden moored boat and found herself wondering about its crew.

NINE

T HAT LUNCH WAS pretty awful, wasn't it?"

Eric entered the lobby of the Hatchery with the others at the end of the day. The group was noisy and laughing, obviously happy to be finished with the hours of ritual, sitting, paying attention, politely applauding.

"It wasn't so bad," one of the other workers replied. "Just wasn't enough of it! I'm still hungry."

Claire was seated at the receptionist's desk. "It's almost time for dinner," she told them. "How was the Ceremony?"

"Fine," someone said. "They got all the way through the Elevens, so there's only the Ceremony of Twelve left for tomorrow morning."

"Good. It went smoothly, then. No children misbehaved or had a tantrum," Claire said, laughing.

"Nope. No surprises at all," Edith told her.

"Except maybe for Dimitri," Eric announced.

"Dimitri?"

Everyone chuckled. "He thought he'd be assigned a spouse. He was on the edge of his seat. But they didn't call his name."

"Oops. That means he has another whole year to wait," Claire said.

"Or more!" Eric pointed out. "There have been people who waited *years* for matching."

"Well, it's for the best," Edith commented. "There probably wasn't a good match for him available this time."

A young man whose name Claire didn't know had been listening. "He only applied for a spouse because he wanted a dwelling," he said. "He's tired of living in the dorm." He turned, seeing Dimitri come through the door. "Even though he gets a special suite, for being director. Isn't that right, Dimitri? You're sick of the dorm, right?"

Dimitri crushed the program he was carrying into a wadded ball, and tossed it at the young man. "I'm sick of living with *you*, that's all!" He grinned, picked up the paper where it had fallen, and tossed it into the trash receptacle.

They hung their jackets on the row of pegs beside the front door. "Everything quiet here, Claire?" someone asked.

She nodded. "A couple of the boatmen came ashore and went for a walk. I saw them strolling along the river path."

"Those guys are so odd," Eric commented. "They never talk to anyone."

"Maybe it's against their rules," Claire suggested.

"Could be. Elsewhere probably has completely different rules."

"Actually, talking to them might be against *our* rules. Has anyone checked?" Edith asked.

Everyone groaned and most of them glanced at the large monitor on the receptionist's desk.

It occurred to Claire that she could check on the rules and answer her own question about whether she could apply for a spouse. But did she care, really? Enough to make her way through the lengthy index and perhaps find her answer in a sub-subparagraph or footnote? Probably not, she thought.

The loud rasp of the buzzer summoned them all to the cafeteria for the evening meal. She rose and found her place in the line. From a window in the hallway, she noticed two members of the boat crew lounging on the deck of the vessel. It was heavily loaded with crates of cargo, and the two young men sat side by side, leaning against a sealed container. Each of them held a small cylinder to his mouth, and it appeared that they sucked smoke from it and then blew the smoke into the air. It was an odd custom that she had not seen before, and she wondered what its purpose was. Perhaps it was a medicinal inhaler of some sort.

The line moved forward. Conversations, laughter, and comments interrupted her thoughts. Claire approached the stack of trays, took hers from the top, and saw that Edith and Jeannette had saved a seat for her at their table. She moved ahead, holding her tray out to the serving person behind the counter, and put the boat crew out of her mind.

"What was the Naming of Newchildren like?" she asked them after she had sat down with her tray of food. "Were there any surprising names?"

"Not really," Jeannette said, "except I was startled to hear that one, a boy, was given the name Paul. That was my father's name."

"But they can't use the same name twice!" Edith said. "There are never two people in the community with the same name!"

"But they do *regive* names," Claire pointed out, "after someone is gone."

"Right. So that means my father is gone. I was surprised to hear it," Jeannette said.

"When did you see him last?" Claire asked. She could remember her own parents, but it had been several years, and details about them had begun to fade.

Jeannette thought, and shrugged. "Probably five years. He worked in Food Production, and I never go over that way. I see the woman who was my mother now and then, though, because she's in the landscaping crew. Not very long ago I noticed her trimming the bushes over at the edge of the recreation field. She waved when she saw me."

"Nice," Edith said, offhandedly. "You want the rest of that salad? Can I have it?" Jeannette nodded, and Edith reached for the half-empty plate that had been set to the side.

"Paul's a handsome name," Claire said, feeling a little sorry for Jeannette, though she didn't know exactly why. "It's nice when they reuse a good one. I remember back when I was a Ten, they named a newchild Wilhelmina, and everyone cheered, because everyone had been fond of the previous Wilhelmina before she entered the House of the Old. So when she was gone, it was nice to reuse her name."

"I remember that. I was there," Edith said.

"Me too," Jeannette recalled. "Nobody cheered when they named the new Paul. But I think there was a feeling of satisfaction. People liked my father," she said. "He was nice. Very quiet. But nice."

They finished their meal in silence. Then, at the sound of the buzzer, they stacked their plates and began to tidy their table.

* * *

It was dusk. The others were tired after the long day of the Ceremony. Anticipating another day of it tomorrow, they had drifted off to their rooms early, after the evening meal. But Claire found herself restless after the day indoors. She decided to take a walk.

The path along the river was shaded and pleasant at this time of day. Ordinarily she would have encountered others walking, and exchanged greetings. But no one was out and about this evening; it had been a long day for them all. Claire wandered beside the water until she approached the huge bridge. It was forbidden to cross it without special permission, and she had no idea what lay beyond, on the other side. There was nothing visible but trees. It was simply Elsewhere. She had heard people say that occasionally, though rarely, small groups were taken to visit other communities. But perhaps it was just a rumor. Claire herself had never known anyone who had seen Elsewhere.

Standing at the base of the massive concrete supports that formed the foundation for the bridge, Claire measured it with her eyes. The barge that was now moored by the Hatchery must have barely fit beneath.

If she crossed the intersecting road here, she would continue along the river path and pass the large barn that housed official vehicles. Citizens made their way around the community only by bicycle, but large deliveries were transported by trucks, and sometimes maintenance required heavy equipment. It was all stored here. Claire remembered a few years back, when she had been a Ten or a Nine, the boys who were her agemates had all been fascinated by the vehicle barn. They had, almost all of them, yearned to be assigned a career involving transportation so that they could be trained to drive the equipment.

But it had never interested Claire, and it didn't this evening. She turned onto the main stretch of road and walked to the northwest, away from the river, with the central plaza spread out on her left. She passed the Auditorium, which stood at the end of the plaza; earlier in the day the community had gathered in throngs on its steps, and they would be there again in the morning. But now, at dusk, the plaza was empty and the large building that dominated its southwest border was quiet and seemed unoccupied.

She realized that she was walking toward the Nurturing Center. She could turn left there and continue on past the

Infirmary and the Childcare Center, making a large loop that would take her back to the Hatchery.

"Hi there!"

The man's voice startled her. The entire community had been so still. But looking up, Claire saw the bicycle stopped at the corner of the plaza. She recognized the nurturer who had been so pleasant to her during her visits. She smiled, waved, and walked toward the corner where he waited, one foot on the ground, balancing his bike.

He put one finger to his lips as she approached. "Shhh." Then he gestured toward the back of his bicycle, where a carrying basket had been attached. As she came near, she could see that there was a sleeping infant in the basket. "Finally he's asleep," the man whispered. "I'm taking him home for the night."

Claire nodded and smiled down at Newchild Thirty-six.

"Were you at the Ceremony?" the man asked.

She shook her head. "I volunteered to stay at the Hatchery. I've been to enough Ceremonies." She kept her voice lowered, as he had.

The nurturer chuckled softly. "I know the feeling," he said. "But it was fun for me today. Part of my job is giving the newchildren to their parental units. The new mothers and fathers are always so excited.

"I'm glad we get to nurture this one for another year, though," he added, reaching to touch the edge of the basket. "He seems pretty special."

Claire nodded in agreement, not trusting herself to speak.

"Gotta go," the man said. He placed his right foot on the uptilted pedal of the bike. "Tomorrow's a big day for my family unit. Our son's a Twelve this year. Lots of nervousness and apprehension."

"Yes, I'm sure," Claire said.

"Come visit us again at the Center? We'll have a new batch of newborns arriving soon. And this guy will be there too, of course! His playmates will all be gone, to their new family units, so he'll enjoy visitors."

"I will." She smiled at him, and he set off again on his bike, toward the area of family dwellings. Claire stood there watching the little basket jiggle gently as the bicycle moved along the path. Then she turned away.

TEN

PPARENTLY THE CEREMONY of Twelve
had concluded with a surprise. When the Hatchery workers
returned at the end of the second day, they were murmuring
about it.

The second day of the Ceremony was always a long day.
New Twelves were called to the stage individually and their
attributes described. It was the first time that the youngsters
were singled out and attention paid to the accomplishments
of their childhood. A boy might be praised for his scholarship,
and the audience reminded of his special abilities in science.
Or the Chief Elder might even call attention to an especially
pretty face—it was always embarrassing when that happened,
because in the community attractiveness was never considered
an asset to be mentioned—and the Twelve thus described

would blush, and the audience laugh. The community was always attentive and supportive; each adult had been through this experience and knew how important it was. But going one by one did make for a long time on the second day.

"The Chief Elder skipped one Twelve," Rolf explained to Claire at the evening meal. "She went from Eighteen to Twenty."

"We all cringed. We thought she'd made a mistake." Edith straightened and tensed, demonstrating with her posture how nervous she and the others had been.

"*Everybody* thought so. Did you hear the murmur go through the Auditorium?" someone asked.

"And the boy she skipped? Number Nineteen? I could see him from where I was sitting. He was completely nonplussed!" A young man at the end of the table grinned.

"So what happened?" Claire asked.

"Well," Rolf explained, "after she finished with the last one—"

"Number Fifty?"

"Yes. But of course she had only called up forty-nine to the stage. Then she apologized to the audience."

"The Chief Elder *apologized?*" It was hard to believe.

Rolf nodded. "She laughed a little. She could see we were all sort of nervous. So she reassured us, and apologized for making us uncomfortable. Then she called the boy, number Nineteen, to the stage."

"He looked as if he was going to throw up," Eric said, laughing.

"I don't blame him," Claire said. She found herself feeling sorry for the boy. It must have been an awful moment for him. "What did she say to him?"

"That he hadn't been assigned—which we all knew, of course. But then—this was the surprise. She said he'd been 'selected.'"

"Selected for what?" Claire had never heard of such a thing before.

Rolf raised an eyebrow and shrugged. "I don't know."

"Didn't she say?"

"Yes, but I didn't understand what she was talking about. Did any of you?" He looked around at his coworkers at the table.

"Not really," Edith said. "It was important, though. It had to do with the Giver and the Receiver."

"Whoever *they* are," someone murmured.

"Yes, it sounded really important," Eric agreed.

"Do you think the boy understood?"

They all shook their heads. "He looked completely confused," Edith said. "I felt sorry for him."

The cleanup buzzer sounded. They began to gather their plates and forks. "Who was he?" Claire asked. She was still fascinated by the idea of the selected boy.

"Never heard of him before. But we all know his name now, don't we?" Eric said with a laugh.

"What do you mean?"

"The whole community called out his name. It was a kind of ceremonial . . . What would you call it? A *recognition*. We all shouted the name over and over. Jonas!"

Rolf, Edith, and some other workers joined in. "Jonas! Joooonas!"

People at all the other tables looked up. Some seemed amused, others a little worried. Then they too called the name. "JOOOONAS! JOOOONAS!"

The final buzzer sounded and they fell quiet. People looked around at each other in the sudden silence. Then they stood to leave the room. Dinner had ended.

ELEVEN

CLAIRE WALKED AGAIN along the river before retiring. Once more she was alone. Usually the workers took walks in pairs or groups, but again tonight the others were tired after the unusual day. One by one they had gone to their rooms, some of them carrying the readers that they were supposed to study in order to advance in their jobs. From time to time Claire turned her reader on and skimmed the material, but she had little interest in it. She had not been selected for this job by a committee that had perceived her fascination with fish. They had simply sent her here because they needed a place to put her after her failure as a Birthmother.

She had read the manual pages listlessly several times, guiltily aware of her own disinterest. She had memorized a phrase: *cleavage, epiboly, and organogenesis*. She could still say it but realized that she had completely forgotten what it referred to.

"Activation of cortical alveoli," Claire murmured, walking. That was another phrase, a heading she had memorized in the manual.

"What?" a nearby voice asked, startling her. She looked up.

It was one of the boat crew, a young man in shorts and a sweater. He wore dark laced shoes made from a kind of canvas, with thick, textured soles that Claire assumed prevented him from slipping on the wet deck of the vessel. She wasn't frightened. He was smiling and looked quite friendly, not at all anyone to be nervous about. But she had never spoken to any of the boatmen before, or they to her.

"Is that a different language?" he asked, grinning. He had the distinctive accent she had overheard.

"No," Claire answered politely. "We speak the same language."

"Then what is 'amplification of corsical alveoli'?"

Claire couldn't help laughing. He had gotten quite close to her words, but still he was amusingly wrong.

"I was just trying to memorize something for work," she

explained. "A phase of embryonal development. It's a little boring, I'm afraid, unless you are fascinated by fish. I work at the Hatchery."

"Yes, I've seen you there."

"You've had to wait to unload because of our annual Ceremony."

He shrugged. "Not a problem. Nice to rest from the work. We'll unload tomorrow and be on our way."

He had begun to walk beside her and now they were approaching the bridge. They stopped there for a moment and watched the turbulent churning of the water.

"Do you ever worry that a bridge might be too low? Do you encounter other bridges? Might your boat be too tall for a low one?"

He chuckled. "Not my job to worry," he said. "The captain has the charts and knows the routes. We're six point three meters. Never bumped a bridge yet, or knocked a crew member into the drink."

"We're required to learn to swim but we're not allowed in the river," she found herself telling him.

"Required? Who requires it?"

Claire felt slightly flustered. "It's just one of the rules of the community. We learn in a pool. When we're five."

The young man laughed. "No rules like that where I come from. I learned when my dad threw me into a pond. I was eight, I think. Swallowed half the pond before I made my way to the dock, and my dad laughing the whole time. I bawled when I got out and so he threw me back in."

"Oh. Goodness." Claire didn't know quite what to say. She couldn't imagine the scene. Her own swimming class had been orderly and precise, with special instructors. No heartless laughing men called *Dad.*

"After that I could swim. Wouldn't want to try in this river, though." He looked down at the fast-moving dark water, how it pounded against some rocks near the bank, then slid splashing over them, so that they disappeared briefly, then re-emerged with foam sliding down their slick, mossy sides.

Some years before, a child named Caleb had fallen into the river near here and the entire community had performed the Ceremony of Loss. Claire remembered it: the shock, the hushed voices, and how parents had kept their children near-by afterward, and warned them, sternly, again and again. She thought she remembered hearing that the parents of the lost child, Caleb, had been chastised. It was the job of parental units to protect their children from harm. Caleb's parents had not performed well.

Yet this boy's father had thrown him into deep water, and laughed; and now he himself laughed at the memory. It seemed so strange.

They chatted. He asked about her job and they discussed fish aimlessly for a while. In a place far away—he gestured—he had seen some almost as large as the boat. She thought he might be joking, but he seemed serious. Could it be true? She wanted to ask him where his boat would go next. Where it came from; where *he* came from. It was Elsewhere, really, that she wondered about. But she felt uneasy. She was afraid that asking such questions might somehow be against the rules. Anyway, it was beginning to get dark, and she knew she must return. "I have to get back," she said.

He turned with her and they walked toward the Hatchery buildings. "Would you like to see aboard?" he asked suddenly.

"I don't think it's allowed," she told him apologetically.

"The captain wouldn't mind. He often has visitors come aboard. We're a sea-river vessel. Very unusual. People like to come aboard and look around."

"Sea-river?"

"Yes. We don't stay just to the river. We can go to sea as well. Most riverboats can't."

"Sea," Claire said. She hadn't the slightest idea what that meant.

He misunderstood her. "Yes, they want to see the galley, and the wheelhouse, all of it. Very curious. The captain is proud to show them around. Or a crew member can. We have a crew of ten."

"I meant that *I'm* not allowed. I have to stay at my work, I'm afraid."

They had reached the fork in the path that meant they would separate, he heading back along the river to his boat. She would turn here toward the Hatchery entrance.

"Too bad," he said. "I would enjoy showing it to you. And you could meet Marie!"

"Marie?"

"She's the cook on the boat." He laughed. "That surprises some people, that we have a woman aboard."

Claire was puzzled. "Why would people be surprised by that?"

"Boating is men's work, mostly."

"Oh." Claire frowned. Men's work? Women's work? Here in the community, there was no such difference.

"Yes, I would have enjoyed meeting Marie, and seeing the inside of the boat," Claire told him. "Maybe when you return.

Perhaps our rules will change. Or I might apply for special permission."

"Good night, then," he said, and turned toward the boat path.

Claire waved and stood watching as he disappeared beyond the overhanging bushes. Then she turned away. "Sea," she repeated to herself, wondering what it might mean. *Sea*.

TWELVE

THE WEEKS PASSED. Except for the secret she carried always with her, the secret of the baby, each day was much like the one before, and the one after. It had always been so, Claire realized. There had been no surprises in her life, or in anyone's within the community. Just the Assignment Ceremony, at Twelve: the disappointing surprise, then, of being named Birthmother. And later, of course, the shock of her failure.

But now it was again the dull routine of daily life in the community. The rasping voice through the speaker, making announcements, giving reminders. The rituals and rules. The mealtimes, and the work. Always the work. Claire had been given increasingly more demanding tasks in the lab, but they were still tedious and repetitious. She performed the work well but often found herself restless and bored.

What was it she had been told about this year's Ceremony? A boy had been singled out. It wasn't clear why, and no mention had been made of it again. Perhaps that boy—she remembered that his name was Jonas—was doing something different, and interesting. But she couldn't imagine what it might be.

She had visited the Nurturing Center again but been turned away. After all the newchildren had been assigned parental units at the Ceremony, the Center was almost empty. Newborns were beginning to arrive to start the year's population. But when Claire stopped by, though she was greeted pleasantly by the receptionist, she was told that they had no need for extra help until the numbers increased.

"It's actually vacation time for nurturers," the young woman explained. "Most of them are volunteering at other places while we wait for more infants." She peered at her computer screen. "We have two arriving next week."

She smiled at Claire. "Right now?" she said. "No need for help. But thanks for stopping by. Maybe in a couple of months."

Claire wanted to ask, *But what about Thirty-six? He's still here, isn't he? He wasn't assigned, remember? You're keeping him another year. He needs someone to play with him, doesn't he? Couldn't I be the one?*

But of course she said nothing. It was clear that the receptionist, however polite, was disinterested and wished Claire would leave. Reluctantly she turned away and left the building.

From time to time, though, she saw the man who worked there, the one who had had a special fondness for Thirty-six. She waved one afternoon when, out for a walk after lunch, she saw him across the Central Plaza, on his bicycle. He was apparently out on an errand; there was a package in his front basket. He smiled and waved back in reply. She noticed that his bicycle now had a child seat on the rear, replacing the carrying basket that had once held Thirty-six. The little seat was empty, but the fact that it was there gave Claire hope. It seemed that perhaps the nurturer was still taking him home at night. And he would be sitting up now. Claire pictured his sturdy little body and how he would grin in delight to feel the fresh air and see the trees.

She began to time her walks, carefully finishing in the lab and cleaning up there so that she could leave work and stroll during shift-change time. She walked to the part of the community that seemed most likely: the northeast corner of the Central Plaza, where the Nurturing Center stood and then the dwellings began, across the main boulevard. She had hopes of seeing the nurturer heading back to his dwelling for the evening meal, with little Abe riding behind him.

Finally her timing was right. There they were.

"Hello there!" Claire called.

The man looked up, recognized her, and eased his bicycle to a standstill, balancing it with his right foot on the path. "How are you?" he asked cheerfully. "It's Claire, isn't it?"

She was pleased that he remembered her name. She wasn't wearing her nametag—it was still pinned to the lab coat she had hung up when she left work. And it had been three months now since they had seen each other.

"Yes, that's right. Claire."

"Nice to see you. It's been a while."

"I stopped by but they said they didn't need me to help out because the newchildren had all been assigned."

He nodded. "All but this one!"

Claire hadn't wanted to look directly at Abe. Not at first. But now, since he had mentioned the infant in the child seat, she turned her attention there and smiled at the child, who was busily examining a leaf in his hands. He must have pulled it from a bush as they rode past. She watched as he held the leaf to his own mouth and tasted it with a puzzled, uncertain look. She could see that he had two teeth.

"You're still taking him to your dwelling at night?"

The nurturer nodded. "He still doesn't sleep well. It annoys the night workers at the Center, especially now that they have some newborns to tend.

"But my family unit enjoys him. My daughter—her name is Lily—tried to convince me that we should apply for what they call a variance."

"A variance? What's that?"

"An exception to a rule. Lily thought we should try to convince them that *three* children would be appropriate for our family."

"And did you apply?" Claire asked.

He laughed. "Nope. My spouse would have applied for an annulment of our pairing if I had! This guy will be assigned to his own family next time around. He'll be fine. But in the meantime, it's fun having him at our dwelling nights." He turned to look behind him at the baby. "Oh, great," he groaned. "Eating a leaf. Well, I've been trained to sponge away spit-up. Part of the job!"

Claire could see that he was beginning to shift his balance and move his right foot toward the bike pedal. "Are you allowed to use his name in public now?" she asked quickly, trying to keep them there for another minute or so. "I remember that you were using it secretly."

The man hesitated. "Actually," he said a little guiltily, "we do use it at home. But we're not supposed to. He's still just Thirty-six until he's assigned.

"So I'm afraid I can't tell you what it is. But it's a good one."

"I'm sure it is. They always choose carefully, don't they? I like your daughter's name. Lily. It's pretty."

He smiled. "I have to be off. He's happy now, with that leaf to chew. But wait till he wants real food. He'll start yowling. And it's almost mealtime."

"It was nice to see you," she told him.

"You too. I'll tell my daughter that you think her name is pretty. She'll love hearing that." He rolled his eyes, as if it were too silly for words. "And of course, just to be fair and equal, I have to tell you that my son has a nice name as well."

Claire laughed. "I'm sure he does."

The nurturer started off slowly on the bicycle. Behind him, strapped into the little seat, his mouth speckled with leaf fragments, the infant looked back and grinned at Claire.

"It's Jonas," the man called, referring to his son, and pedaled away toward the group of dwellings where he lived.

THIRTEEN

SHE ARRANGED HER days so that she would see them often, the man and the infant on the back of his bicycle. She became accustomed to the times, morning and evening, when the two of them made the short journey to and from the Nurturing Center, and she took walks then, after breakfast and before the evening meal. Often she encountered them, and usually the man stopped to chat, though sometimes he was rushed and had to hurry on. Little Abe (though she carefully referred to him as Thirty-six) knew her now, and grinned when he saw her. The man had taught him to wave his small hand when she said "Bye-bye" and they rode on. It became something to look forward to, a pleasant interruption to the long hours of lab work, which held little interest for Claire.

He imitated her. She poked her own tongue into her

cheek, making a bump. He stared at it, then pushed his own small tongue into his own cheek. She wrinkled her nose. So did he. Then she did the two things together, her tongue into her cheek, her nose scrunched; solemnly he did the same, and they both began to laugh.

He was growing. Though he was technically now simply a One—every newchild born his year had become a One at the Ceremony—she calculated the months from the day of his birth. It had been, now, ten months.

"He's trying to walk," the nurturer told her one morning.

"He's strong," she said, gazing at the sturdy small legs dangling from the child seat on the back of the bike.

"Yes. We hold his hands and he takes steps. One day soon he'll be on his own. My spouse will have to put things high up on the counters. He grabs at everything."

"You have to be careful," Claire said, almost talking to herself, thinking about how difficult it must be to care for an infant.

"Of course that was part of my training," the nurturer explained reassuringly. "And I've taught my spouse and children.

"Hey!" he said suddenly, laughing. He turned. The newchild was tugging at his uniform. "Don't mess me all up! This was just delivered from the laundry!"

He turned to Claire. "Could you reach into that carrying

case and get his hippo?" He pointed to a zippered case behind the child seat.

"His what?" Claire pulled the zipper open.

"His comfort object. It's called hippo."

"Oh." She reached in and took out the stuffed toy. All small children had comfort objects. They came in various shapes. Hers, she remembered, had been called badger.

The newchild's eyes lit up when he saw it. "Po," he said, and reached for the toy. Claire handed it to him; he hugged it with a satisfied sigh and began to chew on one of its small ears.

"I think they might be ready to have you stop by and help again," the nurturer suggested. "We have a batch of new ones.

"And the little ones take my time," he added. "You could come play with Thirty-six and keep him out of mischief."

"I will." She waved when they rode on, and called "Bye-bye," but the newchild was preoccupied with his hippo and didn't even hear her.

* * *

She saw Marie for the first time. The cargo boat had come and gone now three times since the day she had met and talked to its crew member. Each month it arrived and remained at dock only a day, long enough for the unloading. She recognized the boy she had walked with once, and waved when she saw him on the deck. He waved back. Claire almost felt that if he repeated his invitation for a tour, she would say yes, though she would ask permission first, she decided. She would check with the Hatchery director.

But they came and went so quickly that the boy (odd, she thought of him as her friend though in truth they had shared only one brief conversation) did not come ashore.

And now they were moored again, but she didn't see him. Other crew members scrambled about, tending lines, lifting crates, but the dark-haired boy wasn't there. Claire glanced over at the activity on the boat through the windows of the lab from time to time, and it became clear that he was no longer part of the crew.

She mentioned it to her coworker, Heather, phrasing it carefully. "There used to be a dark-haired boy who worked on the boat, but—"

"Lots of dark-haired boys. Look. There are three right there, piling those crates."

Heather was correct. Three muscular young men were lifting and straightening some heavy boxes. Each had dark hair.

"Yes, but I meant a different one, one who used to wave to me. He and I talked once."

Heather shrugged. "They come and go. Different ones almost every time. Some stay awhile, others not so much. It's not like here, where we get assigned. I think they can decide about their jobs. If it gets boring, they leave. Or maybe something better comes along."

"Look! Who's that?" Claire pointed. A heavy woman had come from the interior of the boat and stood on the deck, watching the crew at work. She wore a stained apron stretched across her wide middle and tied in back. Her light hair was pulled back into a knot, but it was unruly, and as the girls watched, the woman smoothed and retied it. Then she lowered herself and sat on a thick pile of rope, leaning back against the cabin wall, and took a few deep breaths.

"Mind your feet, Marie!" a crew member called as he passed her on the deck, guiding a thick package that swayed in a net as the winch moved it up and outward.

"Mind your own feet," she called back with a hearty laugh. But she moved her legs aside so that he could get by.

"The boy told me there was a woman aboard," Claire said. "I'd forgotten her name. But now I remember it's Marie. She's the cook."

"Cook?" Heather looked puzzled.

Claire shrugged. "Well, they can't have their meals delivered the way we do. Not when they're on the river." *Or the sea,* she added in her mind. "So I guess Marie prepares the food."

"Her apron has its share of it," Heather said, referring

to the darkened, spattered patches on the cloth, and she and Claire both laughed. Their own uniforms were spotless. Their clothing was collected every morning, laundered meticulously, and delivered each evening.

"Would you go aboard, if they invited you?" Claire asked Heather. "Just for a tour?"

"You mean like when people come to visit the Hatchery and we show them around?"

Claire nodded. Often small school groups came to visit and were given a little lesson on the life cycle of fish.

"I might, if it's allowed," Heather said with a shrug. "But I'm not really that interested in boats."

They watched as Marie rose heavily from where she had been relaxing, reentered the cabin, and disappeared into the dark interior. Claire found herself wondering what it looked like in there. Where did Marie sleep? And how did it feel to be on the river, to stop at other communities? Did people everywhere look the same? The boy she had met wore strange-looking shoes and unfamiliar clothing. He had a different speech inflection, she recalled. And the different hairstyles on the boys was startling; some had almost clean-shaven heads; others, long hair tied back like a girl's. Here in the community, each age had a prescribed hairstyle. But no boy ever had long hair.

Marie, with her oddly light hair, was startling in other ways. She was large, especially broad across her hips, and with a double chin. No one in the community looked like that. They were all of the same proportions. Their food delivery was calibrated to their size. Claire remembered a time some years ago when the weekly report showed that her mother's weight had risen slightly. Her mother had been a little embarrassed, and perhaps annoyed, when the next meal deliveries included special weight-loss meals designated for her. She had eaten them, of course — it was required, and there were no alternatives — until the report showed that her size was under control once again.

"We'd better get back to work," Heather murmured. She turned from the window.

"I'm just going out for a minute. I want to check the temperature in the lower holding pond." Claire could see Heather frown suspiciously.

"Well," Heather said after a moment, "mind your feet. It's muddy by the pond."

"Mind your own feet," Claire replied with a laugh as she left the room.

She had no intention of going aboard, even if they asked her. But the lower pond was quite close to the river. The boat almost grazed the bank there, and she felt a yearning to go close to it. Odd, she thought, but she felt almost *lured* by the boat, in the same way that she found herself drawn to the Nurturing Center and the newchild who had been wrested from her body almost a year before. There was no relationship between the two, but Claire was feeling increasingly connected to both.

Standing beside the pond's edge, she looked up at the vessel's smooth side toward the low railing that edged the deck. The huge crates were all stacked now, and tightly roped in. There were places, near the cargo, where there was no railing. How easy it would be to slip on the wet deck and fall into the river below! *Mind your feet.* She remembered the young man's shoes with their ridged soles. Boat shoes, she had guessed, made specially for the wet deck.

Claire was still standing there when the boat's engine made a sudden low sound. In a moment it was a steady hum and she could see a spurt of dark smoke from a small stack. Some voices called, and she saw a crew member pull loops of rope loose from the moorings. He tossed them to another young man on the deck, and then jumped across and steadied himself as the boat slid away toward the center of the river.

From the building nearby she heard the buzzer that announced the midday meal. She turned and walked back toward the Hatchery as behind her the cargo boat moved with increasing speed toward the bridge and beyond. Behind it, at its broad stern, foam burst; then the river closed around the interruption and resumed its own form again, as if the boat had never been there.

Claire sighed. Returning to her ordinary life seemed so unappealing. She would go tomorrow, she decided, to visit little Abe.

FOURTEEN

ON THE TWELVE-MONTH anniversary of the day he had been born to her, Claire taught him to say her name. He had been officially a One since the previous ceremony, but now, Claire thought secretly, he is truly one year old.

The nurturer chuckled when he watched the newchild toddle over to her, calling, "Claire!" with a grin. "He's a bright boy," he said. "I just wish we could get his sleeping-pattern behavior squared away. If he's not ready to be placed with a family unit by the time of the next Ceremony, well . . ."

"What?" Claire asked when his voice drifted away without completing the thought.

"To be honest, I don't know. They can't give him to parents if he doesn't sleep. It would interrupt their work habits to be kept awake at night. But we can't keep him here indefinitely."

"Not even if he goes home with you at night? He's fine here in the daytime. He hardly ever cries. Look at him!" Together they gazed at Thirty-six, who was seated on the floor, busily arranging wooden blocks in a stack. Feeling their gaze, he looked over. Impishly, he wrinkled his nose and thrust his tongue into his cheek, making the funny face that Claire had taught him. She made the same skewed face in reply and they both laughed.

"I can't keep taking him home forever. My spouse is already somewhat annoyed about it. The children enjoy him, though. He's been sleeping in my son's room. He seems to do well there. But . . ."

Again he failed to finish his thought. The nurturer shrugged and went to the other section of the room where younger infants needed attention.

"I wonder if I . . ." Claire murmured, then fell silent. Of course she couldn't. Unmatched people weren't given newchildren. Even if it were possible, how could she care for him? It was enough to contemplate (and she had) how she could manage a small infant. But now, so well acquainted with this growing, active twelve-month-old boy, she could see clearly that they required more, not less, care as they grew. He had to be watched constantly. Taught language. Fed carefully. Bathed and dressed and . . .

She turned away, feeling tears well in her eyes. What on earth was the matter with her? No one else seemed to feel this kind of passionate attachment to other humans. Not to a newchild, not to a spouse, or a coworker, or friend. She had not felt it toward her own parents or brother. But now, toward this wobbly, drooling toddler —

"Bye-bye," she whispered to him, and he looked up at her and wiggled his fingers. It never distressed him when she left. He knew she'd be back.

But Claire choked back tears as she pedaled her bike back to the Hatchery. More and more she despised her life: the dull routine of the job, the mindless conversation with her coworkers, the endless repetition of her days. She wanted only to be with the child, to feel the warm softness of his neck as he curled against her, to whisper to him and to sense how he listened happily to her voice. It was not right to have these feelings, which were growing stronger as the weeks passed. Not normal. Not permitted. She knew that. But she did not know how to make them go away.

* * *

From time to time she saw the nurturer's son. *Jonas*, she remembered. Months before she had seen his father wave to him one afternoon when he rode by with a friend, the two of them on their way apparently to the recreation field. The two boys had seemed carefree, calling to each other, racing their bicycles along the path.

He seemed different now, to Claire. She saw him one evening walking along the river, alone, deep in thought. Although he didn't know her, and there would have been no real reason beyond politeness for a greeting, it was nonetheless customary for citizens to acknowledge one another with a nod or smile. But Jonas had not looked up as she passed him. It was not an intentional snub, she realized. It was that his mind was somewhere else. He seemed somehow troubled, she thought, and that was rare in a youngster.

She recalled that he had been singled out in some way at last year's Ceremony. Her coworkers, in describing it, had chanted his name — *Jonas, Jonas* — as apparently the audience had. But they had not really known what his . . . What had they called it? Selection, that was it — what his selection had meant.

But his father, the nurturer, spoke of him warmly and without hesitation. *He's been sleeping in my son's room,* he had said cheerfully of Thirty-six. So perhaps she had simply happened on the boy at an unusual moment, when he had something on his mind, probably a school assignment. Claire could remember how troubling her own homework had been at times.

She saw him several more times, always on his bicycle, alone, after school hours. He was a Twelve now, and all Twelves would be working hard this year on the preparation related to their Assignments. Usually after school they would separate from their age-mates and go to the studies required for their future jobs. Sophia had been required to take infant-care classes, she recalled; and in fact Sophia had told her that even now, several years after their Ceremony year, the scholarly Marcus was still studying engineering. One girl in her group had taken up the study of law, as Claire's brother had six years earlier, and still went each day after school to the hall of Law and Justice for training.

One afternoon she found herself watching Jonas as he rode his bicycle away from the school building, which she could see from the front of the Hatchery. He turned left at the end of the educational buildings and seemed to be heading toward the House of the Old. So perhaps, she thought, that was his Assignment: the care of the elderly. But what was so special about that? What would make an entire audience rise to their feet and chant his name?

Later, one day while walking, she continued past the House of the Old, turned down a path, and discovered a very small structure attached at the rear of the building. It had a door, a few windows, and nothing else. Most buildings had an informational plaque explaining the purpose of the structure. HATCHERY LABORATORY. NURTURING CENTER. BICYCLE REPAIR. But this undistinguished rectangle had only an unobtrusive, meaningless label on the door. ANNEX.

Claire had never heard of the Annex. She had no idea what could be housed inside. But she had a feeling that this was where the boy Jonas was spending his training time. She wondered vaguely if what was happening in there was causing him to become so oddly solemn and solitary.

What could Jonas have been selected for?

FIFTEEN

C LAIRE LOOKED AROUND suddenly at her coworkers during the morning meal. Ever since her arrival at the Hatchery over a year earlier, she had felt different from them. They didn't seem to notice. They were friendly enough, and included her in their outings. Everyone was fond of the director, Dimitri, who never allowed his position of authority to make him arrogant. They were able to tease him about his long wait for a spouse.

But those who were young, as Claire was, shared small jokes, sometimes slightly derisive of the older workers, how methodical and orderly they were, how dutifully they went home each evening to their spouses and family units.

Of course they were all diligent workers as well; but

youth was a time when a certain amount of lightheartedness was tolerated. Standing on the edge of the holding ponds, they gave the young fish silly names, and invented personalities for them. "Look at Greedy Gus! He's grabbing all the food again!" "Watch out! Here comes Big-Lips Buster!"

Claire always smiled at the foolishness. The Vessels, during her time at the Birthing Unit, had done the same thing: found things to joke about, ways to pass the time. She had joined in. She had been part of it, and of them, until the end.

But here she had always felt separate. Different. It was hard to identify why.

But today, at breakfast, she suddenly noticed something that she had taken for granted until now. As they cleared their plates, tossed their crumpled napkins into the waste container, and smoothed their uniforms in preparation for another day of work, each worker did one other routine, quick thing.

They each took a pill.

Claire knew about the pills. The pill-taking in the community began at about Twelve—or for some children, earlier. Parents observed their children and decided when the time had come. She herself had not been deemed ready for the pills before her Ceremony of Twelve. It hadn't mattered to her. Those of her friends who took them found it a nuisance. But when she was selected Birthmother at the Ceremony, part of her list of instructions had specified: *No pills.*

If you are already taking the pills, stop immediately.

If you have not yet begun, do not begin.

She remembered now that the pill prohibition had seemed unimportant at the time. Her parents, though, were a little flustered by it. They took the pills. So did her brother, Peter. "I had them here ready for you when the time came," Claire's mother had said with a nervous laugh. "I suppose I'll just throw them away."

"Better turn them in," her father had suggested.

She had asked the other Vessels when she had taken up residence at the Birthing Unit. "Were you already taking the pills?" Claire inquired at mealtime one evening.

Some had shrugged and said no. But several nodded. "I stopped right away when I got my instructions," one girl said.

"I sort of tapered off," another girl explained.

"I think it's because we got switched over to vitamins," Nadia had said. She was referring to the carefully measured dosages of vitamins that all the Vessels dutifully took each morning. "The pills were probably just a different vitamin that we don't need anymore."

"No. The pill was something else entirely," Suzanne insisted. She was the one who said she had tapered off.

"She's right," Miriam said. "The vitamins don't make us feel any different. But the pill—" She hesitated. "Well, *taking* it didn't seem to have any effect. But when I *stopped* taking it, I began to feel . . ." But she couldn't seem to describe what she meant.

"I felt restless," Suzanne explained. "And—well, this is a little embarrassing. I don't even know how to describe it. But I began to be aware of my own feelings. Not just in my head, but—well, *physical* feelings too." She blushed, and chuckled nervously. The other girls, including Claire, felt embarrassed too, but intrigued. Feelings of any sort were not ordinarily discussed.

"Yes, that's it," Miriam agreed, "and you know what? I think they want us to undergo that change. Without the pills, our body gets ready. That's what we're experiencing."

"I kind of like it. I never really wanted anything before. But now I want the Product. When I feel it growing, it makes me happy." She rubbed her belly and smiled.

The other girls agreed, touching their own distended middles. "It's a nice feeling."

"After you give birth, you take the pills again, until you're ready for the next time," Nancy had said. She had produced three Products by then and was waiting for her post-Birth-mother Assignment.

"How long? This is my first time," Claire had asked. "I never had the pills at all."

"You will, though. After you produce, you'll take the pills. Maybe six months. Then you stop, and you get ready for your next Product. See Karen over there?" She pointed to a young woman at a nearby table. "She just produced. She's on the pills now. But in a few months she'll need to start getting ready for her second production."

"It's really boring," Suzanne said in a whisper. "When you're between births, and taking the pills. *Nothing* is much fun. You don't really notice it, though."

Now, looking around in the Hatchery cafeteria, Claire was aware that all the other workers took a pill every morning. And that was why, she realized, their conversation was always light-hearted, superficial, essentially meaningless. They were like the Vessels in the pill-taking time between births — without feel-ing. She was the only one, she could see now, who did not take a pill each day — and she guessed that it was simply a mistake. Her disastrous birth experience, and her decertification, had been so sudden and startling that no one at the Birthing Unit had thought to supply her with pills or instruct her to take them. Perhaps each attendant had thought that someone else had done so.

And so she was the one who *felt* things. The only one! It was why she yearned for the child, and felt her heart melt each time his little hand waved and he said "Bye-bye" to her, calling out her name in his silvery voice, smiling that amazing smile.

She would not let them take that from her, that feeling. If someone in authority noticed the error, if they delivered a supply of pills to her, she thought defiantly, she would pretend. She would cheat. But she would never, under any circumstances, stifle the feelings she had discovered. She would die, Claire realized, before she would give up the love she felt for her son.

SIXTEEN

THE SUPPLY BOAT was once again moored by the Hatchery. Its ropes had been looped over the posts and its slanted gangplank slid ashore. Recalling the delay they had suffered a year ago, this time they had arrived early and would be leaving before the coming two-day event prevented their departure.

The time of the Ceremony was fast approaching. Had it really been that long? Had she been here at the Hatchery for well over a year? It was hard to believe. But when she thought of the child, of little Abe, she was aware of how he had developed from an infant wailing for a bottle when she first encountered him into a giggly toddler who could say her name, wave bye-bye, and imitate the funny face they now made to each other as a greeting that made them both laugh.

Hearing her coworkers mention the upcoming Ceremony reminded her that Abe would be assigned this time. He would move to a dwelling, have a set of parents and perhaps an older sibling. She would have to find a new way of continuing their relationship. Of course his new female parent—Claire could not make herself think *mother*—would have a job in the community as all women did. So the child would go to the Childcare Center each day.

Claire had done volunteer work there when she was young and fulfilling her required hours. She had enjoyed that time and knew that Abe would be well cared for there. He would be given educational toys, fed a balanced diet fortified with vitamins, taken for walks in the big multichild stroller, and introduced to basic discipline: the meaning of *no* and *don't*; how he must not suck his thumb, though he would be permitted to stroke his comfort object if he needed soothing. He would be tucked into a crib at naptime, when the big room's lights were dimmed.

Thinking of the naptime ritual, Claire felt a little concerned. Abe still was not a good sleeper. Most toddlers in the Childcare Center responded to firm discipline and learned quickly to be silent when the lights were dimmed. She re-

membered the rows of cribs with most of the little occupants
sound asleep, and those who were wakeful staring quietly at the
ceiling. The small children had names by then, and she recalled
walking along the row and reading LIAM, SVETLANA, BARBARA,
HENRIK, on the identifying cards. Soon, after the upcoming
Ceremony, he would be officially Abe. She desperately hoped
that the crib with his name on it would not contain a wailing, sleepless little boy who would toss his hippo to the floor
and thump his feet rhythmically against the mattress. Shrieking and kicking, sometimes holding his breath until his face
turned frighteningly dark, was what he was still doing at the
Nurturing Center at naptime. Whatever would they do with
such a child when he entered the childcare system? Failure to
thrive, they wrote on his chart when he was very young. Now?
Failure to adjust? She shuddered. There were very severe con-
sequences in the community for a citizen who couldn't adjust.
Surely they would be more lenient with a very small boy, Claire
thought. But she wasn't certain. It made her nervous to think
about it.

She rode over to visit one afternoon two days before the
Ceremony and could see the cleanup crews working hard outside the Auditorium, obviously preparing for the one time each
year when the entire community gathered. Claire would attend this year. Already they had assigned a different worker

to remain at the Hatchery. It was important to her to see Abe assigned, to know where he would be next. Maybe, since the assignments were so close, she could sneak a look at the paperwork; sometimes there was a clipboard on the nurturer's desk. Perhaps the information was there.

But when Claire arrived at the Nurturing Center, she could feel immediately that something was wrong. Of course, she thought, they are all very busy because of the Ceremony plans. They have to prepare these children, all fifty, for new families. A letter would have to accompany each newchild, a letter with instructions for the parental unit: feeding information, schedules, discipline reminders, health data, and observations about personality. Of *course* the staff was preoccupied and distracted. It accounted, Claire thought, for the heightened tension she felt. The nurturer who had always been so pleasant to her, the one with a son named Jonas who took Abe to his dwelling at night, was oddly abrupt when she greeted him. He seemed angry. She could hear a muttered argument taking place in a corner. No one smiled at her.

Even more distressingly, when she went to pick up Abe, who was playing with a wooden toy on the floor, someone snatched him away.

"Not a good idea to play with this one," a uniformed female worker said. "There's one over there: that girl? She needs to be changed. You could do that if you want to be helpful."

The woman stalked off, holding Abe. She plopped him into an empty crib and he began to howl immediately. Everyone ignored him.

"I could maybe quiet him down," Claire suggested, "and you'd be able to get your work done more easily."

"Leave him," the woman commanded her.

Claire looked questioningly at the nurturer whom she had begun to think of as a friend. She realized, suddenly, that in all these months she had never asked his name. But clearly now was not the time. His face was set in hard lines, and he looked away.

"But I—"

"I said: *leave him*," the woman repeated impatiently.

Claire wanted to argue, perceived that she must not, and fell silent. Dutifully she picked up the baby girl they had indicated and took her to the changing table. In the background, Abe screamed and kicked at the bars of the crib. No one moved toward him.

Claire cleaned and diapered the cheerful female and set

her back down with her toys on the floor. Other babies crawled and played nonchalantly, as if they were accustomed to the shrieking boy in the crib. At the desk, the nurturer whose name she had never thought to learn, the one who (Claire *knew*) cared about Abe, suddenly slammed shut the reader/writer device he'd been working on. He stood. He looked at the clock on the wall.

"I'm leaving early," he said.

"Excuse me?" The uniformed woman looked up. She seemed to have some authority.

"I have a headache," the nurturer said.

The woman glanced at the communication system on the wall. "You can call for medication," she pointed out.

The nurturer ignored her. He went over to the crib and picked up Abe, who was clutching his comfort object and still shuddering with sobs, though his shrieking had subsided. "I'll take him with me now. You know he spends the nights in my dwelling."

"No need," she said sharply. "He might as well stay here tonight. What's the point?"

"The point is that my family is fond of him, and I would like to have him with us this evening." He was speaking firmly to her, and Claire could see that she was trying to decide whether to argue. When she turned back to the papers in her hands, it was clear that she had decided against any confrontation.

"Return him early tomorrow," she said. It sounded like an order.

"I will." He walked toward the door, the toddler in his arms, and then spoke to Claire. "Do you have your bike? Why don't you ride partway with us? You can turn off to the Hatchery at the main road."

Confused, Claire nodded to the woman, who ignored her, and followed the man and Abe. She waited to watch him pack the hippo into the carrying case, then strap the child into the bike seat, then mounted her own bicycle and rode beside him on the path. He didn't speak. The baby glanced at her, smiling now. She lifted one hand from the handle grip, waved to him, and watched him wave back. Both bikes slowed at the intersection where Claire would turn to the right. They stopped.

"Maybe I'll see you tomorrow," she said uncertainly. "I know you have a lot of work because of the Ceremony, but—"

He interrupted her. "I know you didn't attend last year," he said. "Do you plan to go to this one?"

Claire nodded. "I especially want to see Abe get his assigned family."

The man hesitated, then told her. "They're not assigning him. And no more extensions, either. They've run out of patience with him. They voted today."

Behind him, the child began to churn his legs. He wanted the bike to start up again.

"But what, then? Where will he—?"

The man shrugged. "You should say goodbye now. He'll be sent on his way in the morning."

"On his way *where?*"

The child had heard the word "goodbye." He opened and closed his chubby hand toward Claire. "Bye-bye!" he said. "Bye-bye!" Then he thrust his tongue into his cheek and made their secret funny face with its creased forehead and wrinkled nose. Claire tried hard to make the face back to him, but it was difficult; she was breathing hard and could feel tears rising hotly behind her eyes. "*Where?*" she asked again.

But the man simply shook his head. It seemed to Claire that he was unable to speak, that his breath was coming quickly as well. Then he gathered himself, and said offhandedly, "It's just the way it is. It's for the best. It's the way the system works. And by the way, you have his name wrong. It's not Abe."

"Ready, little guy?" he asked, swiveling his head to check on his passenger. "Off we go!" As he started forward, some pebbles spat from the path and stung Claire's ankle.

Stunned, she watched the bicycle set off across the path that led to the family dwellings.

* * *

Years later—many years later—when Claire tried to piece together memories of her last days in the community, the last things she could see whole and clear were the bicycle moving away and the back of the child's head. The rest of the hours that followed were fragments, like bits of shattered glass. No matter how she tried to piece them together, she could never create it whole and unblemished.

She remembered that the cargo boat was still docked. It was loading. They were rushing, for some reason. She heard someone call to another about weather concerns, a phrase she didn't understand. There were the usual complicated sounds of the departure preparations. Whistles and shouts. The thump of the crates being stacked.

But then night came and went and the boat had not left. Something had happened in the night. There were alarm bells. In the Hatchery? Something wrong in the lab?

No. Not there. The boat? Were the alarms from the boat? No. From farther away. From the main building. And from the speakers in each room. Loud announcements. Waking everyone. But why? What had gone wrong?

It was morning now, in her memory. The boat crew had been preparing to cast off the ropes and leave. But they were delayed. Time had passed. Usually the boat was there so briefly. But this time it was longer. Something delayed the boat's departure. Everyone was looking for something. *Someone?* Yes. It was that: Someone was missing.

* * *

Searchers came and looked along the riverbank throughout the day. Then it was dark again. Even at night they searched, with flashlights. They shouted.

She remembered, strangely, that the nurturer had been standing on the path. Why was he there? She had never seen him there before. Now he stood there, but didn't acknowledge Claire, didn't look at her. He was looking at the river. He was calling a name.

Jonas! Jonas!

His son. Yes. That was his son.

So it was his son who had gone missing.

Piecing together the fragments of memory, Claire could feel the cool dirt of the path under her bare feet. Why would she have been barefoot? Everyone always wore shoes. And running! Why had she been running?

Now the nurturer spoke to her loudly. But what had he said? *He took him!*

Jonas took the babe! Was that what he had shouted to her?

Elsewhere! Elsewhere! (But what did that mean?)

Then, through the blurred confusion of the memories, she found that she was on the boat. She had run up the slanted plank, in her bare feet, crying. The heavyset woman, her light hair unpinned, came from the cabin and put out her arms to Claire. She remembered the feeling of enfolding. The smells: sweat and onions from the woman. Fuel and damp wood from the boat itself. A puff of smoke. The scrape of the plank being pulled aboard.

She was with them, on the boat. The engine throbbed. They were leaving. *Why was she, Claire, on the boat?*

They were headed Elsewhere. They said they would help her find the boy, and the baby.

My son, she had told them, sobbing.

Her next blurred memory was of *sea,* which she had never seen before. *Rain:* something she had never felt. *Storm. Lightning. Waves. Fear.* The men were shouting. She was in the way; they shoved her aside and rushed to tie things down. She couldn't stand. It was wet and slippery even inside the cabin. She fell. Sprawled on the floor, she heard things slide loose and break.

She felt a rush of water, suddenly; it pulled at her clothing. Cold. *So cold.* And then: *Quiet. A hollow, rushing kind of quiet. Darkness.*

And that was all Claire remembered of those last days, no matter how hard she tried over the hard and lonely years that followed.

BOOK II

BETWEEN

ONE

———

THE SLATE GRAY sea roiled, scraping the narrow
strip of sand rhythmically, tugging at beach grass, digging
and sucking loose the rocks at the shore's edge. Spray stung
the men's eyes when they went to tighten the ropes holding
their boats secure. Salt coated their beards and eyebrows. They
pulled their woven hat brims low.

Old Benedikt cupped his hand above his eyes and peered
upward, assessing the sky through the pelting rain.

"It won't break for a while," he called. "Not till night."
But his words were carried off by the stiff wind, and the others, tugging and twisting at the coarse ropes, didn't hear him,
didn't reply.

The women remained in their cottages. Fighting the
weather was men's work. The women listened to the wind as it

roared in the chimneys, to the ripping sounds of torn thatch, and to the whimpering of frightened children. They tended the fires, stirred the soups, rocked the babies, and waited. This storm would pass. The sea would calm. It always had.

* * *

In the time that came after, the story of Water Claire took different forms. It was told and retold; things were forgotten, or shaped and changed. Always, though, there was this truth: that she came from the sea, flung in by that fearsome December storm years before.

Some said she was found, later, when the scudding clouds pulled aside and showed low sun in early evening: that she was there on the strip of beach, her clothes half torn from her, and they thought she was dead till she stirred and her eyes opened to show the deep amber-flecked green that later all remembered the same.

Others said no, it was Tall Andras who saw her in the waves, who threw himself in and grabbed her by her long hair as she clung to a thick wood beam, that he swam with her till he could stand, and when they looked he was there in the churning broth of sea with her in his thick arms, her head against his beard, and that he said but one word: "Mine."

Children said she was carried in by dolphins and they

made games of it, and rhymes, but all of that was just tale-spinning and fun, and no one took it to be true.

Others murmured "selkie" from time to time when she was remembered, but only as a fanciful tale. The selkie stories of seal creatures were well known, oft told, and in all of them there was a shed skin. Water Claire had come in clothing, though it had been shredded by the gritty winter sea. She was human. There was no seal to her.

Or mermaid, either.

She was a human girl sent to them by the sea, who stayed among them for a time, became a woman, and went away again.

It was actually Old Benedikt himself who carried her in, once she was seen. Several, including Tall Andras, swam out, but it was Old Benedikt who reached her first, slicing his way through waves with his burly, muscled arms. He pried her loose from the wood spar, for her fingers were locked there. He knew how to wrap her lifeless arms around his neck and to hold her pale chin high above the foam and spray. He had brought wounded sheep in from the field this way many times, holding them against his chest.

He stood, finally, in the shallow surge and suck of water, walked forward, his feet heavy in the drenched, icy sand, and laid her there. He could see that she still lived, and he covered her with the thick woven coat that he had thown aside as he entered the sea. Then he turned her wet, pale face to the side. He pressed upon her through the coat until she spewed frothy brine onto the sand, and coughed.

Tall Andras was there, it is true, and he thought, gazing down, that he wanted the girl for his own, but did not give voice to it.

Old Benedikt looked up at the surrounding men. "Run ahead," he directed Gavin, who was fastest. "Tell Alys. We'll carry her there."

Hastily the men gathered poles and coats and made a carrying litter, knowing how to do it for they had done it many times before. Their children fell from boats and cliffs. Their sons and brothers were wounded by hooks and rope. Their women died giving birth, and the newborns died too. They used such a litter for the slow journey to graveside.

But this girl was alive, though her eyes stayed closed and her fingers clenched as if she still felt the splintery mast in them. When they rolled her onto the litter, she coughed again, and when they lifted it to carry her up the hill, a cold breeze picked up a strand of her long wet hair, drawing it across her cheek. Her eyelashes fluttered then, and she began to tremble and whimper.

Carefully, in the increasing darkness, for twilight was brief here in winter, they moved with her up the ridge and felt with their feet for the worn path that would take them to the village and to Alys's hut at its edge. Four men carried the girl. The others walked behind. Now and then one stopped, turned, and looked out toward the sea and the horizon with its darkening sky as if searching for the silhouette of a vessel that might have thrown this astonishing gift their way. But there was nothing there but what had always been there: empty ocean the color of pewter, tarnishing to black now as night fell.

✳ ✳ ✳

The village nestled at the foot of a forbidding cliff in the curved elbow of an arm of land. The peninsula jutted out from the main coast in an isolated place where time didn't matter, for nothing changed. No newcomers had ever appeared, not in anyone's memory, and only an occasional discontented man climbed out (for that was what they called the leaving) or tried to. An overgrown, root-tangled path meandered upward at the foot of the cliff but then disappeared at the base of a sheer rock wall, and after that there was no way to go farther but to climb. Several had fallen to their death. One, Fierce Einar, had climbed out successfully but returned, embittered by what he had encountered at the top.

He had quarreled with his father and climbed out on a winter night with a sack of his own belongings, and some he had stolen, tied to his back. When he returned, climbing back in, it almost killed him, for he was maimed by then, bloody and in terrible pain. He dropped from the final rocks onto the snowy path at the base, howling in agony and with a knowledge of failure. Then he fell silent. He crawled to a place where he could pull down a narrow tree. He stripped it of branches, broke the trunk into two pieces, and used them to haul himself upright. Then he leaned on the sticks and dragged himself home to face his father. He lost the title Fierce, and was renamed Lame Einar. Still only eighteen, still silent, he tended sheep now, and nursed a deep despair.

The best route away from the village was by sea. But the ocean was turbulent and unpredictable, with dangerous currents and constant wind. Each fisherman had found himself in peril more than once, and all had lost friends or brothers.

Alys, toothless and wrinkled though with piercing eyes and a sharp tongue, told the men roughly: "Leave us be!" when they carried the trembling creature in to her. She tended the girl through the night. Alys was childless herself but had been midwife to many and was no stranger to damaged young. She stripped the girl of the drenched, ripped clothing, setting it aside, then rubbed her dry with rough cloth, and wrapped her in soft wool. She did all this in flickering light from a smoky oil lamp. When the girl stopped shaking, Alys stirred the herb-flavored broth that had been simmering on the fire in an iron pot. She poured some into a bowl, and fed the girl from a spoon held carefully lest she thrust it away in her fear.

But the girl sipped, wary at first, then opened her mouth for more.

"Go slow or you'll puke," Alys told her.

"What brung you?" she asked when the soup bowl was emptied. The girl's head turned and she half rose, listening to the murmur of the sea, but she did not answer and the old woman did not urge her. Instead, Alys found a comb carved of bone on the shelf nearby, and began to unsnarl and smooth the wet, salt-stiffened hair.

The wind howled through the thatch on the roof. It was deepest night now. The girl dozed, half sitting. Finally, Alys lowered her to the bed and pulled the length of wool cloth up around her bare shoulders. She watched for a few moments as the girl slept, her hair fanned about her head. Alys had always yearned for a daughter and felt that the sea had sent this one to her. After a bit she lowered the flame in the lamp so that the hut was dim, with dark shadows on its walls. She wrapped her own self in a woven blanket, sank into a nearby chair, and slept too.

In the morning the girl woke and wept softly. When she saw her clothing, all rags now encrusted with drying salt, she clutched the tatters, feeling the ruined cloth with her fingers, and then relinquished it all, turning her face to the wall. After a bit, with a resigned sigh, she took the coarse woven shift that Alys offered her, slipped it over her head, and stood. Her bare legs and arms were bruised and scraped; one ankle was badly swollen and she favored it, limping to the table where Alys had set a bowl of porridge.

Her hair was red-gold, burnished copper in the early light of winter that came through the small window and fell over her as she ate. The day was fair, as it was often after storms.

"What brung you to this place?" Alys asked her again. "What carried you and threw you to the storm?"

But again the girl did not answer, though she stared at Alys with her gold-flecked eyes. She had a puzzled look.

"Do you not understand our tongue?" Alys asked, knowing that the question was foolish, for if the answer were to be no, then the girl could not understand in order to give it.

"I am Alys." The old woman pointed to herself. "Alys," she said again, and patted her own chest in explanation. "I have no child, none ever, but I have birthed many among our women and few died in the birthing; they say I have the firm hands and the feel for it, and I also lay out the dead and sometimes can heal if the sickness is not beyond healing.

"That's why they brung you to me, for they felt you

needed healing, or if not healing, then I would clean and wrap you for the grave."

The girl was watching her. Her bowl was empty, and she raised the cup of milk beside it and drank deeply.

From outside they could hear, suddenly, the giggles of children. Alys pushed a window open, peered out, and called to them. "She's alive! She eats and is whole, with no parts broken. Go and tell. And stay off now till she's rested good! She don't need the likes of you laughing and shouting about!"

"What be her name?" a child's voice called.

"Go now! We'll know her name soon enough, or give her one!" the woman called, and then there was the sound of the little ones scampering away.

With her gnarled hand she smoothed the girl's hair. "It's just the curiosity comes on them. Them three little ones are always together—best friends, they are. Delwyth, Bethan, and Eira be their names—I midwifed each one, same year. Six, they are, and full of the mischief, but they have good hearts and mean no harm."

Then the girl spoke. "My name is Claire," she said.

—

TWO

THEY CALLED HER Water Claire.

People came to Alys's hut during the weeks that passed and brought gifts to Claire, knowing she had nothing of her own. They were a generous people, as a rule. Gareth, his bald head and round cheeks pink with shyness, made shoes for her, leather sandals with straps that she fastened around her ankles over thick knitted socks when the swelling lessened and she could walk without pain. Bryn, the mother of little Bethan, stitched a linen petticoat and took the time to embroider flowers on its edge, a fanciful touch beyond the ordinary clothing of the people, but no one scorned Bryn for it, for the girl seemed worthy of such a gift. Old Benedikt carved her a comb, which she carried in her pocket, and to the surprise of everyone, since he was fierce in his anger and solitude, Lame Einar came in from the sheep meadow, hobbling on his two sticks, and gave her a hat he had woven her from straw.

As spring came, children brought her early wildflowers in small wilting bouquets and they helped her weave the stems into the straw of the hat's brim.

She wore the brimmed hat to keep the sun from her eyes but even so needed to hold her hand there when she looked to sea because the light reflecting off the gray-white waves was blinding. She stood often on the shore with the wind blowing her hair and molding her skirt against her legs. She watched the horizon as if she waited. But she had no knowledge of what she waited for. The sea had drunk her memories away, leaving only her name.

"How old do you be, Water Claire?" asked a half-grown freckle-faced boy named Sindri. He measured himself beside her and she was the taller. But she shook her head, not knowing how to answer him. Alys was there; they were gathering herbs.

"Sixteen year or so," Alys said, telling Claire more than the boy. And they knew Alys to be true in her guess, for it was she who tended the bodies of them all, and knew the signs that each year brings.

"Sixteen," Water Claire repeated in her soft voice, and though she said no more, they knew that she was mourning the knowledge of the years that the sea had gulped away. She watched the little girls at play, laughing as they ran through the meadow, quick and colorful as butterflies, but there was sadness in the watching, for Claire's meadow days had been taken from her. They did not come back, even in dreams.

"Sixteen?" Tall Andras repeated when he heard of it. The boy, Sindri, had told everyone, and most had shrugged. But Tall Andras rubbed his hand across his thick blond beard, looked across the marketplace to where Water Claire stood fingering ribbons at a stall, and said to his mates, "She could be wed."

It was true that in this place there were often girls given as brides at that age. Even now the village was preparing for a wedding; Glenys, shy and sparkle-eyed, would soon wed horse tender Martyn, she not yet seventeen and he barely twenty. But Old Benedikt and Alys both said no. Not this girl. Not Water Claire. She must not wed, they said firmly, until the sea gave her back what it had stolen, until she knew what her life had once been.

Tall Andras, frowning with disappointment, asked brusquely, "What if it never do?"

"It will," Old Benedikt replied.

"Bits and pieces, they'll come," Alys said, "over time."

Tall Andras glowered. He had a fierce want for the girl. "The sea pukes up dead fish," he said. "It won't give her back anything. What the sea coughs up smells of rot."

"You smell of sweat yourself, Andras," Alys told him, laughing at his misery, "and should bathe if you want the girl to come close. Wash your hair and chew some mint. Maybe then she'll give you a smile some morning."

Tall Andras stalked away, but she could see that he was headed to the freshwater pond beyond the thick trees at the edge of the village. Old Benedikt, watching, shook his head and smiled. "I told him she'll come back to herself, but truly I don't know," he told Alys. "It's as if the sea sucked away her past and left her empty. What does she say to you?"

"She remembers only waking in my hut. Nothing before. Not even being in the sea."

They walked together along the rocky path bordering a wide meadow, each of them with a stick to lean on. Old Benedikt was strong still, but bent. Alys, too, walked with her back hunched. They had been friends for more than sixty years.

Alys carried the basket she used for gathering herbs; she was in need of raspberry leaf on this morning, to steep for tea to give Bryn. Since birthing Bethan six years before, Bryn had lost three babies and had fallen into despair. Now she was again with child, and Alys would prepare the raspberry leaf infusion for her to drink three times a day. Sometimes it tightened and held a pregnancy.

"Is there no herb for memory?" Old Benedikt asked her as she leaned to strip the raspberry leaves from the thick thorned bushes where they grew.

Alys chuckled. "Aye," she told him. "Try this." She reached to a nearby tree, peeled a tiny shred of bark, and placed it in his hand. "Chew, and think back."

Frowning, puzzled, Old Benedikt placed the shred on his own tongue. "Think back on what?"

"On a time you choose. Far back." She watched him.

He closed his eyes and chewed. "Bitter," he said, making a face.

She laughed.

After a moment he opened his eyes and spat the chewed bark from his tongue. "I thought back to the day we danced," he told her with a wry smile.

"I was thirteen," she said. "You were the same. A long way back. Was the memory clear?"

He nodded. "You had pink flowers in your hair," he said.

She nodded. "Beach roses. It was midsummer."

"And bare feet."

"Yours were bare too. It was a warm day."

"Aye. The grass was warm and damp."

"Dew," he said. "It was early morning." He looked at her for a moment. "Why were we dancing?" he asked, his brow furrowed.

"Mayhap you need to chew the bark again." She chuckled. "To remember why."

"You tell me," he said.

Alys added the last of the raspberry leaves to her basket, straightened, took up her stick, and turned on the path. "Back to the hut," she said. "My kettle's aboil, and I must steep the leaves." She began to walk away from him.

"Shall you take some of the bark for the girl? For Water Claire?" he asked.

She turned back to him and crinkled a smile at him. "The bark does naught," she said. "It's only the turning your mind to it. Making your mind go back.

"She'll do that when she's ready," she added. "I must go now. Bryn is in need of the tea."

He called after her as she walked away on the path. "Alys? Why were we dancing?"

"Take your mind there again," she called back. "You'll remember!"

To herself, she murmured, shaking her head with amusement as her eyes twinkled at her own memory. "Only thirteen. But we was barefoot and flower-strewn and foolish with first love."

THREE

CLAIRE WAS THERE, at the hut. With her coppery hair tied back by a ribbon, and a cloth tied around her waist to protect her simple homemade skirt, she was chopping the long pale green stems of early onions fresh from the garden. Newly picked greens lay heaped on the table with a thick mutton bone near them, ready to add to the pot of water that was already simmering over the fire. When Alys entered, she smiled.

"I'm starting soup," the girl said.

"Aye. I see that." Alys emptied her basket of raspberry leaves into a bowl. "I'll just take some of the water first, for my brew." With a ladle she slowly poured hot water from the pot over the leaves. Steam rose as the leaves began to steep and tint the liquid.

"For Bryn?" The girl looked at the darkening tea.

"Aye. To lose another will surely make her heartsick."

Claire leaned toward the bowl. As Alys watched, she closed her eyes and breathed the steam. At her forehead, tendrils of hair curled from the moisture, framing her pale face. For a moment she stood there, motionless, breathing. Then she gasped, drew her head back, opened her eyes, and looked around with a puzzled gaze.

"I cannot——" she began, then fell silent.

Alys went to her and smoothed the damp hair. "What is it, child?" she asked.

"I thought——" But the girl couldn't continue. Moving tentatively, she sat down in the nearby rocker and stared into the fire.

Alys watched her for a moment. Then she went to the trunk against the wall. Unopened for years, it bore an iron clasp that was rusty and worn. But Alys's strong fingers pried it loose, and she raised the heavy, carved lid. Her father had made this trunk for her mother almost a century before, a bride-gift when they were wed. It had come to Alys when her mother died. Her mother had stored things in it: linens and baby dresses, sprinkled with dried lavender blossoms. None of those things remained, though the scent of the lavender lingered. Alice used the trunk only for treasures, and there were few enough of those in her life.

Now she reached through the things within and took from near the bottom a fragile bit of folded cloth. Holding it, she went to the rocker and said to the girl: "Watch now."

Gently she unfolded the cloth and showed her bits of torn brown shreds. "Smell," Alys told her, and held it to the girl's nose.

"Old," Claire said. "Sweet." She leaned back in the chair and sighed. "What is it?"

"Beach roses from sixty years ago."

"Why—"

"To hold memories. Scents do that. When you smelled the tea—"

"Yes. For a moment something came back," the girl acknowledged. "Like a bit of breeze. It drifted past. I couldn't keep it with me. I wanted—" But she couldn't say what she wanted. She sighed and shook her head. "It went away."

"It's waiting," Alys said. Carefully she refolded the cloth around the dried petals and leaves and replaced the little packet in the carved trunk. Then, while Claire watched, she strained the dark tea and poured it carefully into small bottles, which she corked tightly. "I'll take this now to Bryn," she said.

"Add a raspberry leaf or two to the soup. And some of that sorrel from the garden. It'll give flavor," she added. "Those greens you have give bulk, but their taste is ordinary."

Claire nodded. Alys watched as the girl pushed the chopped onions into a neat pile with the side of her hand.

"Did you cook once, mayhap?" Alys asked.

The girl looked up. She frowned and furrowed her brow. "I don't think so," she said, finally.

"But something come back to you a minute ago," Alys said, "when you breathed the tea."

Claire stood thinking. She closed her eyes. Then, finally, she looked up and shrugged. "It wasn't the tea," she said. "It came from something else, I think."

"You talk elegant," Alys said with a chuckle. "Probably somebody done your cooking for you, once."

Claire took a deep breath, still thinking. Then she picked up the stirring spoon and turned toward the pot of simmering soup. "Well," she said, "those days are gone."

❋ ❋ ❋

The three little girls, Bethan, Delwyth, and Eira, barefoot and grass-stained, smoothed and tidied the little corner of meadow that they called their Tea Place. A flat rock there became their table; they decorated it with blossoms from the clumps of wildflowers nearby. With a leafy branch acting as a broom, Eira swept the ground around the rock. "Sit down, dear ladies," she said. "Now that it's tidy here, we'll have tea."

It was a game they often played, serving imaginary tea to one another, pretending to be grown women.

"Your hair's a wee bit straggled, Miss Bethan," Eira said haughtily as she set the broom aside. "Was you rushed? I'd expect you'd be more primped up, and maybe brush some, when you've got a tea invite."

Bethan giggled and pulled at her unruly curls. "So sorry, Miss Eira," she said. "This baby in my belly makes me forgetful." Dramatically she pulled her frock away from her own thin middle.

"Can I have a belly baby too?" whispered solemn-eyed Delwyth.

"Yes. Let's all." Eira tugged at her own skirt. "Oh, I do hope mine is born soon, because I'm so weary of being fat."

"Yes, fat is hard," Delwyth agreed in a serious voice. "It makes you breathe all puffy.

"When do you expect yours?" she asked the others. "Mine's coming tomorrow. I do hope for a boy. I'm going to name him . . ." She pondered briefly. "Dylan," she decided. "Tea?" Delicately she sipped from her own imaginary cup.

"Oops!" Bethan announced. "Mine just be born. A little girl." She cradled an invisible baby in her arms.

"Mine too!" The other two little girls announced. Rhythmically they rocked their invisible infants.

"My mum be cross with me if she knowed we did this," Bethan confided. "She says it be bad luck to pretend about a baby."

Delwyth stopped her rocking motion. "Bad luck?"

Bethan nodded.

"Better we don't do it, then. We can pretend tea, though." Delwyth smoothed her skirt. "Want a teacake?" She offered the other girls each a twig.

Eira pretended to chew. "You be a fine cook, Miss Delwyth," she said.

Delwyth nodded solemnly. "I learnt it from the queen," she said, "when I be'd a helper in her kitchen."

✳ ✳ ✳

Claire, listening from where she stood in a small grove of trees nearby, smiled at the sweetness of the children. But their conversation troubled her, as well, because it reminded her of what she had lost. It was more than the loss of memories. She had no knowledge. She wondered what a *queen* might be. Had she known that once? Had she played this way, once?

This baby in my belly makes me forgetful, one little girl had said. Claire, working now with Alys, preparing the herbs for Bethan's mother, understood what the child was pretending. Why did it make Claire feel so unbearably sad?

She straightened her straw hat and walked slowly back to the hut with the herbs she had been sent to find and gather. She resolved that she would learn. She would learn everything—about queens, whatever they were; and herbs, and birds, and how the men farmed and what they thought, and the women, too, how they spent their hours, and what they talked about, what they dreamed, what they yearned for.

It would be a start, Claire thought. Perhaps somehow she would learn her own lost life.

* * *

From a field higher up, where he was prying weeds from the rocky soil with his hoe, Tall Andras stopped his work, wiped sweat from his glistening forehead, and watched the mysterious girl walk along the path. She had favored one leg for some weeks, until the bruise and swelling disappeared. He had worried for her, that she might become hunched and lame, as people did when their wounds went unhealed. Andras's own father, flung years before against rocks when a boat swung around and tipped, still held one arm locked into a curved and crooked shape.

But he could see that Water Claire strode easily now along the path, her legs strong and equal, her feet sure in the soft leather sandals she wore. He watched her make her way easily to the turning; then she disappeared into the woods, heading back to the hut she shared with Alys.

A shadow crossed the ground in front of him, and Tall Andras looked up and waved his arm at the crows that circled the field. His weeding was turning up bugs and worms, morsels that the crows wanted, he knew, and it put his seedlings at risk. He couldn't afford to lose the crops. Winter was long here, and in the good weather seasons they prepared for it: growing, catching, storing things away. His father was getting old and his mother had been unwell for months, with fever that came and went. Tall Andras was young, just seventeen, but the family depended on him. He would make a bird-scarer, a *mommet*, he decided. Last summer that had helped. And he had a large gourd in the shed that he could use for a head, with a face carved on it: a fierce face. He twisted his own face, practicing, pushing his lips up against his nose, and then flapped his arms, the way the cloth of his mommet might flap in the wind to frighten away the crows.

Then he stopped, feeling childish and foolish, and glad that the girl had not seen. For her, he wanted to seem a wise and hard-working man, worthy soon of a wife.

FOUR

———

THEY NOTICED THAT creatures frightened her. A chipmunk, tamed by the little girls, sat on Eira's hand nibbling at the seeds they gave to it. But Claire backed away with a startled look.

"You never seen one before, then, Water Claire?" Bethan asked her. "They not be harmful."

"You can touch him," Delwyth suggested. "He don't mind."

But Claire shook her head no. She was fearful of the smallest of creatures—a mouse, scurrying across the floor of Alys's hut, almost caused her to faint—and fascinated in a worried sort of way with birds. She found frogs amusing but strange. And she was completely, utterly terrified of cows.

Claire held her breath and looked away when she had to pass the place where a scrawny milk cow, its wrinkled mouth moving as it placidly chewed on the rough grass, was fenced beside the cottage where Tall Andras lived with his parents.

"I must try to learn creatures," she said to Alys apologetically. "It's not right to be so fearful. Even the smallest of the children feel at home with the creatures."

"Mayhap you had a run-in with a creature once." Alys was in the rocker, knitting with gray wool in the dim, flickering light.

Claire sighed. "I don't know. But it's not a feeling of a bad memory. It's as if I have never seen them before."

"Fish neither?"

"Fish are familiar," Claire said slowly. "I think I have known of fish somehow. They don't frighten me. I like how silvery they look."

"Nary birds?"

Claire shook her head and shuddered. "Their wings seem so unnatural. I can't get used to them. Even the littlest ones are strange to me."

Alys thought, and rocked. Her wooden needles clicked in her gnarled hands. Finally she said, "Lame Einar has a way with birds. I'll have him catch us one, for a pet."

"Pet?"

"A plaything. A pretty. He'll make a cage for it, from twigs."

Claire cringed at the thought, but agreed. It would be a start to the learning.

* * *

One afternoon she stood barefoot on the beach, watching the trio of little girls. Using sticks, they had outlined a house and were furnishing it with debris they found in the sand.

"Here's my bed!" Bethan announced, and patted an armful of seaweed into a shape.

"And cups in the kitchen!" Eira set five scoop-shaped shells in a row. She lifted one daintily and pretended to drink from it.

Delwyth ran to fetch a branch she saw beside some rocks, and dragged it back. Torn from a nearby tree by the constant wind, it was crowned with a thicket of leaves. "Broom! I found us a broom!" the little girl announced happily, and scraped the sand with it. "Wait. It needs fixing." Carefully she tugged at a thin side branch, broke it loose, and tossed it aside. "There. Now it's a proper broom."

Claire, watching, leaned down and picked up the slender

branch that Delwyth had discarded. The sand was damp and she saw her own footprints in it. With the tip of the branch, she poked a round hole in each of her own toeprints, then laughed and scribbled the footprints away with the stick. A gentle surge of seawater moved in silently, smoothed the roughened sand, and receded.

She leaned forward and wrote the first letter of her name.

C.

Then *L.* And *A.*

But a foamy inrush of seawater erased the letters.

Claire moved back slightly, farther from the sea's edge, and began again. *CLAIRE,* she wrote.

"What be that?" A shadow fell across her letters. It was Bethan, looking down.

"My name."

The little girl stared at it.

"Would you like to do your name beside it?" Claire offered her the stick.

"How?" she asked.

"Just make the letters."

"What be letters?"

Claire was startled at first. Then she thought: *Oh. They haven't learned yet.* She had a sudden image of herself, learning.

Of a teacher, explaining the sounds of letters. There was a place she had gone, a place called school. All children did. But she looked around now, at the cliff and hills and huts, at the sea—she could see the boats bobbing in the distance, and the men leaning in with their nets—and she was uncertain.

"Will you go to school soon?" she asked Bethan.

"What be school?"

She didn't know how to answer the child. And maybe, she realized, it wasn't important. Six letters; they made a name. What did it matter? She looked again at the word she had written, then erased it with her own toes, stamped the sand firm, and tossed the stick into a pile of glistening kelp nearby.

✳ ✳ ✳

Alys had sent Old Benedikt to ask the favor of Lame Einar. Not long after, slow on his ruined feet, the young man made his way laboriously down from his hut on the hillside, carrying the twig cage on his back, with the bird inside.

"Here it be," he told Alys.

Einar was not one for talking. His failures had made him a recluse, but people remembered the vulnerable boy he had once been. Though he had stolen from his father, they forgave him that; his father had been a harsh and unjust man. That he

had climbed out, many admired, for the cliff was steep and jagged and the world beyond unknown; few had the courage that
Einar had had. They regretted his failure, but they welcomed
his damaged return. Einar, though, had never forgiven himself;
he lived in self-imposed shame and stayed mostly silent.

"It sings," he said. He leaned his two sturdy sticks against
Alys's hut and hung the cage on a tree branch near the entrance.
He watched for a moment until the carefully crafted perch
inside stopped swaying and the little finch stilled the nervous
flutter of its bright-colored wings. Then Lame Einar took up
his sticks again; he righted himself between them, for balance,
and went slowly away.

The bird was chirping when Claire returned from the
beach, carrying her sandals. She stopped in surprise, looking
at the cage and the bird within. "It can't get out, can it?" she
asked nervously.

Alys laughed. "Were you to take it in your hand, child, it
would tremble in fear. Have you never been near to a wee bird
before?"

Claire shook her head no.

"You'll feed it each day. Seeds, mostly, and some of the
bugs from the field."

"I don't like the bugs," Claire whispered.

"It will help when you learn them. Fear dims when you learn things."

The bird chirped loudly, and Claire jumped. Alys laughed at her again.

Claire took a breath and calmed herself. She went closer and peered into the cage. The bird tilted its head and looked back at her. "It should have a name," Claire said.

"Name it, then. It be yours."

"I've never named a single thing."

Alys frowned, and she looked at Claire with her squinted eyes. "Do you know that, then?" she asked.

Claire sighed. "I feel it, that's all."

"Naming is hard. Someone named you once."

Claire looked away. "I suppose," she said slowly, and then turned her attention again to the cage. "Look! It cleans itself!" She pointed. The bird had raised one wing and pecked fastidiously at its feathers beneath. "Isn't that a lovely patch of color on his wing?" She hesitated, then asked, "What is it called? I know *red*. You taught me red from the berries. It's a pretty red there around his eyes, but what is that bright color on his wing? I can't think of its name."

Alys was troubled by this, for she knew by now that the girl was clever, and filled with knowledge of many things. But she seemed lacking in so many ways, and the realm of colors was one. The names of the various hues were one of the first things small children learned. Yet when Alys had sent Claire on a simple errand some days ago, asking her to fetch some jewel-weed, which Alys needed to treat a painful poison ivy rash on one of Old Benedikt's grandsons, Claire had not known how to find the flower that grew in such profusion by the stream. "The bright orange blossoms," Alys reminded her. "We gathered some the other day."

"I forget *orange*," Claire had said, embarrassed. "We gathered several things that day. What does *orange* look like?"

And now she could not name the color that decorated the wing of the little singing finch.

"Yellow," Alys told her. "The same as evening primrose, remember?"

"Yellow," Claire repeated, learning it. Yellow-wing became the bird's name.

✳ ✳ ✳

On a cool foggy morning, she climbed the hill to find Lame Einar and thank him. It had taken a while to accustom herself to the bird, to end her fearfulness around it. But now it hopped to the side of the cage when she brought seeds to it in a little shell dish and waited, head cocked, while she set the dish down. It would have hopped onto her finger, she knew, if she had held it still and waited. But she wasn't ready for that, or for the feeding of live insects. The little girls took on that task, happy to find beetles and hoppers in the grass and bring them to Yellow-wing.

She found Einar near his hut. He was seated on a flat rock, cleaning a wooden bowl, scrubbing the cracks in the rounded poplar with a rag dipped in fire ash. Nearby, through the fog, she could hear the sheep move in the grass, and an occasional bleat. She approached the young man. She was nervous, not to be with Einar, who was always silent and unknowable, but because of the sounds of the animals.

He was startled to see her, and lowered his eyes to the bowl. Had he heard her coming, he would have fled into the fog and disappeared. But Claire had been silent, appearing without warning from the swirling gray mist, and his maimed feet made it impossible for him to jump and run.

"Good morning," she said, and he nodded in reply.

"I came to thank you for the bird," she told him.

"It's nought but a bird," he muttered.

Claire stared at him for a moment. A word came to her from nowhere. He's *lonely*, she thought. People say he's angry, and hermitlike, but it's loneliness that afflicts him.

She looked around, and saw a log nearby. "May I sit

down?" she asked politely. He grunted an assent and scraped
some more at the spotless bowl in his hands.

"I know it's just a bird," she told him, "but you see, I have
been afraid of birds. They're strange to me; I don't know why.
And so the little bird you brought me—I call him Yellow-
wing . . ."

She saw his puzzled look and laughed. "I know. It's just
his color. But I'm only learning colors. They're as strange to
me as birds. And so it's a help, to call him Yellow-wing. I say
his name when I put his dish of seeds in the cage. And you
know what? He's singing now. He was afraid at first, but now
he sings!"

Einar looked at her. Then he arranged his mouth, gave
a small sound as a trial, and then reproduced the sound of
the small bright-colored bird, with its trill and fluttering whistle.

Claire listened in delight. "Could you do the songs of
other birds?" she asked him. But he ducked his head in embarrassment and didn't reply. He set the bowl aside and reached
for his sticks.

"Sheep need me," he said brusquely. He rose and moved
with his awkward gait into the edge of the foggy meadow. He
was no more than a blurred outline when she heard him call

back to her. "Greens!" he called. "Not the color. But he needs greens. Willow buds be good, and dandelion!"

Then he was gone, but as she gathered herself to leave, she heard him whistle the song of the bird once again.

* * *

Alys and Old Benedikt stood watching the preparations for the marriage of Glenys and Martyn. Friends of the couple had built a kind of bower from supple willow branches and now they were decorating it with blossoms and ferns. Beyond, on tables made of board and set outside for the occasion, the women were arranging food and drink.

"It's a fine day," Alys commented, squinting at the cloudless sky.

"I was wed in rain," Old Benedikt said with a chuckle, "and never noticed a drop of it."

She smiled at him. "I remember your wedding day," she said. "And Ailish, all smiles. You must miss her, Ben."

He nodded. His wife of many years had died from a sudden fever the winter before, with their children and grandchildren watching in sorrow. She was buried now in the village graveyard with a small stone marker marking her place, and room beside her for Old Benedikt when his time came.

"Look there, at Tall Andras, watching the girl," Old Benedikt said with a chuckle, and pointed. "He's bent near double with longing for her, isn't it so?"

They both watched with amusement as the young man's lovesick gaze followed Claire, who was helping with the flowers. She hardly noticed him.

"She puzzles me, Benedikt."

"Aye. She's a mystery. But a splendid one!" While they watched, Claire lifted one of the little girls and helped her weave daisies into the twigs of the bower. The other little ones waited eagerly for their turns. "They follow her like kittens after the mother cat, don't they?"

"Do you know she fears cats? Even kittens? As if she never see'd such before," Alys told him.

"And birds, I hear."

"Lame Einar caught a bird for her, and wove a cage for it. She's learning to like it now, for it sings nicely. But, Ben—?"

"Aye?"

"I had to tell her the colors of it. She don't know the names! Yellow, and red: it's as if they are new to her. And yet she's clever! Clever as can be! She creates games for the little girls, and helps me with the herbs, but—"

"I never knowed one who couldn't say the colors. Not even one who is weak in the mind, like Ailish's nephew, who's like a young boy though he's thirty! Even he cries for his blue shirt instead of the green," Old Benedikt said.

"Not Water Claire. She may long for the blue but don't know its name. She's learning now. But she's like a babe about it."

"So you've got you a wee babe to tend, after all these years without," he teased her.

He patted her hip through her thick skirt, and she pushed his hand away. "Let me be, you old fool," she told him fondly.

———

FIVE

TELL ME ABOUT weddings," Claire asked as she and Alys carried the nutcake they had made to the feast table, where it would be placed with the festive puddings and sweets. "Does everyone have one? Did you?"

Alys laughed. "Not me," she said. "But most do, when they reach an age, as Martyn and Glenys. When they choose each other, and the parents say aye, then we have the Handfasting. Always in summer, usually at new moon."

Summer. Claire had learned, already, from Alys that summer is a time of year, the time of sunshine and crops and the birth of young animals. It had been one more thing she had not known.

She waited while Alys rearranged some of the other foods

in order to make room. Then she set down their cake and together they decorated its edge with yellow daisies.

The village people were gathering. No one, not even the fishermen, was at work today. Babies perched atop their fathers' shoulders. Claire saw Tall Andras with his parents, the three of them scrubbed and dressed in their best clothing. She could see that his mother was not well; she leaned on her son, and was flushed with fever, though she smiled and greeted the others.

Bryn waved to Claire. She was holding Bethan's hand. For once the three little girls were separate, each with their families. Claire could see that beneath her lace-trimmed apron, Bryn's body had thickened with the coming child. Alys thought the time of danger was past and that this one would survive.

"Oh! What's that?" Claire asked, startled at a sound. From the path, several young village men approached and the crowd opened to make way for them. One was blowing into a carved flute. Another kept time on a small drum made from an animal skin stretched across a hollowed gourd. The third plucked at strings stretched across a long-necked instrument made of wood. Moving in time with the melody, they entered the circle that had opened to admit them as Claire watched from where she and Alys stood at the edge.

"It's so lovely! Listen! How they make the sounds go to-gether! I've never heard anything like that before!"

Alys frowned. "It's music, child. Have you never heard music? Have you forgotten it?"

"No, never," Claire whispered. "I'm quite sure."

* * *

The Handfasting ceremony ended as Martyn and Glenys kissed each other, and the red ribbon that had been wound around them unfurled, loosened, and freed them. The musicians began again, with a louder, rollicking tune, and the villagers cheered and turned to the waiting feast.

Claire stood silent, awed by the music, puzzled by the concept of love, and moved by both the solemnity and the celebration of the occasion. When she turned to look through the noisy, laughing throng for Alys, she suddenly noticed Lame Einar standing alone on a small rise at the edge of the meadow. While she watched, he adjusted the two sticks that support-ed him, turned, and hobbled slowly away. For a moment she thought of running over to invite him back, to entice him to join in. But her attention was drawn by the music. Never had she heard such an enticing thing as music, she was sure of it! And now the villagers were choosing partners, forming lines, and moving in time to the cheerful melody. Surely Einar would enjoy watching, even if he couldn't do the quick hopping steps that they all seemed to know. They could watch together. But when she looked back for him, it was too late. He had disappeared into the woods.

* * *

Back to daily tasks after the excitement and holiday of the Handfasting, Tall Andras knelt in the field and meticulously tied together the thick branches that would form the body of the mommet. Then, after he had decided on a spot, in the center of the young, sprouting crops, he pushed the main branch into the earth and patted the dirt firmly around its base so that it stood upright without tilting. He dressed it, carefully fitting the wide sleeves of a ragged coat over the two stick arms. He tied a sash around the middle to hold the coat closed, but loosely, so that the breeze would lift and sway the fabric. He stood back and watched with satisfaction as the cloth moved. The ends of the arm branches, extending from the sleeves, looked like beckoning, skeletal hands.

Claire, approaching on her way to the stream, watched with a smile. She understood what he was doing, though she had never seen a mommet before. She stopped, watched, then called to Andras: "Do you have a ribbon? If you added a long ribbon, it would wave in the wind."

He shook his head.

"I'll bring you one, if you like," she suggested, coming closer.

He stood back and looked at his creation. "A ribbon would be good," he acknowledged, "around the neck."

Claire laughed. "The neck?" she asked. There was only the gnarled branch end protruding upward from the patched coat.

Andras laughed as well. "I'll make the head now," he told her, and showed her the large gourd waiting on the ground. He knelt beside it and with his knife carved a hole at one end. He dug out several inches of the pulpy flesh within, then placed the gourd atop the neck, fitting it down so that it sat firm. Claire could see that it looked, indeed, like a head, and that from a distance the entire mommet would seem a frightening, flapping creature. The crows would surely avoid it and the crops would be protected.

He lifted the yellow gourd off the neck and set it on the ground again. "It needs a face," he told her.

She sat on the soft earth and watched him begin to carve. First he gouged two circles near each other in the center of the gourd, then scraped at the rind between and below the eyes, to create the impression of a nose.

Impulsively Claire tore some handfuls of grass from the earth and handed them to him. "Hair," she said.

He laughed and draped the hair over the gourd. It slid away and he looked around. "Wait," he told her. "I can make it stay." He left her with the gourd lying on the ground and went over to the edge of the woods. As she watched, he found the pine tree he had in mind, and pulled a length of one supple branch loose. "Oh, aye," he murmured. "This is good." He brought it back to where she was sitting and showed her the wetness from the torn end, where the bark glistened. He held it for her to sniff the woodsy pine scent.

"Alys makes a pillow filled with the needles," she told him.

He nodded. He was smearing the oozing resin on the gourd. "Aye, it soothes the sleep," he said. "Look now!" He picked up the torn grass and pasted it on the gourd's head, where it settled in tufty clumps, held tight by the sticky sap. They both laughed as he held it up. "Some mommet!" Andras said with pride.

"Needs a mouth," Claire reminded him. She pictured a grin on the odd creature.

"Aye, it does." He bent over it, carving meticulously. She watched as he worked. Now and then he drew back, examined his own efforts, and then leaned forward to correct the shape, to trim the curves. She saw him smooth the mouth edges with his finger. He flicked away some tiny shreds of gourd.

"May I see?" she asked him.

"Wait." He moved his blade to the expanse of yellow rind above the gouged eyes, and she could see him make three deep rippled cuts across the broad forehead. He looked at it and laughed in delight. "There!" he said. He stood, holding it, and placed it carefully over the wooden neck, easing it down into place.

"There!" he said again proudly, and turned with a grin to see her reaction.

Claire stared. The grotesque face stared back at her. Its forehead was wrinkled by the wide cuts, which made it looked puzzled, and the eyes squinted above the twisted nose. The mouth was a tortured smile, a leer. She caught her breath and felt her heart pound. Andras was laughing. She turned to him, horrified, not knowing why, and cheerfully he twisted his own face into a mimicry of the mommet. He thrust his tongue into his cheek, wrinkled his nose and creased his forehead. He made a chortling sound.

The skewed face, the laughter with it, made something flood into Claire's memory, surging upward in her like a wave about to break. She had made that face once, and thought it funny. Someone had made it back to her. But why? *Who?* She pulled herself upward from the place where she had been sitting in the grass so cheerfully a moment before. She felt sick, suddenly, and began to cry.

"I'm sorry," she gasped. "I'm sorry. I'm sorry——"

Then she turned and ran, sobbing and breathless, down the hillside as Tall Andras stood uncomprehending beside the wretched, ragged stick figure with its bulbous head. High above him, two crows wheeled in the sky and cried out.

∗ ∗ ∗

Alys had been busy sorting and separating her dried plants when Claire burst through the door, her face wet with tears, and threw herself onto the bed. It was clear that this was not a thwarted romance or a quarrel with a friend, the usual cause for the weeping of young girls. This was raw and deep. The old woman poured steaming water from the kettle over a few pinches of blue vervain and chamomile, then put the mug of herbal tea into Claire's hands. She watched with concern as the girl sat huddled and shaking in the dim light of the hut.

"Something's come back, then," Alys said. "Something cruel."

Claire nodded. She took a few shuddering breaths and sipped the soothing drink.

"It helps to say it," Alys suggested.

Claire looked up at her. "I can't," she said. "It was so close! It was there, so close! And I can feel it, still, but I can't grasp what it is."

"What brung it? Where be you, when it come so close?"

"Over on the hillside, with Andras. I was helping him build a stick figure to frighten the crows away."

"A mommet."

"Yes. That's what he called it."

"Tall Andras is a good lad. Surely it was nothing he done?"

Claire hesitated. "I don't think so. I can't remember, exactly. We were laughing, and then—well, everything changed. I can't think why."

"Something brung it. Want I should ask Andras?"

Claire closed her hands around the mug and breathed the tea's steam. "I don't know." She whispered, after a moment, "I feel so sad."

Alys watched her, and knew that the herbs in the mug would soothe the panic that had afflicted her, that soon she would calm and likely sleep for a bit. But they would not heal her. It would be hard to heal a girl as desperately wounded as this one.

SIX

THE GOOD-WEATHER DAYS continued. The sun turned the wave tips to sparkling jewels, and the fishermen filled their nets each day with their glistening catch. In Tall Andras's field the mommet flapped its loose fabric arms and the crows, made timid by it, called out harshly and went to other fields, other crops. The gourd head began to rot in the sun and collapse upon itself, oozing and purple like a bruise. A bold starling swooped and grabbed some of the browning grass that had been its hair. One day it fell sideways into the field. When Claire walked past on her way to gather herbs, she saw only the toppled, ruined remains. The memory it had brought her was no longer there.

Andras's mother, Eilwen, weakened and no longer left her

bed. Alys tended her there, holding her head so that she could sip warm liquid made from chopped wild sunflower roots simmered in spring water. The medicine eased her cough. But it was a comfort, not a cure. "She'll not live," Alys told Claire.

Claire had learned about death already in her time here, for they had buried an old fisherman earlier, and she had helped Alys wash and wrap the gaunt body before his sons lifted it into the box they had built. The fisherman's death had been sudden, though, in his sleep. Now Claire watched, day by day, as Eilwen drifted in her mind, woke less often, and seemed to shrink. Finally, early one evening, with Andras and his father there, her breath slowed and stopped.

The father and son touched her forehead gently as a goodbye and went away.

Alys squeezed cloths that she lifted from the pail of water, handed one to Claire, and together they began to wash the thin body. Clean wrappings were folded nearby, waiting.

"The day they brung you from the sea," the old woman said, "I washed you like this."

"Did you think I would die?"

Alys shook her head. "I could see you was strong. You fought me some." She chuckled softly as she patted Eilwen's arm dry and laid it back gently on the bed.

"I don't remember."

"No, you wasn't yourself yet. It was your sleep self what fought me."

"Here." She handed Claire a dry cloth and together they dried and tidied the dead woman, folding her arms finally across her gaunt chest. Alys brushed her thin hair and they carefully wrapped her. They could hear the two men moving outside, readying the box.

"They'll be needing a woman here," Alys said, glancing around the crude hut. The cooking vessels were unwashed and a blanket thrown across a chair was stained and in need of mending.

"Yes," Claire agreed. "Men don't tend houses well, do they?"

"Tall Andras is of an age to wed," Alys said pointedly.

Claire shrugged. "He should, then."

"It's you he wants."

Claire knew it to be true. She blushed. "I'm not of a mind to wed," she murmured.

Alys didn't hear, or pretended not to. "He'll want sons."

"All men do, I expect." It was something Claire had observed, in the village. Sons carried on the outside work; they took on the boats and the fields as their fathers grew old.

Alys busied herself with tying the cords that held the wrappings firmly in place around Eilwen's remains. Claire, silent now, helped her. She thought how proud Eilwen must have once been, to have birthed a strong boy like Andras.

They sat back. Their work was finished. In a moment they would call the men, father and son, to lift the woman into her coffin. The village would gather in the morning to place it in the earth.

"On that day, the day I tended you," Alys said to Claire, "I saw your wound."

"Wound?"

"Your belly."

Claire placed her hand there protectively. She looked at the ground. "I don't—" she began, then faltered.

"It's a grievous wound. Someone tended it, stitched it up. There are the marks."

"I know," Claire whispered.

"One day it will come back to your mind, like everything else."

"Perhaps."

"But I fear this: that you will not be able to give birth. I think it has been taken from you."

Claire was silent.

Alys leaned forward and turned the flame higher in the oil lamp. It was darkening outside. "There are other ways a woman finds worth," she said in a firm, knowing voice.

"Yes."

"Come. We'll bring the men inside to be with her now."

They rose and went out into the evening where Tall Andras and his father waited in a light rain, their faces resigned.

* * *

In her mind, Claire made a list of what was new to her.

Colors, of course. She was grateful for knowing them now: the red of hollyberries, and the red ribbon of the Handfasting—she marveled at the vibrancy and vigor of it. And she had come to feel bathed in contentment when the sky was blue, as it was on these late-summer days. Sometimes the sea was quiet and blue as well, but most days it churned dark graygreen, with spumes of white blown and dissolved in the air. Claire liked that darkness as well, with its relentless motion and mystery, though she blamed the sea for hiding her past in its depths.

Yellow she loved for its playfulness. Yellow-wing, her little bird, came to her finger now when she poked it between the twigs that formed his cage. He hopped onto it and tilted his head at her with a questioning look. She wondered why she had ever been so frightened of birds.

They were added to her list of newly learned things: birds, and animals of all sorts. She still skirted the cow uneasily when she walked past, but she had become fond of Lame Einar's sheep, especially the small ones, who frolicked in the tall meadow grass and showed their pink tongues when they bleated in excitement.

Einar told her of wolves, but she had not seen one and did not want to, ever.

She took joy in butterflies and scolded the little girls for catching them. "You've ruined it now," she said, looking sadly at the crumpled spotted wings in Bethan's outstretched hand. "It deserved to live, and to fly." Together they buried the dead creature, but later she saw the child chasing another.

She feared bees, and most bugs.

"You're like a wee child," Alys said to her, laughing when Claire backed away nervously from a fat beetle on a bush where they were gathering large leaves of goldenseal. Infusion of goldenseal eased the sore throat that sometimes afflicted fishermen after long days in the boats.

"I've just never seen them before," Claire explained, as she had often, of so many things.

Her list included lightning, which astonished her; thunder, which terrified her; and frogs, which made her laugh aloud. A rainbow one morning made her almost faint with delight and surprise.

SEVEN

CLAIRE JOINED IN the harvesting at the end
of summer, and the rejoicing after. The crops were brought in
and stored, and in the fields the birds picked at the strewn leavings. Apples were ripening still, but the early ones were picked
and pressed into cider.

She could see that the days were shorter now. In summer
the children had played barefoot into the evening, chasing one
another until their shadows grew long. The men fished until
there were stars, and still the sky did not darken until they
brought their catch ashore. Now, though, the air turned brisk
late in the afternoon. The sun seemed to topple down to the
edge of the horizon and colored it crimson there until it was
gulped by the sea and gone. The wind rose then, taking the

brown leaves in a whirl from the trees, and smoke wafted from the chimneys of cottages as fires were fed. The smoke carried with it the scent of soups and stews: nourishment for chilly nights. Women unraveled the sweaters their children had outgrown. They rolled the yarn and started again with it, forming new patterns, bright stripes, in larger sizes. Nothing was wasted. Boys carved buttons from bone.

Tall Andras gave Claire a fringed shawl that had been his mother's. Most days were still sunlit and warm, but in the evenings she wrapped the soft shawl around her. Lame Einar, seeing how she tied the ends to fasten it closed, created a clasp from willow twigs that he'd soaked to soften and then twisted into a curled design. Carefully he attached the two pieces to the green shawl and showed her how to fit them into each other and hold the thick fabric tight together.

She noticed one morning, early, that her breath was visible in the cold, clear air. "Like mist," she said to Alys.

"Steam," Alys replied.

They were on their way to the cottage at the edge of the woods where Bryn lived with her fisherman husband and their little girl. Bethan had burst into their hut just before daybreak, shivering with the cold because she had forgotten her sweater, and breathless with excitement.

"My mum's pains have begun and my dad says come because he wants no part in it!"

"Run back, child, and tell her we'll be there shortly." Alys spoke in a calm voice while she rose, prodded the fire, and reached for her clothing.

"You'll come too, won't you, Water Claire?" Bethan begged. Claire had sat up and yawned.

"I will. Go tell your dad he's a big baby himself." Claire knew Bethan's father, that he was gentle and loving. But men were not good at this.

The little girl giggled. Claire swung her bare feet to the floor and winced at the cold. She reached for the knitted socks that Alys had made for her. "Go now! Scat!" she said, and Bethan, gleeful, left the hut and scampered back along the lane.

Yellow-wing, whose cage had been brought inside at the end of summer, shifted on his perch and chirped. Alys rolled a leaf tightly and slipped it between the bars for him to nibble. Claire finished dressing. She fastened her leather sandals over the warm socks and watched as the old woman gathered things from the shelves in the corner. Suddenly, watching, she shuddered.

"Why do you need a knife?"

Alys placed the knife carefully beside the corked containers of herbal infusions. She rolled them all in a soft leather skin and placed the bundle inside her bag. She added a large stack of clean folded cloths to the bag and pulled its drawstring tight.

"Some say it eases pain to lay a knife beneath the bed."

"Is it true?"

Alys shrugged. "Likely not. But if the person thinks it, then the thinking eases the pain." She wrapped her thick knitted shawl around her and hefted the bag over her shoulder. "And I need the knife for the cord."

Claire pulled her own shawl tight and fastened it with the willow clasp.

"Bring the lamp," Alys told her.

Together they hurried along the path. Claire held the lamp high and it made their way easier. But the sky itself was lightening now. The moon was a thin sliver against the gauzy gray of earliest morning. Bryn's child would be a daylight baby.

They could see when they arrived that Bethan in her excitement had dashed about in the shadowy dawn and wakened her friends. Now all three little girls, still in their sleeping garments, were giggling nervously in the small room where Bryn groaned and twisted on the bed. Alys firmly shooed them back outdoors.

"Don't come back till the sun is full up. And then you come with your arms filled with flowers from the meadow, to welcome the babe."

"They'll find some dried asters still," she told Claire, "and late goldenrod. And it will keep them out from underfoot."

The coming baby's father was nowhere in sight. Alys had told Claire that men were frightened by birthing.

She had watched Lame Einar, though, help his ewes to bear young in early spring. He was both firm and gentle with them, and unafraid. Einar hadn't minded that she stood watching when she came upon the scene. It was the first time she had ever seen him smile, when he unfolded the damp legs of a newborn and set it wobbling on its feet so that it could nudge its mother for milk.

"They don't really need me," he told her gruffly. "They can birth alone unless there's trouble."

"But it's nice you're there to help," Claire said.

Einar had shrugged, patted the rump of the nursing ewe, and reached for his sticks to hobble away. Claire watched him for a moment after he turned his back. Then she too walked on.

But that had been months before. The spring lambs were tall now, playful, and thick with wool. Einar was no longer so shy with her. Once he startled her by making a harsh cackling sound, suddenly, and then a series of soft clucks. She looked at him in surprise.

"You asked me once could I do other birds. That's a pheasant," he explained.

Then he looked up at something very large, soaring above the sea. He gave a long, hoarse call. "Black-backed gull," he said.

Now he let her help when he gathered the sheep in for the evening. Together they counted. He had never lost one to wolves, he told her, and was proud of that. He loved the new lambs.

"Wash the knife," Alys directed her, and her thoughts returned to the cottage, where Bryn gasped and gathered herself now as the child emerged. Claire saw it was a girl. She heard it cry as she turned and dipped the knife into the water that simmered on the fire. The blade was hot when she wiped it carefully dry with a clean cloth.

"Don't cut Bryn!" she implored suddenly.

Alys frowned at her. "No need to cut the mother," she said brusquely.

She knotted a string around the pulsing cord. The baby waved a fist in the air and wailed. "Sun's rising," Alys said to Bryn. "And you've got you a fine girl." She waited a moment, then reached for the knife that Claire held, took it, and separated the newborn from its mother with a careful cut.

Bryn was watching wearily, and smiling. Suddenly Claire stepped forward without thinking, toward the baby that Alys was wrapping now in a cloth, and cried out, "Don't take it from her!"

Alys frowned. "Take what? What's troubling you, girl?"

"Give Bryn her baby!"

Alys looked puzzled. She leaned forward and placed the swaddled infant in Bryn's arms. "And what did you think I was to do, child? Put it out for the wolves? Of course it goes to its mum. Look there. Wee as she is, she knows what to do."

Like the lamb wobbling forward to suckle, Bryn's baby turned its head against its mother's warm skin and its mouth opened, searching. Claire stared at it. Then she began to sob, and stumbled out of the cottage into the dawn. Behind her, Alys, her face folded into puzzlement and concern, began to replace her birthing tools into the woven bag. The new mother dozed while her tiny daughter nuzzled and sucked. Outside, in the distance, the little girls were moving about in the gradually lightening meadow, their arms filled with flowers. But for Claire, who stood on the path weeping, the sunrise, perhaps all sunrises to come, was ruined by memory and loss.

EIGHT

HALTINGLY, PAUSING TO weep, Claire told her remembered story to Alys. Astonished, the old woman asked to examine her scar. Her gnarled hands touched the raised pink flesh and followed the map of it with one finger.

"Aye," she said, "this is what I saw the day you came, and I knew you'd had a terrible wound. But never did I see until now that it's the size to remove a child. Imagine: to cut a woman like that! Or a girl! You was just a girl! The pain would have been so fierce. It would have killed you."

"No," Claire explained. "I felt nothing when they cut. Before, there was pain—like what Bryn had, with the squeezing of the baby. But when they cut, I felt only pressure. The pushing of the knife. No pain."

Alys shook her head as if in disbelief. "How could that be, then?"

"There were special medicines. Drugs. They took away pain."

"White willow brings relief," Alys murmured. "But not for *cutting!* We have no herbs for that."

"I felt nothing."

"And what of the blood?" Alys again touched the scar. Her finger, its knuckle bent and thickened by age, ran the length of the wound. "I've seen wounds like this. A fisherman caught and ripped apart by the gaff. A hunter clawed and torn open by an animal. I've been called to tend them. But I can do nought but to soothe and comfort. The blood pulses away and they die from it — from the blood and the pain. They scream from the pain and then weaken as the blood flows. Their eyes die first." The old woman's own eyes seemed to look into the distance, thinking of the terrible things she had seen and could not heal.

Claire looked down, herself, at the scar. "I couldn't see. My eyes were covered." She shuddered a bit, as the memory of the mask came to her. "But I felt them cut. And you're right: of course there must have been blood. They had tools, I think, to deal with that. I remember a small sound —"

She thought, and then tried to reproduce it. "*Zzzzt!* And I smelled a burning smell. I think it . . ."

Alys, puzzled, waited for her to continue.

Claire sighed. "They had something that we don't have here. Electricity. It's hard to explain. I think they had an electric tool that burned and sealed the blood vessels. *Zzzzt. Zzzzt.*"

Alys nodded, as if it made sense to her. "I burn a wound, sometimes, or a snakebite. I use a firestick. To kill the poison. Not for bleeding, though. Not for a huge wound like this one."

Claire drew her clothing across the scar, covering it, and the two of them sat together in silence, one with her new and troubling memories, the other puzzling over what had happened to the girl, and why.

"I must find him," Claire whispered, finally.

"Aye. You must."

"*How?*"

Alys stayed silent.

✳ ✳ ✳

She told Bryn. Watching the woman hold and tend her infant one afternoon, Claire confided in her and described the return of the memories. Bryn listened with shock and sorrow. She clutched her own baby tighter as Claire answered her horrified questions. Neither of them was aware that just outside the cottage, beside the door that had been left partly open for fresh autumn air, the little girls, wide-eyed, were listening.

They scampered away to tell others. "A terrible secret," Bethan called it, enjoying the attention she received as she retold the embellished story. *Water Claire had had a baby! Yes, young as she was! No, no husband at all. And they took the baby from her—just stole it away, and she never saw it since!*

The secret was murmured throughout the community. Older women lowered their eyes in sympathy; many of them had lost children in cruel ways and they knew what strong, lasting grief came with such a loss. Younger ones, jealous of the pretty stranger, tossed their heads in judgment. *No husband! Wanton thing! We suspected something like that! So she was tossed out of where she lived!*

Glenys, who had welcomed Claire's attentions at the handfasting ceremony in early summer, now smoothed her skirt smugly over her newly rounded belly. "I'll have Alys come to midwife me when my time comes," she said with a toss of her head, "but I don't want *her*."

* * *

Tall Andras, his face set in hard lines, turned away when he saw her.

"Is something wrong?" Claire asked him, puzzled by his cold look. He had always been so friendly.

"Is it true, what they say?"

"Who? And what is it they're saying?"

"Everyone. That you've had a child. And no husband."

Claire stared at him. The knowledge was still so new to her that it seemed secret. She had yet to think it all through. It was still fragments, some of it, though from describing it to Alys she remembered the birth now, clearly and with horror. But *child?* She had no sense, yet, of a child. Only something small and newly birthed.

"It was different, where I lived. There weren't weddings. And yes, I gave birth." She found herself speaking tersely to him. She was angered. "You can't understand. I was *selected* to give birth. It was an honor. I was called *Birthmother.*"

He raised his chin and looked at her with a kind of contempt. "You live here, now. And you're stained."

"*Stained?* What are you talking about?"

"Women who couple in the field, like animals. They have a stain to them. No one wants them, after."

Oh. Now she understood what he meant. She had watched the sheep mating. Einar had had to explain it to her, how it created the lambs. He had laughed, finding it strange that she knew nothing of the process.

"That has nothing to do with me," she told Andras defiantly.

"Or with me," he said coldly. He turned his back and resumed his stacking of wood. Claire watched for a moment, then continued striding on, but her morning was tainted by the encounter. Later, troubled, she told Alys of it while they were having lunch.

"It's the way here," Alys explained. "Foolish, mayhap. But it has always been so. Girls must come to the Handfasting untouched, or pretend to be. Otherwise . . ."

"Otherwise no one wants them?"

Alys shrugged, and chuckled. "People learn to overlook. Sounds to me as if Andras was hopeful to have you. He'll overlook, with time, if you don't remind him."

"Hmmppph." Claire stood. She fed a piece of spinach to Yellow-wing, who hopped happily back and forth on his perch. Then she scraped the leavings from the plates into the bucket. "I don't care about Andras. And I never wish to wed. *You* didn't," she pointed out.

Alys grinned. "I was a willful girl," she said.

"Willful?"

"Some said wild." Now Alys laughed aloud. "And wanton."

Claire found that the laughter was making her own anger subside. Looking at Alys, wrinkled and bent, it was hard to imagine her as a willful, wild girl. But in the unrestrained laughter Claire could hear a hint of the carefree creature she must once have been.

The children, curious about what seemed a mystery (for people spoke of it in whispers) but too young to judge her, were open with their questions to Claire. They were on the beach, gathering driftwood to dry for the fireplace. The wind was sharp and snapped at Claire's skirt.

"Did it grow in your belly, like my mum's?" Bethan asked.

Claire nodded, resigned to their knowing. She added a bent stick to the pile.

"Were it a boy?" Delwyth's eyes were wide.

Claire nodded again. "Yes," she said. "A male." She startled herself. Why had she called it that? Everyone knew a baby was either a girl, like Bethan's new sister, or a wee boy. Why had she said that odd word, *male*, as if she had given birth to a creature of woods or fields?

"Where did it go, then, your male?" Solemn little Eira looked worried. "Who took it?"

Claire smiled to reassure the child. "Someone else needed it," she explained. "Just as your mum needs these pieces of wood! Let's drag that big one over here and see if we're strong enough to break it, shall we?"

"I'm strong!"

"Look at me, how strong I am!"

"As strong as a boy! As a male!"

The children strutted and shouted as they ran about in the wet sand. Claire glanced toward the high bank that bordered the beach and saw Einar watching. He balanced a wooden yoke across his wide shoulders, and two buckets hung level from either side. He was coming from the spring where he got fresh water. With his shoulders bearing the weight, he was able still to use his walking sticks. Now, seeing her watching, he lifted one hand and waved to her.

Claire waved back, and smiled. *So,* she thought, *there's one young man who doesn't think me stained. Or is it that I'm now ruined, as he is?*

She watched him make his way along the path, his feet dragging, one after the other. Beside her, in the sand, the laughing children imitated Einar, dragging their feet and limping dramatically, and then watching the furrowed ruts they made fill with seawater and smooth over.

NINE

WINTER DESCENDED SUDDENLY, with
bone-chilling cold. The damp, raw wind swept in from the
ocean and entered through cracks in the walls of the hut. It
made the fire flicker and hiss. Claire wore a thick furred vest
that Alys has stitched for her from an animal hide, and warm
boots from the same hide, laced with sinew.

She accompanied Alys one morning to Bryn's cottage,
where the baby girl, now named Elen, was swaddled in layers
of woven cloth and warmed in her cradle by wrapped stones
made hot in the fire. Alys chuckled after listening to the shrill
cry of the infant. "Summer babies fare better," she told Bryn.
"But this one sounds to be strong."

Bryn poured tea into thick mugs. Outside the wind blew,
and on the floor near the fire little Bethan, humming tune-

lessly, sorted acorns into families. Claire excused herself and slipped away.

Outside, she wrapped her shawl tightly over the fur vest and pulled her thick knitted hat down to protect her ears. She started up the hill, following the deserted path as it wound among the wind-tossed trees. No one was about. The cold weather was keeping people indoors. But perhaps, she thought, Einar would be in the meadow, tending his creatures, and would welcome her company. Climbing, she held her mittened hands to her mouth and breathed into them for warmth. Her feet slipped now and then on mud frozen to ice.

* * *

It was hard for Claire to understand seasons. Her returning memory had told her nothing of the way the leaves in summer showed their undersides as a storm approached, then withered and dropped when the nights were chill. Now there was the cold, and she could not remember it. She had never had a coat before, or shawl, she was sure of that. And rain! It had been new to her in summer, and now, with the cold, it was mixed with spits of ice, and who was to guess what might follow! Each day came as a surprise, though Alys, realizing, tried to prepare her and explain.

Claire knocked at the door of the wood-slatted shed

where Lame Einar lived, but there was no answer. She pushed the door open, peeked in, and saw that the ashes of his fire were still hot; wisps of smoke drifted from the chimney and disappeared with the wind into the gray sky. He would be up in the field, she knew. She closed the door tight, pulled her shawl closer around her, and climbed the path.

She found him rubbing salve into the leg of a sheep that had caught itself in a thorny bush.

"Here—help hold him still, would you? He keeps pulling away."

Claire wrapped her arms around the neck of the impatient creature and tried to soothe him by murmuring meaningless sounds. "Shhhh, shhhh," she said, as she had heard Bryn whisper to the baby when she cried. She leaned her head against the matted fleece of the sheep's neck. It felt like a pillow, though its smell was strong.

"There." Einar released the leg, and the sheep shook itself and pulled loose from Claire's grasp. It bounded away through the high, dry grass, and she could hear the nasal bleats of greeting from its flock.

He looked at her and said, "You're cold." Claire laughed at him because he had said the obvious. She was shivering, and breathing again into her own cupped, mittened hands. "Come down to my shed," he told her. He looked out over the flock, saw that they were huddled together, heads hunched low, out of the sleet. Then he went down the path and she followed.

She sat on the heap of skins that he used for sleeping while he poked the ashes into a red glow and then added a thick piece of oak branch. She could feel the warmth expand.

"Tell me why you've come out on a foul day like this," he asked her.

She hesitated, uncertain how he would react. Finally she said carefully, "They tell me you climbed out, once."

He glanced over, then turned back to the fire and rearranged it a bit, though it seemed to Claire unnecessary. She thought that perhaps he simply needed to look away.

"Aye. I did," he acknowledged. "Do you want to know the why of it?"

"The how. I want to know the how. I look at the cliff and it looms there, unclimbable."

Einar sighed. He rose with an effort from where he knelt on the ground, then moved over to sit beside her on the skins. They both stared at the fire.

"I best tell you the why, first, so you understand."

Claire nodded, knowing she would need to tell him her own why when the time came.

Spatters of sleet tapped against the roof of the shed. But they were warm inside.

"I never knew my mum," he began. "She died when she birthed me. Alys came, they said, and helped, but I was big and she labored too long, and bled, and she died. It happens sometimes."

Claire nodded. Alys had told her that it did. She remembered how interested Alys had been, hearing her tell her own story, of the cutting. "It be different here," Alys had said.

"My father was a fisherman, and he was out with the boats. It was this time of year, with the cold and the wind. He likely had a bad time of it too. But he was a hard man, my father. Strong. Used to the weather."

He shrugged. "As I am," he added.

"But you're not *hard*, Einar."

"Hardened to the weather, I am. I must be, for the creatures."

She knew he meant his flock of sheep.

"I don't feel the cold as you do," he told her.

"You've always been here. You've learned to live with it."

They sat silently for a moment. Then he began again to talk. "They say he came in from the sea that evening, and emptied his nets and tied his boat. All who saw him fell silent, for no one wanted to be the one to tell him that his son was birthed healthy but his wife was already stiffening and being readied for a coffin."

He looked away. Then he said, "They say he had wanted a son. But not the one what took his wife."

Outside, a branch broke in the wind, skittered across the dooryard of his shed, and slammed against the wall. Claire could picture the fisherman arriving home in weather just like this to find a squalling infant and a wife turned blue and lost.

"It was Alys kept him from flinging me into the fire. Others came and held him down. He roared into the night, they say, cursing all flesh and the wind and the gods, even cursing the sea that be his livelihood.

"He was a hard man to start, they say. My mum, she softened him a bit, but when she was gone he turned to stone. And the stone had an edge to it, sharpened against me, for I had killed her."

"But it wasn't—" Claire began, then stopped. He hadn't heard her.

"Others raised me. Village women. Then, when I was old enough, he tooken me back. Said it was time for me to pay for what I done."

"What did that mean, 'old enough'? How old were you?"

He thought. "Six years, mayhap? My front teeth had fallen out."

She shuddered at the thought of a little boy expected to atone for his mother's death.

"I didn't know him. It was as if a stranger took me. I went to his cottage, for they said I must, and that night he gave me food and drink, and a blanket to wrap around me as I slept on a pile of straw. In the morning he kicked me awake before it was light and told me he would make a fisherman of me, for I owed him.

"After that, every day, until I was growed, I went with him to the boat and on the boat out onto the sea. He never spoke a soft word. Never told me about the kinds of leaves, or creatures, or pointed to the stars in the sky. Never sang a song to me, or held my hand. Just kicked me across the deck if I be clumsy, laughed when I be twisted in the ropes and sliding pure froze in the water that washed aboard. Slapped me in the head when the sea was rough and I puked over the side. He hoped I would wash overboard and drown. He told me that.

"He made me climb the mast to untangle the lines and he laughed when my hands slid from the salty wood and I fell onto the deck. When I broke my arm he kept me on the sea all day, hauling nets, then sent me to Alys that night and told her to have it fixed by morning or he'd break the other."

"You should have killed him," Claire said in a low voice.

He didn't speak for a moment. Then he said, "I had already killed my mother."

He stood suddenly, leaning on his stick. He went to the

door, cracked it open, and breathed the wind. She was afraid he was going to go out into the bitter cold, that telling her his past had now forced him to punish himself in some way. But after a moment he pulled the door tightly closed and came back. He sat down again, leaning his stick against the wall, and took several deep breaths.

"I growed very strong," he said.

"I know."

"I growed taller than my father and so strong, I could have picked him up and flung him into the sea. But I never thought to do that. I stayed silent. I obeyed him. I cooked for him like a wife and washed his clothes and was a wife in other ways too terrible to mention. I made myself into stone. I willed myself deaf when he cursed me and blind to the look of hatred in his eyes. I waited."

"Waited for what?"

"To be old enough, strong enough, brave enough, to leave. To climb out."

"What went wrong?" she asked him.

"Naught in the climbing out. I trained for it. I was ready. I knew I could do it and I did. It went wrong *after*." Einar moved one damaged foot slightly, staring at it. His tone was bitter. Then it changed and became more gentle, and curious. "Why do you be asking about this?"

"I must try," Claire told him. "I must try to climb out."

He stared at her. "No woman ever done so," he said.

"I must. I have a child out there. A son. I must find him."

She had known he wouldn't be scornful, for that was not his nature. She had thought, though, that he might laugh at the impossibility of her plan. But he did not. And she realized that he already knew of the child, that he had heard the talk of it.

He looked at her thoughtfully for a moment, then said, "Push against this." He extended his arm toward her, his hand held out upright at if to shove something away.

"Like this?" Claire held her hand up against his.

He nodded. "Push."

She did, summoning her strength to try to move his hand, to bend his arm. It was firm. Rigid. Immobile. Her own arm trembled with her effort. Finally she gave up. Her hand dropped back into her lap. It ached.

Einar nodded. "You're strong, at least in the arms. Can you climb?"

Claire pictured the vertical rock cliff that hung over the village and hid the sun for half the day. She shook her head. "I climb the path up to the meadow where you keep the sheep. You've seen me do it often enough. And sometimes, gathering herbs, I go up into the woods near the waterfall. I never get tired. And it's steep there. But I know that's not what you mean."

"You must start to harden yourself. I'll show you. It won't be easy. You must want it."

"I do want it," Claire said. Her voice broke. "I want *him*."

Einar paused, and thought, then said, "It be better, I think, to climb out in search of something, instead of hating what you're leaving.

"It will be a long time," he told her, "to make you ready."

"I know."

"Not days or weeks," he said.

"I know."

"Mayhap it will take years," he told her. "For me, it was years."

"Years?"

He nodded.

"How do I start?" Claire asked.

TEN

"EINAR SAYS I must do this every single day. It strengthens my belly, where the scar is. Watch."

Alys glanced over from the fire, where she was stirring a pot of onion soup. She watched for a moment as Claire, lying on the floor of the hut, wedged her feet under a slab of rock that jutted from the base of the wall, and then lifted the upper half of her body and held herself at a slant, taut, for a moment before she lowered herself slowly back down and took a breath.

"Surely you didn't show that lad your scar?"

"Of course not. But I told him of it." Claire bit her lip, held her breath, and raised herself once again. Then down, slowly. And again.

"There," she said, gasping, after a few moments. "That's ten. He told me to do it ten times every day."

"Here. Have some soup and bread now," Alys told her. "I'll start bottling some strengthening brews for you, as well." She glanced up at the dried herbs hanging from the beams that supported the hut's roof. Claire could hear her murmuring the names—white willow, nettle, meadowsweet, goldenseal—and knew she was pondering what combinations to create.

She had told Alys of her plan. No one else knew.

Claire thought of Alys as the calmest person she knew, the person who had seen the worst of things over her long life and was not surprised or distressed by any of it anymore. Claire had watched her stitch the flesh and wrap an astringent poultice around the leg of a small child gashed by a fall on the slippery rocks, soothing both the terrified mother and the screaming toddler at the same time with her reassuring voice. She had seen her, quiet and commanding, attend the most difficult births, with the babies upside down or sideways and the mum begging for death and the dad puking in the dooryard. Claire had been there at deaths—Andras's mother from fever and cough; a fisherman with his skull crushed by a broken mast; a young boy racked by fits from the day of his birth, finally at five dead with foam on his lips and his eyes rolled back to white. Alys had tended them, tended their families, weighted the eyelids and folded the arms, then returned to the hut to wash her tools, cook supper, and wait for the next frantic villager who would come to the door begging for help.

She had never seemed alarmed—until the day Einar and Claire told her that Claire must climb out.

"That canna be," she had said loudly, and began to rock back and forth in her chair as if to try to soothe a deep pain. "Oh, no. Canna! You'll die!"

She turned to Claire fiercely. "You'll die on the cliff. You'll fall and be broken to pieces! I've seen the others who was! And look at him, who was once fleet and sure-footed—look at him now, ruined by climbing out! I'm sorry, Einar, you're a good lad and I loved your mum, but you're bloody ruined by that mountain and I won't have you do it to my girl!"

"It was not the mountain ruined me, Alys," Einar said firmly. Claire, listening, was startled by the sudden sureness of him. He had always been so shy and halting in his speech. But now he spoke with certainty to Alys. "I strengthened myself for it and did it. I climbed out. It was *after*. And I'll teach her of that. But for now I'll make her strong. That's how we're starting, and we need you to help, Alys, for she wants her son and must have a way to find him."

"Boat," Alys wailed. "She can go forth on the sea, surely, if she must go."

"No. Not by sea. I won't." As much as she feared the cliff

and the climbing she must learn to do, Claire feared the sea more.

"It's winter now," Alys said to them, weakening a bit. "Mayhap in spring we can toughen her up. The sun, and air. That'll be good for strength."

Einar laughed. "We'll start now, Alys," he said, "and spring will come before we know it. It always does."

* * *

It did. Spring came. Through all the months of winter she had, each day, lain on the hut floor, put her hands behind her head, and raised herself. Her scarred abdomen had become tight and smooth, and she no longer breathed hard at the effort.

She told Einar, "I'm ready."

He laughed. They were standing beside the door of the hut, and he told her to run up the hillside path, up to the waterfall, and back down to where he stood.

There was a fine rain falling, as there had been all week. The path was slick with spring mud. Claire made a face.

"It's too slippery."

"It's smooth and dry, if you think on it compared to the mountain."

"Yes, well —"

"Run up it. Grip with your feet."

Claire looked down at her own feet, encased in thick wool socks under her coarse leather sandals.

"Take them off," Einar said.

Claire sighed and obeyed. She pulled her sandals off, and the socks. The ground was very cold, still. Spring was young and the drizzle was chilly. She wiggled her toes into the cold, wet earth, to get the grip, and then began to run.

The path steepened partway up and she slipped, scraping her knee on a rock. She righted herself and now her hands were thick with mud and a red trickle of blood patterned her leg. Catching her breath, she eyed the wet path above; then she took a breath and continued. *Run*, Einar had said. She had climbed this path often before, but always slowly, placing her feet carefully. Now she ran. She tried to dig her toes into the ground, but they slid and she fell again and righted herself again. By the time she reached the top of the hill and stood by the rushing waterfall, she found herself in tears. She was coated in mud, shaking with cold, and her knee was swollen and sore. From where she stood, she could see him below, looking up, watching her. She hoped he couldn't see her crying.

"Now down!" she heard him call.

Sliding partway, grasping tree roots to keep from falling, she stumbled down the treacherous path to the bottom. She wiped her tearstained face with muddy hands and hurried to where Einar was waiting.

"Good," he told her. "Now do it again."

* * *

Each day through the summer she ran the hill path. On fine days, the mist of the falls made rainbows, and she began to smile when she reached that place, instead of weeping as she had the first time. It began to feel not easy, but doable. She began to come down grinning and proud.

Einar grinned back at her. "You're growing strong," he said, then added, "for a girl."

She glanced at him and saw that he was teasing her. His look was fond. He turned away quickly and tried to hide the fondness, but Claire knew. She had seen him look that way at a half-grown lamb prancing in the meadow on a midsummer afternoon, admiring its agile charm. She had seen him look that way at her, and knew there was a longing to his gaze.

When she felt she had mastered the path, he made it harder. He tied her hands together so that she couldn't use them to steady herself. When the spring moisture had dried, the path became gritty and treacherous in a different way. She couldn't grip it with her toes. When she fell, bruising her shoulder because she couldn't break the fall with her tethered hands, he taunted her. When she wept, he ignored her. She dried her tears and ran.

One afternoon Bryn, her baby in a sling on her chest, stopped by the hut to get a remedy for a spider bite on her ankle. Alys and Claire looked at the hot, swollen sore. "Comfrey root oil," Alys told her. "I have it here. Sit while I heat it."

Bryn handed little Elen to Claire. "I'll take her outside," Claire said, and she carried the sturdy, curly-headed girl to the dooryard to show her some black-eyed Susans in bloom.

Einar appeared. He came every day now, if Claire didn't run to the sheep meadow and meet him there.

"It's Bryn's baby," she told him. "Isn't she sweet?" She handed a picked flower to Elen, who grasped it in a fist and waved it in the air.

"Run with her," Einar said.

Claire was startled, but she laughed. Then, holding the baby, she ran around the small dooryard. Elen waved her arms in delight.

"Let me feel her weight." Einar took the baby from Claire. She could see that he had no experience with a human infant, though he was sure and facile with lambs. She watched as with his large hands under her, Einar assessed how heavy Elen was.

"You must start running with weight," he said, and handed the baby back. "I'll bring it tomorrow."

The next day he was back with a crude leather sack half filled with rocks. He tied it to Claire's back and told her to run the hill path. She did so, and arrived panting at the waterfall. She was tempted to throw a few of the rocks into the rushing torrent, to ease the burden for the run back down. But she didn't. She ran with the weight, and then ran the path again, and found that her breathing changed, to accommodate the heaviness. After a few runs, the longer breaths she needed came naturally, and it was as if she had always carried it. Alys told her that it was the way of women, to tote a newborn and then adjust as it grew until by the time the child was plump and heavy, the weight seemed naught. Einar left a pile of rocks beside the base of the path and told her to add one more to the sack each day.

Her legs grew muscled and firm. She showed him, one day, how strong and sure they had become. He felt where she showed him, pressing his large hand against the taut, smooth skin above her ankle, and nodded. Then he left his hand there, encircling her leg, and they looked at each other for a moment before he took it away. She felt his fondness again, and her own for him, and the futility of it for them both. She could not stay here.

One morning Einar set a thick log on end. It reached to her knee.

"Step up on that," he said.

She reached for his hand, needing it for support, but he backed away. Claire checked the log to be certain it was firm on the ground. Then she measured the height with her eyes, raised one leg up, placed it on the top of the log, shifted her weight, and picked up her other foot. But she lost her balance and fell back.

"Try again."

All afternoon she stepped onto and down from the log. At first she held her arms wide, using them for balance. Then Einar approached with the coarse rope he had used to restrain her hands on the steep path.

"Wait," she told him. "I don't need my arms tied." Firmly she held her own hands at her sides. Wobbling at first, she tested herself again and again until without moving her arms she could maintain her balance as she mounted the log.

"Good," he said. The next day he brought a higher, narrower log.

* * *

Winter came. Outdoors, she ran and climbed on ice. He began to teach her to use a rope, to knot it and twirl it and fling it so that it caught on a rock or a branch. At first it caught things at random. Then, after a bit, she found she could aim with the noose of the rope, that she could choose a log or a bush and catch it precisely on most of her attempts. Then he made the noose smaller. He directed her to capture smaller things: a seedling pine reaching upward from a crevice; a stone balanced on a tree stump. He took away the thick, coarse rope and gave her a thin, woven cord that whistled when she spun it out into the cold air and snapped a twig with its tiny noose.

Inside the hut, in a corner that Alys had cleared for her, she walked back and forth on a piece of rope stretched taut between two posts, her toes gripping the rope, her breath even, her eyes focused, her arms at first stretched for balance, and then, as spring approached, her hands at her side and her movement steady and controlled. She walked the rope forward and backward. She stood on it still as a post: on one leg, then the other. Slowly she bent one knee, lowered herself, remained there poised, then rose again.

Yellow-wing twittered and pranced on his perch, excited as he watched her. Alys, watching, held her breath and then gasped at each new move.

But Claire was calm. She felt strong. She felt ready.

"Now?" she asked Einar.

Einar shook his head. "Next, we begin to strengthen your arms," he said.

* * *

By the following spring, Bryn's baby, Elen, was sturdy and walking. Bryn was expecting another and hoped for a boy. Bethan, Delwyth, and Eira were tall now, with long legs and secrets that made them whisper and giggle.

Most of the village had lost interest in Claire. She was no longer new and mysterious. The scandal of her child was forgotten; there had been more recent disgraces—a woman who took up with her sister's husband, a fisherman who was caught stealing from his own brother. The villagers took little note of Claire's odd new hobby; the hill paths were not visible, and Alys's hut was separate.

She continued her everyday chores, helping with the gathering of plants, accompanying Alys to births and deaths. Sometimes Alys sent her alone to tend a simple cough or fever or rash. The old woman was increasingly bent over, and her walking now was slow. Her eyesight was dimmed. She needed more rest.

Claire teased her gently and told her that she should train to climb out. "Look how strong Einar has made me!" she said, and held out her bare arm, tightening the muscles with pride.

Each evening, after she had cleaned up the hut from dinner and while Alys sat knitting in her rocker, Claire took up her position, lying on her side on a mat near the wall, and breathed deeply. Then, legs straight, she raised her body on one arm, held herself there, hovering, and then eased herself slowly down. Again and again. First one arm. Then the other.

Her sack of rocks was so heavy now that an ordinary person groaned, trying to lift it. But for Claire it was easy. She swung it onto her back each day and wore it while she tended the garden or gathered the herbs. She ran up and down the hill path with the sack on her back and another in her arms. Steep, rutted places that had once made her stumble and slip were now familiar and easy.

He had her run the path at night. Things felt different in the dark. She trained her feet and hands to know the shapes of things and her mind to sense when she neared an edge and must back away lest she fall.

He wanted to blindfold her so that she could practice the dark in daytime. But she said no.

"I'll do it at night, even in the middle of the night, when there's no moon and when it's bitter cold. But I can't have something tied over my eyes. It's like being on the sea. It's a fearsome memory that I can't—"

She turned away and couldn't finish. But he seemed to understand. "You must learn the dark, though," he told her. "Part of the climbing out will be in dark. You'll start before the sun comes up."

"Why?"

"It's too long a climb to do it all in daylight. If you wait and go at dawn, at sunup, then the dark part will come near the top. You'll be making your way up and around places where a mistake will bring death on you. I'll teach you to feel every bit with your feet, but even so you'll need your eyes as you near the top."

Together they looked up at the shadowy cliff. Claire had to lean back to see the top. Mist swirled there and she could see hawks circling.

He had said he would teach her to feel with her feet, and after some time she became aware, amused by it, that even her toes were supple now. With astonishment she realized that she could perceive the smallest of pebbles—and pick them up, if need be, with individual toes. She could grasp a twig between the third and fourth toe of her left foot, or carefully feel her way around the sharp edge of a flat rock by her right big toe, which was as sensitive now as a fingertip.

She told this to Einar with delight. "Imagine that!" she said. "Toes!" He nodded in agreement but looked sad.

"What's wrong?" she asked him.

But he turned away and didn't reply. Guiltily she realized it had been cruel to be so gleeful over the strength and agility of her feet to someone who had lost his own.

ELEVEN

TWINS! TWO BOYS with bright red hair. Bryn, exhausted as she was, lay laughing at the surprise and the sight of them. Claire held one in each arm and then laughed herself as she realized she was raising and lowering them slightly, the same way Einar had her raise and lower heavy rocks to strengthen her forearms.

It was almost winter again. She moved Yellow-wing's cage indoors. It had hung all summer and into autumn from a tree branch in the dooryard. Now, in the warmth, he fluffed his wings and chirped. Bethan was there, and Elen. Their mother needed quiet to tend her two new boys, and sent the girls off to amuse themselves. Now little Elen, squatting on the floor, twisted twigs into a bird shape and pretended she had made a wife for Yellow-wing. Bethan was busily helping Alys sort some dried herbs to be packed into bags and stored. Claire, watching, realized that Alys was beginning to teach the young girl in the same way that she had taught Claire for these past years. The village would need someone to take Alys's place. It was clear that it could not be Claire.

She wrapped her hands around the thick branch that Einar had peeled and set firmly in place above the door. She lifted herself up until her chin was level with the peeled wood. She hung poised there and counted to ten, then lowered herself slowly. Doing this still hurt. That meant she needed it. She must do this each day until it stopped hurting. Then, she knew, Einar would tell her to put on her backpack filled with rocks and begin doing it again.

Briefly, on a day when she was exhausted, she thought of Einar with frustration, of how demanding he was, how relentlessly he made her do the exercises again and again. Then she thought of how he watched her, assessing and admiring her strength, and she knew that his gaze was also that of someone who loved her.

Tall Andras had married in midsummer, his new wife a fresh-faced, quick-smiling young girl named Maren. Standing at the ceremony, Claire felt no sadness; she had never wanted to be his wife. But once he had hoped for it, and now he had moved on and seemed happy. She thought sadly of Einar, alone in his hillside hut, and knew that a part of life was passing both of them by.

"Soon?" she asked Einar, after she showed him how she could hold herself raised on the branch with her arms taut and unshaking, even while wearing the sack of rocks at its heaviest. He ignored her question.

"One arm now," he said. While he watched, she struggled to lift herself with just one. He wanted her arms to be equally strong on both sides, as her legs now were. On either leg she could hop up onto a rock slippery with damp moss and stand balanced there with the other tucked up like a waterbird. After rain she could slide, standing on one foot, down the steep muddy path and stop herself at any point by pressure on her heel or toes.

She could hold a pebble on her raised foot and then move it by concentrating on it until it was between two toes, then under. From there she could move it from toe to toe, under and over. It made little Elen laugh uproariously to watch and then try the same feat with her own chubby toes.

"Why do I need to spend time learning foolish tricks?" Claire asked Einar. "This seems a waste."

"It won't be. It's important. You'll see."

She was eager to go. She had waited such a long time.

But she had come to trust Einar, his wisdom and caring, deeply. So she sighed and nodded.

* * *

In the winter she slept beside Alys. When the fire died late one night, with wind howling outside, the old woman shivered and Claire embraced her, trying to send warmth from her own body into the frail limbs that could no longer hold on to their own heat.

"You're a good girl," Alys murmured. "Your own mum must miss you fierce."

Claire was startled. When she tried, in response to Alys's words, to think of her mother, there was little that came forth. Parents. Yes. She had had parents. She could remember their faces, and could even recall the sound of their voices. But there was little else.

"No," she told Alys. "I don't think she loved me."

Alys turned in the bed and through the dim light of the last embers that glowed in the fireplace, Claire could see her bright eyes, open in surprise. "How could that be, child?"

Claire chuckled and hugged her. "I'm not a child anymore, Alys. Maybe I was when you found me. I was a young girl, then. But so much time has passed, Alys. I'm a woman now."

"To me you're a child, still. And a mum always loves her child."

"It should be so, shouldn't it? But something stood in the way of it. I think it was a—well, they called them *pills*. The mothers took pills."

"Pills?"

"Like a potion."

"Ah." That was something Alys understood. "But a potion is meant to fix an ill."

Claire yawned. She was achy and exhausted.

"My people—" ("My people"? What did that mean? She didn't really know) "They thought that it fixed a lot of ills, not to have feelings like love."

"Fools," Alys muttered. Now she yawned too. "You loved your boy, though. That's why you're soon to climb out."

Claire closed her eyes and patted the old woman's back. "I did," she said. "I loved my boy. I still do."

TWELVE

IN LATE SPRING, Tall Andras had a plump newborn son, and there were lambs prancing in the upper meadow, their soft fleece warm in the changed, gentler weather. Early wildflowers were in bloom, and lavender butterflies with lacy-patterned wings darted from one to the next. Bryn's twin boys grinned and showed two teeth apiece. The fishermen folded freshly knotted nets they had mended in winter while their wives, beside them at the fire, made the sweaters they would wear on their boats.

Even the wind seemed new. It wasn't the same brutal wind that had ripped the roof thatch and swirled the snow. Now it pulled the warm scent of brine-washed sea urchins, mussels, and kelp from the rocks and carried it gently across the beach and up the hill. It lifted Claire's long curls as she knelt and filled a basket with nettles. The rigid stems and heart-shaped leaves were covered with stiff hairs that were painful to touch, but she was wearing the special protective gloves Alys had made. The plant would be a valuable pain reliever for Old Benedikt, who was suffering from gout.

"Don't touch," she warned Bethan, who had come with her and wanted to help. "It stings. You gather the elder bark, over there. Your mum needs it for your brothers."

Bethan peeled bits of the bark and added it to the basket. The twins were fussy from teething.

"When I leave, you'll be in charge of the gathering, then. Alys will make gloves for you. You must be careful with these nettles."

Bethan hung her head.

"Do you think you can't do it? You've learned so much," Claire reassured her.

"I can do it. But I don't want you to leave."

"Ah, Bethy." Claire hugged the slender girl. "You know why I must go."

"To find your baby." Bethan sighed. "Yes, I know."

"Not a baby anymore. He's a boy now. If I don't go soon to find him, he'll be a man!"

"I fear for you, Claire." Bethan's voice was low.

"Why is that? You know how strong I am. Look!" Claire

reached up with one arm and grasped a limb of the elder tree. She raised herself until she balanced, unwavering, from the one muscled arm. Then, slowly, she lowered herself back to the ground. "Not even your pa can do that, can he?"

Bethan smiled slightly. "No. And Pa's getting fat, too, Ma says."

"You mustn't fear for me, then. You can see that I'm strong, and swift, and . . ."

"Smart, and sly, and . . ." Bethan giggled. It was a game they often played, with the sounds of words.

"And silly!"

"And sleepy!"

"And slugbucket!"

"Swatbottom!"

As it always did, their word game dissolved into nonsense and they laughed as they carried the basket back down the hill.

✳ ✳ ✳

Time passed quickly now. The seasons flowed into one another and Claire was no longer surprised as the changes came. Like the other villagers, she bundled herself against the increasing cold as each winter approached, and welcomed each new spring. The growth of the children made her aware of time passing. Bethan and her companions were no longer giggling, exuberant children; they were becoming taller, quieter, preparing for womanhood to come. Elen, no longer a baby, was the small, mischievous one now, playing the imaginative games that her sister once had. The redheaded twin boys scuffled and scampered together while Bryn, their mother, fretted over their misbehavior and laughed at their antics.

Each spring the snow melted and Claire took Yellow-wing's cage outside to hang it once again from the tree. Each fall, when the wind swept in from the sea and the leaves fell rustling on the ground, she brought her little companion into the cottage once again.

"How long will he live?" she asked Einar one day when she was feeding the bird. Suddenly she was aware that each life had a beginning and an end.

"Birds have a long life. He'll be here to keep Alys company when you be gone."

Claire glanced at him. He had not mentioned it in a long time, the fact of her leaving. He tested her strength, still, and kept her working at it, but he had not spoken of the climbing out for many months. It had been six years now since the day she had been carried in from the sea, and five since the morning that Elen's birth returned the memory of her son to her. Somewhere he would be a half-grown boy: running, shouting, playing.

Einar saw her questioning look.

"Soon," he told her.

* * *

With summer approaching, plants coming into flower, and Alys in need of more help as her strength began to ebb, there was a great deal to do. The daily exercise had long been part of Claire's routine. She rose before dawn each day and lifted sacks weighted with stones many times with each arm before she put the kettle over the fire. Then, while she waited for the water to boil for tea, she practiced the lifting of her legs, and the raising of her upper body as she lay flat. She could now do these things with great ease. It made her laugh to remember how difficult they had been when she started. Now she tied heavy rocks to her ankles and wrists but still performed the familiar motions without effort.

She cleaned Yellow-wing's cage as she did each morning. It had been raining for some days, but now the rain seemed to have ended; it was a simple cloudy spring morning. She carried the cage outside and hung it from the willow tree beside the hut. She whistled and chirped back at the bird, who was excited at being outdoors. Then she heard a familiar answering whistle and turned to greet Einar, who was approaching from the meadow path.

"Alys baked bread yesterday," she told him cheerfully. "And she made extra. We have a loaf ready for you."

"Look at the sky," Einar said.

She did. Above the looming cliff, the pale wadded clouds reminded her of Einar's sheep when, after the snowmelt, they still huddled for warmth but with heads down moved across the meadow nibbling at new shoots. But somehow she knew that wasn't what he meant.

"What?"

"There's sun behind. The rain's done for a while."

Those who tended stock, like Einar, or who farmed, like Andras, or all of the village fishermen — they knew the sky. Claire nodded cheerfully at what he said. "Good. I can do the washing and hang it out on the bushes."

"No," Einar said. "No more washing. It's time to climb out."

THIRTEEN

THERE WERE STILL stars visible in the night sky. A sliver of spring moon was low, just above the quiet-moving sea. In the meadow, the huddled sheep were silent. The only sound was the rush of water from the falls above, through the woods to the side.

They stood there together. Then Claire said, "I'm sorry for what happened to you."

"Aye. I know."

He had told her, at last, how he had been damaged. It was worse than she could have imagined. But she knew she must not think of it now. When she reached the top would be the time. She would have to plan, then, and what he had revealed to her would be part of her planning. But for now she must concentrate only on the climb.

"He'll be there at the top, do you think?"

"Not at first. You'll wait there and he'll come. Don't think on it now."

"But I will know him?"

"Aye. You will."

"Do you think I'll make it, Einar?"

"You will." He laughed and touched her cheek. "I've given you what's been in my mind for all these years, since I climbed out. Every night since then I've climbed out again. I've felt again each rock, each bit of moss, each twig and hollow and cleft and turn: at night, when other men are mending their nets or sharpening their tools or making love to their women — I've been remembering the climbing. I have a map in my mind and I've given it to you and you'll be safe."

He chuckled and hugged her. "You must. If you don't, I'll be made a fool of, for I was the one what made you strong! Let me see your pack now, to make it tight against you."

Claire knelt on the path at the base of the cliff while Einar leaned his walking sticks against the rock wall and adjusted the pack on her back.

"Knife?" he asked her.

She showed him how it was firmly knotted onto the cord that hung around her neck.

"Rope?"

It was coiled neatly and wrapped around her shoulder.

"The water gourd's in your pack. Don't try to reach it when you're on the rock, even if you thirst fierce. There are places where you can stop and rest. Ledges, they're called. If you climb steady you'll reach the first one at midday. You can stop to drink there."

"Yes, I know. You told me."

"What's this?" He was feeling her pack. "Down by the water gourd, with the gloves?"

"Alys put that in. Herb salve for healing."

"Aye, that's good. Mayhap when you use the rope, you'll burn your hands, even with the gloves. If you slip on the rope, it pulls against your skin. But don't let go."

"I won't. You know I won't."

"Don't put on the gloves lessen you use the rope. You need to feel with your fingers."

"Einar?"

"What?"

She showed him. "Alys made this. You can't see it because it's too dark, but feel."

She handed him the flat, round object and waited while he felt it.

"It's just an ordinary rock. But Alys sewed a piece of cloth around it. It's bright red. She made it from the woolen hat I wore last winter."

"Whyever?"

"When I get to the top? You told me there's a very steep place just before. The place I must be so careful . . ."

"Aye, the place with the rock steps. Don't look down."

"No, I won't. I'll do it just the way you told me, feeling for each step, being so careful, not looking down, not being gleeful because it's the top."

"What, then?"

"When I finish climbing all those steps and am at the top, and feel my feet in the solid earth? Then I'll fling this rock out into the air and down."

"The sun will be setting."

"Yes. I'll fling my rock out into the sunset. You look tomorrow. Look on the ground down here for the bright red. Then you'll know that I did it. That I climbed out."

"Aye. I'll look. It'll be a sign."

He touched her cheek and held his hand there tenderly for a moment. "I will miss you, Water Claire," he said.

"I will never forget you, Fierce Einar," she replied.

They both smiled at the long-ago names. Then he kissed

her, turned away, and reached for his sticks. She would not see him again. It was time for her to start.

* * *

The base of the cliff was large boulders, some of them slippery with damp moss on their shadowed sides. They were easy for her to climb; she had practiced here occasionally, after dark. So her feet (bare, though her sandals were in her pack for later) knew the feel and shape of them. But it would be too easy to dismiss the dangers even of this familiar beginning place. A slip on the moss, a misplaced step, a turned ankle, and her mission would end before it began. So she reminded herself to be vigilant. She focused on each move, placing each foot meticulously, feeling the surface with her toes, assessing the texture, shifting her weight before she took the next step. Once she jostled a small rock in passing and sent a shower of stones clattering down. She scolded herself for that. It was a small misjudgment and caused no harm. But she could not afford a single mistake this day.

Einar had told her to think of nothing during the climb but the climb itself. But now and then, during this early section that she could maneuver with ease, she found her thoughts straying from the cliff. *If only,* the voice in her mind whispered. *What if.*

If only I had taken the baby that day. What if I had brought my little son here, and he could have grown up with Einar teaching him about the birds, and the lambs . . .

He would have died in the sea. She shuddered, thinking of it.

What if Einar had not tried to climb out? What if he had stayed whole? Then he and I could go together, and find my son, and . . .

She willed her thoughts to stop. *Concentrate,* she told herself. *Concentrate only on the cliff. On the climb.*

There were plants here, in places where wind-borne seeds had dropped into the rocky crevices and been nourished by melted snow, sprouting now in this early spring, their stems reaching up. By daybreak she would be able, perhaps, to see them move as they sought the sun. Now, in the dark, she could only feel them there, tendrils brushing against her bare legs. She tried not to trample their fragile growth.

Ah. Here. This was why Einar had told her not to let her thoughts wander. Here was the place he had described, where suddenly, in this massed section of boulders, was a rift, a deep gap in the rocks, a place where she must jump to the next foothold. He knew it would still be dark when she reached it.

"Why don't we go there now, in daylight, just for practice?" she had asked him. "Then I'll know exactly the length of the jump, and—Oh." She caught herself, realizing that it would be impossible for him. He struggled each day, making his way with difficulty down from the sheep pasture in order to teach and help her. He could not scramble up this mass of uneven rocks.

But he had helped her to create the practice place. He measured the distance and height; they built the shapes from mud and let it harden. She jumped it again and again. It was not difficult. She was to leap from the top of a jagged boulder across the gap to a flat granite surface. He had her do it repeatedly on moonless nights, so that she could not see, and she began to feel the distance so accurately that her feet found the same landing place every time.

"You'll come to a place where you must squeeze betwixt two rocks as high as your shoulder. Matched. Same size, like Bryn's boys," he had told her. "When you get yourself through—mind you don't catch your pack in the squeeze—then you go upward to the top of the next rock. It slants up, and there's a sharp edge you'll feel. That's where you plant yourself, on that edge, and jump outward and down."

It was just as he had described. The twin rocks were as high as her chin, and the space between them narrow. Carefully she used her hands and felt the surface all the way down each one, to make sure there would be no rough places to scrape and injure her as she squeezed herself between them in the dark. Then, arching her back to accommodate the lumpy pack — it would be a disaster should her water gourd be crushed — she slid through.

The next rock was what she expected, a sharp upward slant with jagged outcroppings. She mounted it inch by inch, avoiding the daggerlike places that might gash her soles. She used her trained toes like fingers, feeling the way. It was slow going because she took such care. It was what he had taught her to do. Finally she reached the top of the slant, the sharp edge where he had instructed her to plant her feet for the jump. She balanced there, took a deep breath, recalled in her mind the feel of the distance she must cover, then made the leap into darkness with certainty. She landed on the flat granite, balanced perfectly. It had been her first challenge, really, and a small one. But even the small ones could be disastrous if they went wrong, and it was satisfying to have it behind her. She took her water gourd from the pack, sipped, and rested there for a moment, thinking through the next part of the climb. On the horizon, looking out across the sea, she could see a thin pink line of dawn emerge.

FOURTEEN

MIDDAY. THE SUN was directly overhead now. Claire could see, below her, that the tops of the trees were moving slightly. So there was a bit of a breeze. But it didn't reach here. She wiped sweat from her forehead and pushed her damp hair back. She retied the cord that held it bunched at her neck, then wiped her sweaty hands carefully on the woven cloth of her garment. She could not afford the least slip of her hand on the rock face of the cliff. Earlier, farther down, she might have recovered from a falter or stumble, might even have bound up a twisted ankle and continued on. But here, now, an instant of missed footing or a lost grip on a handhold would mean certain death. She blew on her hands and dried them again.

She was balanced now on a narrow ledge. Einar had

told her she would reach this place at midday and it would be safe to stop here and drink from her gourd. She had done so already, once, at dawn, on the lower rocks, when it was still easy to stand and rearrange her pack. Here it was much more difficult. The hours of learning balance were helping her now. Turned sideways on the ledge that was no wider than her two feet side by side, she wriggled the pack around so that she could reach in and grasp the gourd. She held it carefully with both hands while she drank, then replaced it and withdrew the gloves from the pack. She would need them next.

If she had needed her arms for balance on this precarious perch, she would not have been able to drink. But her body needed the water, and he had prepared her for this. After she moved the pack again to its place between her shoulders, she stood with her legs steady and firm and pulled a glove onto each hand. Then slowly she uncoiled the rope.

It was amazing, really, that having made this climb only once — then down again, so perhaps that counted as twice; but he was injured then, and could hardly have been memorizing the ledges and grasping places — Einar had been able to recreate it for Claire. She imagined him alone in his hut, all those years, making the climb again in his mind, creating the map of it night after night.

Here you must stop and look carefully ahead and slightly up, for the next hold.

At this place there is loose rock. It deceives. Do not place your foot on the ledge here. It won't hold.

A gull has nested here. Feel under the nest, through the twigs. There's a place to grasp.

Use the rope here.

Feel with your toes now.

Don't look down.

She was now at the place where he had said to use the rope. She must find the spot up and ahead where a gnarled tree jutted from a slice in the rock face. There would be a small ledge beneath it. Between here, where she stood balanced on this ledge, and the one below the tree, was nothing she could grip or hold. So she must capture the tree with the noose of her rope and use it to get across the wide expanse of vertical rock.

She formed and knotted the noose. Across and above, she saw the stunted tree. She measured it with her eyes, to know how large the noose should be. Einar had said it may have grown in the years since he had done this. She might have to make a large noose, he had told her, to whirl it over the crooked branches, then tighten it around the twisted trunk.

But she could see from here that it had not grown at all. Instead, it was blackened, and one of the branches hung crooked and dead, split from the trunk. *Lightning,* Claire thought. *It has been struck by lightning.*

She tried to see where the roots emerged from the rock. Were they split as well? Would they hold? But they were hidden from her sight by a thick knob on the trunk itself.

He had warned her not to look down here. She was tempted to do so, in order to know what would happen if the tree failed her, if it broke from her weight and she fell. But she could hear his voice: *Think only on the climb. Think on what you control.*

She could not control the tree, or its blackened, split trunk. She could not control the strength of the gnarled roots that held it to the cliff.

But he had taught her how to control her body: her arms, her hands, her fingers, her feet and legs. And with them she could control the rope. She let it out, looping between her gloved hands, until it seemed the length was right. Then she began to twirl the noose. She had practiced this with Einar so often.

Now. She sent it loose and the loops unwound between her gloves as the rope shot out like a snake she had once seen unwind itself in pursuit of a mouse frozen in terror. The snake had killed the mouse in a split second. Claire's aim was just as accurate, but she had made the noose too small. It caught the end of the tree but didn't encircle it entirely; it was caught in the Y of a small forked branch.

She jerked at the rope and to her relief the twig on which it was caught snapped and the rope fell loose. She brought it in, hand over hand, and coiled it again. She remade the noose, slightly larger this time, and looped it for a second time between her gloved hands.

She called back the image of the snake: its eyes, its aim, the swift accuracy of its strike. One more time she twirled the rope and sent it out. This time, snakelike in its precision, it encircled the tree.

Claire tightened the noose, pulling it in close around the trunk by its base near the rock wall. Then, still balanced on the tiny ledge where she stood, she knotted the rope around her own waist. Her next move must be to leave the ledge, to steady herself with the taut rope and walk herself across the expanse of vertical veined granite, feeling for tiny protrusions to grasp with her bare toes. If the tree uprooted and fell, she would fall with it and die.

Think only on the task. On the climb.

She reached out with a foot, pressed it into the wall, and anchored it there. She tightened her grip on the rope and lifted her second foot from the ledge. For a breathless moment she dangled there in space. Then she placed her foot on the wall and steadied herself. The tree was holding. She moved her first foot an inch, then another. The tree still held. She tightened the rope, moved her second foot, and then the first again. She took in more rope through her gloved palms as she moved herself slowly across.

When at last she reached the small ledge below the tree and felt her feet firmly in place there, she took a deep breath. From here she would go upward though a diagonal crevice, but there would be footholds—she could see the first ones just above her—and at the top, another resting place. With difficulty she pulled the rope loose from the tree and rewound it. There was no way to return her gloves to her pack here on this tiny precarious place, so she fixed them under the rope on her shoulder. Then she reached up for the first wedge of rock and lifted herself by one arm into the crevice.

It was cooler here in the shadows. She realized she was getting tired. And it was only early afternoon. There was still a long way to go.

✳ ✳ ✳

It took Claire longer than she had expected to make her way through the narrow shadowed tunnel that the crevice had formed. It was not life-threatening, as the rope-assisted passage across the cliff face had been. There was no sheer drop here. She was moving upward at a slant between two walls of rock. It was cool, which helped, for it had been very hot on the cliff face, and the sun had made it hard to see at times, shimmering as it did on the granite. Here, it was hard to see for the opposite reason: the shadowy darkness that made it cool. But it was like the night climbing at the bottom. She did it by feel.

The chill had also made it wet. Snowmelt had seeped into the rock tunnel, and the small opening had not allowed the sun in to evaporate the water. So the rock walls were damp and slippery. Twice Claire's fingers slid loose from their holds and she went backwards, sliding down into the space she had just climbed through. She wiped her hands firmly again on her clothing, but the fabric too was now soaked through. Finally she thought to put on the gloves that she had wedged under her coiled rope. But when she pulled at them, there was only one. The other glove had slipped free and fallen someplace. For a moment she despaired. Then she remembered what Einar had told her: When something went wrong—*and it's sure that something will*, he had said—you stopped to think, then found a way around it.

She lay at a slant in the tunnel, holding herself there with her legs taut against the walls, and thought. Then she put the remaining glove on her right hand, turned, grasped the next handhold, the one she had slipped from, and held herself there. The glove made it easier. It was thick and coarse. Even damp, it held fast. So she was secure for the moment. She worked her legs up an inch at a time, on either side, until they held her.

Then slowly, carefully, she took the glove off, put it on her other hand, and reached up farther for the next handhold. She grabbed, held on, and began again to inch her legs up. In the darkness she felt the wall with her ungloved hand, trying to find the next holding place; when she had found it, she carefully switched the glove again so she could hold fast. It was painstakingly slow, but she was moving upward instead of sliding down. Far up and ahead she could see the sunny opening where she would emerge back onto the side of the cliff. This, she remembered, was where she would find a large nest. She was to reach under the thick twiggy construction for a place to grasp. From there she would move onto a series of outcroppings that formed something almost like steps.

"Nest. Steps. Nest. Steps." She began to murmur the two words, giving them a sort of rhythm that helped her move upward and forward. It gave her something to focus on as she continued the agonizingly slow ascent between the dark, damp walls.

FIFTEEN

EMERGING FROM THE tunneled cleft in the cliff wall, Claire was once again faced with the sheer drop of it, the certain death if she were to fall. Just in front of her, she was reassured to see the large nest that Einar had told her she would find. She caught her breath, then stretched forward and pulled loose some dried seaweed that formed part of its construction. She used it to dry her perspiring hands, then tucked it into her sleeve.

Reach under the nest, he had told her. *There's a place to grab on to, there.*

She began to follow his instructions, leaning against the cliff toward the nest. *Nest. Then steps.*

The attack was swift, painful, and without warning. From behind and above, something huge swooped and stabbed her viciously behind her ear. She could feel the blood flow down her neck.

She retreated with a gasp back into the tunnel, supporting herself with her feet pressed against the side walls. She held the wad of seaweed against her wound but could feel the blood pulsing.

Immediately she understood what she was facing. Einar had made the climb in winter. The nest had been empty then. Now there must be new chicks. Yes. She listened and could hear the tiny squawking cries. Peering out, she could see the shadow of the parent gull, circling.

The neck of her shirt was wet with it, but the flow of blood gradually eased. Tentatively she lifted the homemade bandage. Good. The wound was only oozing. The sharp pain had subsided. She knew that she would be bruised and sore later, but that was not a concern now. Her urgent need was to figure out how to get past the nest, using its important handhold, and to the steplike rock protrusions that would be the means of her final ascent to the top.

After testing her legs and feet against the walls to be certain her perch was secure and she wouldn't slip back down into the tunnel, Claire reached back into her pack and took out her water gourd. She drank deeply. Then she remembered the healing salves that Alys had placed in the bottom of the pack. If she returned the gourd, she wouldn't be able to reach the medicine. But she had no place to put the water container. She shook it, and realized there was little water remaining. Finally, knowing there was a risk in this, she gulped the remaining liquid and dropped the empty gourd into the tunnel she had just climbed through. She could hear its single hollow thud against the wall as it fell, and then silence.

Now she was able to reach into the pack. First she removed her sandals, the laces of which were tied together. She hung them around her neck and removed the container of salve. It opened easily, and she smeared the healing paste thickly on her wound. She returned the small clay pot, and the wad of bloody seaweed, to the pack, which now dangled, near empty, from her shoulders.

She felt ready to try again. The shadow of the gull had stopped passing over the opening. She hoped it had soared to the sea and wouldn't return until it had a beak full of fish for its young. She would be fast. She planned it in her mind. She would lean from the opening, throw herself across the steep rock, and make a quick grasp of the hold beneath the nest. From there she had only to pull herself across quickly and to find the first step on the other side. He had told her it was quite close. Easy to reach. She thought it through.

One. Move quickly out of the mouth of the tunnel.

Two. Reach with her left hand, arm stretched across the rock, under the nest and grab the handhold firmly.

Three. Push with her legs. Holding on with the one hand (how grateful she was now for all those months of arm strength exercises!), move across the cliff side. Feel with her toes for small ledges; they would help.

Four. Find the first step and reach for it with her right hand. Then she could move her left arm away from the nest and go beyond the place where the gull would see her as a threat.

Time to start. From her brief glimpse of the sky when she had tried to reach the nest before she was attacked, she guessed that it was now very late in the day. She must do this quickly. Once she passed this danger, the end was in sight and she could reach it before darkness.

Go!

Claire hoisted herself up until she was kneeling at the lip of the tunnel. She reached across with her left arm quickly, into the debris that formed the thick base of the nest. She found the knobby handhold there and grasped it. The squawking from the chicks became louder. They were frantic with fear.

Holding tightly with her left hand, feeling the strength in her arm, which would now briefly be her only support, she planted her feet firmly to push off and propel herself across the rock.

From the sky, its black wings folded tightly against it, the parent gull, summoned by its young, dove at her. She could see its pink legs folded against the white underparts, and the red spot at the tip of its razor-sharp yellow bill. But it was just a split second. The gull speared her arm, ripped at it, wrenched it loose from its hold. Claire screamed and fell back into the tunnel, instinctively using her feet once again to wedge herself against its walls.

She was bleeding badly. She could see the bone of her arm exposed by the huge gash the bird had made when it tore at her with its beak.

She leaned her head as low as possible and took deep, shuddering breaths. If she fainted, she would slide all the way back down the tunnel that it had taken her several hours to climb.

She would not allow herself to faint.

She would not allow herself to be killed by a bird.

It came to her what she must do.

She removed the container of salve again from her pack, opened it, and applied it thickly to the gaping slice in her flesh. She used the salve as a paste to compress the wadded seaweed against the wound. Still it bled. The little pot was empty now and she let it drop, hearing it fall as the water gourd had. She reached into the pack again and found nothing remaining there but the red-covered rock intended as a signal when she reached the top. She held it between her teeth while she used her knife to cut through the fabric of the pack itself and made a strip of the leather. Then she placed the flat rock over the seaweed and held it fast there with the leather strip wrapped tightly around her injured arm. She tested it, moving her arm in several ways, and the dressing stayed firm. Then she dropped the ruined pack down into the tunnel and it disappeared into the darkness.

Next she moved up to the top opening of the tunnel. The gull was circling, waiting. Claire ignored it. She uncoiled the rope that she had been carrying looped around her shoulder. She made a noose.

Then once again she planned what she was about to do. She did it in her mind, rehearsed it: this motion, then that. She knew she must be very, very fast. Another successful attack from the black-backed gull would bring about her death. She could not let that happen.

When she was ready, she thought: *Now.* She lifted her upper body from the tunnel lip, spun the noose, and let the rope fly. It was just a short distance, and her aim was accurate. She lassoed the nest, tightened the noose, and pulled. It was startlingly heavy for something made of twigs, seaweed, and grass. But it crumpled, folded upon itself, and she ripped it from the rock, flinging it outward into the air. She watched it, and the chicks, falling for a moment, and the enormous gull swooping toward it and shrieking.

Then she lifted herself, reached across, grabbed the now visible handhold with her uninjured arm, and pulled herself triumphantly across the cliff face and to the steps that would lead her to the top.

SIXTEEN

C LAIRE LAY PANTING upon the solid earth. It was dark now. The attack of the gull had consumed precious time, and when she reached the steps that would be the final climb, dusk had come. He had said "Don't look down" because this very last section, although it was made relatively easy in its climb because of the odd outcroppings that formed footholds, was sheer in its vertical drop. It could have been terrifying to look down and realize the distance that a fall would be. To lose your grip out of terror after such a dangerous and difficult day, to fall at the very end of it — that was what Einar feared. But she rose and looked down now from the edge at the top and saw nothing but darkness. Above her, the sky was filled with stars.

She felt the wound on her neck. It was encrusted with

dried blood and very sore, but she thought it was not a serious wound; she had seen worse on children who had tumbled on rocks. Her arm was a greater concern. Gingerly she untied the tight leather strip and let it fall away. The flat rock was stuck to the seaweed, and she pried it loose carefully. Its red covering had been meant as a sign that she was safe. She wondered if Einar would be able to see that it was stained with her blood as well. She held it to her lips briefly, trying to impart a message, a thank-you, a goodbye; then she threw it as hard as she could out into the night beyond the cliff.

She left the seaweed on the throbbing gash and retied the leather strip around it, using her teeth and her right hand. Then she put on her sandals. She was to wait here, Einar had said, for dawn. At dawn the man would come, a strange man wearing a black cloak. He was the one who would take her to her son. Einar did not know how. He only knew that the man had special powers. He came to people who needed help, and offered himself.

Claire was to say yes to the man. There would be a price. She must pay it, Einar said. There would be no choice. To decline the man would bring terrible punishment upon her. Einar knew. The man had approached him, assessed how desperately cold he was after the climb, seen that his toes were white with frostbite, and offered—for a price they would agree upon—to provide him with warmth, comfort, and transportation to whatever his destination might be. It was tempting. But Einar was both willful and proud. He had said no.

"I don't need you," he had said. "I'm strong. I climbed out alone."

The man had offered again. "One more chance," he said. "The price will be something you can afford, I assure you. A fair trade." But Einar, suddenly mistrustful, had again said no. Without warning he had found himself on the ground, struck down and weakened by a mysterious power summoned by the man. He lay there unable to move, watching in horror while the man reached under his cloak, withdrew a gleaming hatchet, and chopped off half of his right foot. Then the left.

This was the person Claire was to wait for and say yes to.

＊　＊　＊

She moved carefully away from the cliff's edge, feeling her way in the dark to a mossy patch beside some bushes. She arranged herself there and fell into an exhausted sleep. When he came, it was morning, and she was still sleeping. He touched her arm and she woke.

"Exquisite eyes," he said when she opened them. Claire blinked. She stared at him. He was not what she had expected. He was ordinary. Somehow she had thought he would be pow-

erful in appearance. Large. Frightening. Instead, he was nar-
row-shouldered and thin, with a sallow complexion and neatly
trimmed dark hair. And for such a desolate place — she looked
around and saw nothing but a barren landscape — he was oddly dressed, in a fashion that was unfamiliar to her. Behind the
cloak that Einar had described she could see that he wore a
tightly fitted dark suit with sharp creases in the trousers. On
his feet were highly polished shoes of a fine leather. There were
gloves on his hands, not knitted gloves such as those she was
accustomed to wearing in winter, or the coarse gloves that had
helped her grip the rope as she climbed. The man's black gloves
were of a thin, silky fabric and molded to fit his slender fingers.

The gloved hands frightened her. He was reaching for
her arm, and Claire didn't want to be touched by those sinuous, silk-encased fingers. She shrank back and rubbed her eyes
("exquisite eyes"? What did that mean?), then rose without his
help and stood.

He moved back slightly, facing her. Then he bowed, and
his lipless mouth stretched into a mirthless smile. "Your name,
I believe, is Claire," he said. "And perhaps my presence comes
as a surprise? Allow me — "

She interrupted him. "No. I was told you would be here."
She could tell that the interruption annoyed him. But she felt

vulnerable and humiliated, standing there in her shredded clothing, bleeding from wounds and in need of his help. She wanted to assert herself in some way.

"Indeed. I am here at your service, prepared to offer a fulfillment of your wishes, at a price to be negotiated to our mutual satisfaction."

Claire drew herself up. "I understand that," she replied, and could see him stiffen with annoyance again. He wanted her to be weak, and needy. She swore to herself that she would not be. "You realize," she went on, "that I have nothing of value to give to you."

"Shall we let me be the judge of that?" He spoke now in a threatening whisper.

"If you wish," Claire said.

"Let us begin, then. Let us commence. Let us undertake to establish what it is that you hope to achieve or acquire, what it is that I may provide to you for this yet-to-be-determined price."

She could feel her resolve weaken, and her voice faltered as she told him. "I have a son," she said. "I want to find my son."

"A *son!* How sweet. Maternal love is such a delicious trait. So you don't want riches, or romance, but simply . . . your *son?*"

The way he said the word, hissing it, sneering it, made her feel sick.

"I was told that you could help me."

"You have been informed correctly. Accurately and precisely. But! We must agree on the price to be paid. The trade, do you see? A son in return for—"

She made her voice as firm as she could. "I have nothing. You can see that. I was hoping—"

To her horror he reached forward and grasped a thick handful of Claire's long hair. She flinched.

"What is this, then? You have beautiful hair. Luxuriant tresses, I would say. Sweet-smelling despite your recent ordeal. Do you call this nothing?"

He put his face into her hair and inhaled. His breath was foul-smelling, and Claire willed herself not to step back in disgust. He was twisting the hair he held and hurting her, but she stood her ground. Was that what he wanted? Just her hair? He was welcome to it. It was dirty and tangled and she would be glad to free herself of it, Claire thought.

But he opened his gloved hand, released the handful of curls, and stood back to look at her with his slitted, close-set eyes. Her first thought on meeting him had been: *ordinary*. Now she saw that he was not ordinary at all but darkly sinister. It was not just his breath that smelled. Suddenly he was enveloped in a rancid aroma so thick that it was almost foglike. His words seemed to ooze from his lipless mouth.

"Hardly a fair trade, is it? A head full of coppery curls in return for a living boy? A son?" Had she imagined that his tongue darted in and out, like that of a snake, when he hissed the word?

"No," Claire agreed. "It doesn't seem an equal trade. But as I told you, I have nothing."

"*Nothing* is such a pathetic word, isn't it? But then, *you* are pathetic. Your clothes are rags and you have a pustulous scab on your neck. Still . . ." He hesitated. "My calling, my mission, my motivation and my very existence, is to create trades. This for that! Reciprocity!"

The tongue flickered again as he drew out the word "reciprocity." Claire shuddered but maintained her composure.

"So you want your boy. Your son. Tell me his name."

"I'm sorry—I'm not certain. My memory has been damaged. I think he was called Babe."

"Babe?" His voice was contemptuous. Claire felt as if she were failing a test.

"Wait!" she said. "Maybe it was Abe! It was so long ago. It might have been Abe!"

"Abe, Babe . . ." The man's body swayed as he repeated the

words in a singsong voice. Then he fell silent, moved close to her, leaned forward, and whispered harshly. "I offer you this trade. I make the offer only once. Take it or leave it. Ready?"

Dreading what he was to say, Claire nodded. She had no choice.

He grabbed her neck with his eerily smooth gloved hand, pressing into her wound so that pain sliced through her, and drew her face close to his. She could smell his foul breath again. "I want your *youth*," he said harshly into her ear, and his warm saliva sprayed across her cheek.

"Trade?" he murmured, still holding her in his awful embrace.

"Yes," Claire whispered.

"Say it."

"*Trade,*" she said loudly.

"Done." He released her then and shoved her away from him. When he turned and walked away, she understood that she was to follow. Surprisingly, she found it difficult to walk. Her legs were weak. She couldn't straighten her body easily. Had it been only twenty-four hours before that she had leapt from rock to rock, had climbed and grasped and pulled herself up the sheer cliff? Now she was shuffling and bent, and it was hard to catch her breath. She struggled to keep up with the man, who was striding quickly ahead. Her hair fell forward over her face, and when she reached up to smooth it back, she saw that her hand had changed, had become veiny and spotted; and she saw, too, that the loosened hair was no longer the thick red-gold curls he had admired a few minutes before. Now it was a sparse handful of coarse gray.

He paused, looked back, and smirked at her confusion. "Get a move on, you old hag," he said. "And by the way . . ."

He watched her contemptuously as she made her way, shuffling around a boulder in the path. "Your son's name is *Gabe*," he said.

"And mine? My name," he added, with a superior and hostile smile, "is Trademaster."

BOOK III

—◆—

BEYOND

———

THE OLD WOMAN appeared frequently. Suddenly she would be there, standing in the thick pines beside the river, watching him as he worked. Gabe would catch sight of her, would see her dark homespun clothing, her stooped posture, and the fierce, knowing intimacy of her gaze. But then she would withdraw and disappear into the shaded grove of trees. If he turned away and then looked back, there was no longer a sign of her, not even a whispering motion in the needled branches she had moved through. She simply went away. Sometimes he thought of calling after her, asking who she was, why she watched him. But for some reason he felt shy.

He saw her in the village as well, but noticed her less there because he was generally in the company of friends. He and the other boys, the group he lived with, would be wrestling and joking, vying to be cleverest, or strongest, as they made their way together to or from the schoolhouse. Sometimes the people of the village complained about them and their horseplay, said that they were a noisy, inconsiderate group, worse than any bunch of adolescents that had ever lived in Boys' Lodge. One neighbor had called them "louts" after they wrested plums from the tree beside her cottage, then squashed them in the path.

This particular old woman, though she was often nearby, never glared at the group of boys, as others did, or chided them for their behavior. She simply watched. She had been doing it for a long time. And Gabe thought that she watched *him* most of all. It puzzled him.

Occasionally he thought about using his power—well, he never knew exactly what to call it, but he thought of it as *veering*—to try to learn more about who she was, why she watched him. But he never did. His power made him nervous. He found veering tiring, painful, and a little frightening. So though he tested it now and then, seeing if it was still there (and it always was; sometimes he found himself wishing it wouldn't be), trying to understand it (and he never did, not really), he rarely called it into full use.

Anyway, she was gone. He was annoyed at himself for

the time he had wasted, wondering about her, when he had so much to do, still. Sighing, Gabe looked around the clearing on the riverbank, the place he had claimed for his task, the place where he was now spending hours every day. His bare feet were deep in wood shavings. He smiled at himself, realizing there was sawdust on his face, stuck there by his own sweat. He licked his lips and tasted powdered cedar.

The boards that he had crafted so carefully were neatly stacked, but his tools were scattered about, and it looked from the graying clouds as if rain was on the way. He heard a rumble of thunder. Time to get things into the shed. But even as he moved his tools, trudging back and forth to store them in the primitive little structure he had built between two trees, he found himself thinking again of the old woman.

There were so few mysteries in the small village. When new residents arrived, there was always a ceremony of welcome. Their histories were told. He remembered none for her, but he would have been a child then; he had seen the strange woman for years now, had felt her eyes on him since he was a young boy. And he rarely attended the ceremonies. Some of the histories were interesting, Gabe thought, especially if they involved danger and narrow escapes. But people rambled on, and sometimes they wept, which embarrassed him.

I'll stop being shy, he thought. *Next time I notice her staring at me the way she does, I'll simply introduce myself. Then she'll have to tell me who she is.*

The rain began spattering suddenly. Gabe closed the crooked, hastily made door of the shed he had built from old boards. Briefly he glanced back through the increasing downpour, at the grove of trees where the woman stood from time to time. Then he closed the latch on the door of the shed and ran through the rain toward the village.

* * *

"How's the boat coming?" It was Simon, one of his friends, standing on the porch of Boys' Lodge as Gabe climbed the steps and shook his head to try to get some of the wetness out of his curly hair.

"All right, I guess. Slow."

He went inside to change into dry clothes. It would be time for dinner soon, he thought. There were no clocks in the village, but the bell tower rang at intervals, and the midafternoon bell had sounded some time ago. On a shelf in his cubicle Gabe found a clean, folded shirt and put it on. He tossed his wet one into a bin in the hall.

He lived in Boys' Lodge with twelve other adolescent orphaned boys. Most of his lodge-mates had lost their parents to illness or accident, though one, Tarik, had been abandoned as an infant by an irresponsible couple who had no interest in raising a child. All of the boys had a history to tell. Gabe did too, but he didn't enjoy the telling; there were too many I-don't-knows to it.

He had asked Jonas again and again. It was Jonas who had brought him here years before, when Gabe was just an infant. "Why did my parents let you take me?" he had asked.

"You didn't have parents," Jonas had explained.

"*Everybody* has parents!"

"Not in the place where we lived. Things were different there."

"How about you? Did you have parents?"

"I had people I called Mother and Father. I'd been assigned to them."

"Well, what about me?"

"You hadn't been assigned yet. You were a bit of a problem."

Gabe had grinned at that. He liked the idea of being troublesome. It seemed to give him a certain superiority.

"I had to have parents, though. People don't just get born from *nothing*."

"You know what, Gabe? I was just a boy then. Babies appeared from the infant-care building and were given to parents.

I accepted it. I never knew anything else. I never asked where the babies had come from."

Gabe had hooted with laughter. "Hah! *Where do babies come from? Every kid asks that!*"

Gabe was laughing, but Jonas had looked serious and concerned. "You're right," he said, slowly. "And I do remember that there were young girls chosen each year to be what was called 'birthmothers.' They must have been the ones who . . ."

"What happened to the birthmothers? What happened to *my* birthmother?"

"I don't know, Gabe."

"Didn't she want me?"

Jonas sighed. "I don't know, Gabe. It was a different system—"

"I'm going to find out."

"How?"

Gabe was very young then, no more than nine. But he swaggered when he replied. "I'll go back there. You can't stop me. I'll find a way."

✳ ✳ ✳

Now that the boys had moved out of the Childhood Place where they had spent their first years, now that they were in Boys' Lodge, their interests had changed and they rarely talked of their earlier years. It was girls who did that, Gabe thought. At Girls' Lodge, he heard, the girls talked long into the evening, retelling their own tales to each other. For the boys, though, talk now was of school, or of sports, or of the future, not the past.

Boys' Lodge was a congenial group. They did their schoolwork together in the evenings, and shared meals, their food prepared by a staff of two workers in the kitchen. There was a lodge director, a kindly man who had a room within the building, and who mediated the infrequent disputes among the boys. One could go to him with problems. But Gabe often wished that he lived in a house with a family, the way his best friend, Nathaniel, did. Nathaniel had parents, and two sisters; their house was noisy with bickering and laughter.

Glancing through the window, through the rain that had now almost stopped, he could see the house where Nathaniel lived, farther along the curved path. Its little garden was thick with summer flowers, and as he watched, a door opened and a gray cat was sent outside, where it assumed a pose, in the way of cats, on the little porch and licked its paws. It was Deirdre's cat. Gabe tried to remember its name; he could picture Nathaniel's sister laughing when she had told it to him, but the whimsical name eluded him. Catacomb? Cataclysm? No. But something like those. Deirdre was good with words.

Pretty, too. Gabe flushed briefly, a little embarrassed at his own thoughts. He watched the cat, hoping that Deirdre would appear at the door. Maybe she would sit down and stroke the gray fur. *Catapult!* That was its name. He pictured her there, stroking Catapult, gazing into the distance, maybe thinking about—him? Maybe? Could that be possible? Of course, he realized suddenly, he could veer, and find out. But maybe he didn't really want to know? And anyway, there wasn't time. The dinner bell was about to ring. The other boys, laughing and noisy, would soon be rushing down the hallway.

Also, Gabe reminded himself, shaking off the thoughts about Nathaniel's pretty, dark-haired sister, it wasn't fair to her, even if he found that she *did* care about him. She shouldn't. Very soon he would finish his boat. And then he would be gone.

———

TWO

Y OU KNOW HE'S building a boat."

Kira nodded. She had just gotten the children to sleep. They were so lively, into everything. Now that Annabelle could walk, she followed her two-year-old brother, Matthew, into all kinds of mischief. Kira was exhausted by evening. She brought her cup of tea, set her walking stick aside, and sat down beside Jonas, who looked troubled.

"I know. I was here when he came for the books, remember?"

Jonas glanced at the walls of the room. Shelves of books extended from the floor to the ceiling. And not just this room, but all the others in the house he shared with his family. It was one of the things they were trying now to teach the children: not to pull and grab at the books. So tempting, for babies: the bright colors. He remembered when the dog, as a puppy, had indulged in the same mischief, and again and again they had found corners of the lower volumes chewed. Now Frolic was middle-aged, overweight, lazy, and no longer needing to chew. He slept, snoring, on his folded blanket most of the day, and it was the toddlers who grabbed and gnawed.

"I always knew this time would come," Jonas said. "He told me when he was much younger that he would go looking for his past."

Kira nodded again. "Of course he wonders," she pointed out. "It will be the next generation, the ones like our children, who were born here, who won't feel that pull."

Both of them, like almost everyone in the small village, had come from another place, had fled something, had escaped from hardship of some kind. Jonas stood. He stared through the window out into the night. Kira recognized the look. Her husband had always had that need, to turn his gaze outward, trying to find the answers to things. It was the first thing she had noticed about him: the piercing blue eyes, and the way he had of seeming to see beyond what was obvious. In their earlier days together, when Jonas was Leader, he had called on that vision often for answers to problems. But the problems had fallen away, the village had thrived, and Jonas had relinquished leadership to others so that he could take up an unburdened life with his family.

Now he was the protector of the books and the knowledge. He was the scholar/librarian. It was Jonas to whom Gabriel had come not long ago, looking for books with diagrams and instructions, so that he could learn to build a boat.

He sighed, turning away from the darkness that was enfolding the village. "I worry about him," he said.

Kira set aside the needlework she had picked up. She went to him, circled her arms around his waist, and looked up into those solemn eyes that were as blue as her own. "Of course you do. You brought him here." It had been years before that Jonas, hardly more than a boy himself then, had brought Gabriel—a toddler with no past, a child who deserved a future—to this village, which had welcomed them with no questions.

"He was so little. And he had no one."

"He had you."

"I was a boy. I couldn't be a parent to him. I didn't know what that meant. The people who raised me did their best, but it was just a job to them." Jonas sighed, recalling the couple he had called Mother and Father. "I remember that once I asked them if they loved me," he said.

"And?"

He shook his head. "They didn't know what that meant. They said the word was meaningless."

"They did their best," Kira said, after a moment, and he nodded.

"Gabe's older now than I was when I brought him here," Jonas mused. "Stronger. Braver."

"Not as handsome, though." She reached up, smiling, and smoothed a strand of his hair. Ordinarily he would have grinned back at her. But his face was worried and his thoughts were elsewhere.

"And I'm pretty sure he has a gift of some sort."

Kira sighed. She knew what that meant. She and Jonas both had a gift. Sometimes it was exhilarating, but it was demanding, too, and burdensome, to know how to use it well, and when.

"I worry about what he'll find, if he goes searching," Jonas went on. "He wants a family, and there won't be one. He was a—" Frowning, he searched for the right description. "He was a manufactured product," he said at last. "We all were."

Kira sat silently. It was a chilling description. Finally,

thoughtfully, she replied. "All of us came here from difficult places," she reminded him.

"But you had a mother who loved you."

"I did. Until she died. Then I was all alone."

"But you had her, at least, for — how many years?"

"Almost fifteen."

"That's close to Gabe's age now. He feels such a longing for something, and I worry that he'll never find it. That it never was there. But — " Jonas rose and went to the window. Kira watched him as he stood there, looking out into the darkness. Beyond him, she could see the outline of trees moving slightly in a night breeze against the dark starless sky. "But what?" she asked, when he had stood silently for a long moment.

"I'm not sure. I can feel something out there. Something connected to Gabe."

"Something dangerous?" she asked in an apprehensive tone. "We must warn him, if there's something dangerous out there."

"No." Jonas shook his head. He was still focusing on something beyond the room. "No. He's not in danger. At least not now. But there is a presence. It seems benign. I think . . ." He paused. "I think something — some*one* — is looking for him. Or waiting? Waiting for him? *Watching* him?"

He didn't tell Kira what else he felt, because he didn't comprehend it himself, and because he didn't want to alarm her. But there was something *else* out there, something vaguely at the edges of his awareness, something not really connected to Gabe. And the something else was vaguely familiar, and very dangerous.

THREE

———

AT FIRST, HIS friends had helped him. But that time had passed. Now they were off fishing, playing ball, indulging in all the usual summer pastimes during this brief holiday from school. The excitement of Gabe's project was short-lived, and their interest waned when they realized he was not just hammering together a primitive raft that they could paddle along the riverbank.

Gabe hummed to himself as he measured his boards. He had a vague picture in his mind of the way they should go together. But though the books he had borrowed from Jonas had shown boats of all kinds, from ones with billowy sails to long, narrow vessels with rows of seated men at oars, none had provided instructions for the building. His would be small, he knew. Just big enough for him and his supplies. It would have a paddle; he had already begun carving one, crouched in his little shed during rainy days.

"Any chance you'd like to go fishing?"

Gabe looked up at the sound of the voice. Nathaniel, tall and brown from the sun, was standing on the path, holding his gear. Often they had fished together, usually from a huge rock on the bank farther along. The river was easy to fish, slow moving and somewhat shallow there; the silvery, sinuous trout were eager for the bait, and made good eating later.

It was tempting. But Gabe shook his head. "Can't. I'm behind. This is slower going than I thought it would be."

"What's that?" Nathaniel asked, pointing to the edge of the clearing where a leafy stack of thin poles waited.

Gabe looked over. "Bamboo."

"You can't build from that. You need real planks for a boat."

Gabe laughed. "I know. I'm using cedar. But I need the bamboo for . . . Well, here; I'll show you." He wiped his sweaty hands on the hem of his shirt and then went and got the large book from the shed.

"Jonas let you bring it here?" Nathaniel asked in surprise.

Gabe nodded. "I had to promise to keep it clean and dry." He set the book on a flat rock, squatted there, and turned the pages. "Look," he said, pointing to a page.

Nathaniel looked at the picture of a large vessel with its many sails unfurled. The rigging was complicated, with countless lines and winches holding the billowing sails in place, and a large crew of men could be seen on deck. "You're crazy," Nathaniel said. "You can't build that."

Gabe chuckled. "No, no. I just wanted to show you. It's not for rivers anyway. They sailed them once on oceans. I think we learned about it in history class."

Nathaniel nodded. "There were pirates," he recalled. "That's the part I paid attention to."

Gabe turned the pages slowly.

He smiled. "Here's mine," he said, and he rifled the pages until the book opened to a page near the end, a place that had clearly been opened to frequently. "Don't laugh."

But Nathaniel did, when he leaned down to look at the picture. Gabe, watching his face, chuckled as well. The picture was of a tiny boat, with one lone man, huge waves surging around him, shark fins visible in the foam. There was endless sea and sky. The man looked terrified, and doomed.

"So you're planning your own death? Where is this guy, anyway?"

"Ocean. But that's far from here. I don't need to think about ocean, just river. And I'm not going to end up like him. I'm just copying his boat, sort of. Mine's smaller, and doesn't have that cabin part. Mine will be little, and sturdy. That's all I'll need. It'll be easy to build."

Gabe looked around at the piles of boards, the sawdust, the mess on the ground. "Well, I *thought* it would be easy."

"How will you steer it?" Nathaniel asked, still peering at the picture of the lone man cowering in the boat as the waves approached.

"Paddle. Anyway, the river will carry it. I won't need to steer much. Just to go ashore when I want to."

"So what's the bamboo for?"

"It'll hold it together. I invented this system myself. Once I get the cedar all arranged in the right shape, I'll use the bamboo—first I'll wet it, so that when it dries, it tightens—it'll be like rope."

Nathaniel looked around. The cedar planks were lying haphazardly about, a few of them hammered together. He could see that Gabe had been preparing the bamboo, peeling and slicing it thin. It was a huge task for a boy to do alone.

"Does anybody ever come and help you?"

Gabriel hesitated. "Not really. Some old woman comes and watches me, though." He gestured toward the grove of pines. "She stands over there."

"An *old woman?*"

"Yes. You've seen her. She's all bent over and you can tell

she has trouble walking. She sort of follows me. I don't know why. Someday I'm going to yell at her to stop."

Nathaniel looked uneasy. He gave a nervous laugh. "You can't yell at an old woman," he said.

"I know. I was kidding. Maybe I'll just growl, and scare her a little." Gabe made a face and growled loudly, imitating a beast of some kind.

Both boys laughed.

"Sure you don't want to go fishing?" Nathaniel asked.

Gabe shook his head and picked up the book to return it to the shed. "Can't."

His friend gathered his things and turned away. "Deirdre says she misses you," he remarked with a sly grin. "You're never around lately."

Gabe sighed. He looked up the path as if he might see Nathaniel's pretty sister there. "Will she come to the feast to-morrow night?"

Nathaniel nodded and shouldered his fishing pole. "Everyone will. My mother's at the gathering place now, helping to get things ready."

"Tell Deirdre I'll see her there." Gabe gave his friend a wave and turned again to his work as the other boy walked away.

———

FOUR

F EASTS WERE FREQUENT in the village. Some-
times there was an excuse: Harvest, Midsummer, or a marriage.
But often, no reason was necessary. People just wanted a time
of merriment, laughter, dressing up, eating—and overeat-
ing—and so a feast was planned.

Kira dressed the children in bright-colored embroidered
outfits that she had designed and stitched. She was a mas-
terful seamstress. Many people sought her out to create their
wedding clothes; and they still talked in the village about the
hand-woven cloth adorned with intricately patterned birds
of all kinds in which she had wrapped the body of her father before his burial. Kira's father had been blind, and sound
had been his life. He knew—and could imitate—each
bird's call and song; they came from the trees, unafraid, to

eat from his outstretched hands. The entire village had gathered to sing a farewell as he was laid to rest, but the only song that day was theirs; the birds had fallen silent, as if they mourned.

Her own garment for the feast was a deep blue dress; she entwined blue ribbons through the straps of her sandals and in her long hair. Jonas smiled at her in admiration and affection, but his own clothing, even on Feast Night, was simple: a homespun shirt over coarse trousers. With a roll of his eyes, he let his wife attach a blue flower from the garden to his collar. Jonas was not fond of decoration. His tastes were plain.

Annabelle and Matthew scampered about the large room, giggling, while Kira wrapped the pie she had baked and placed it in a basket she had adorned with daisies and ferns. Frolic yawned and rose from the blanket where he'd been napping. The dog sensed excitement and wanted to take part. Noticing, Kira laughed, and leaned over to wind a stemmed flower around his neck. "There," she said. "Now you're in your party outfit too!" Tail wagging, Frolic followed the family as they set out from their house. Jonas carried the pie basket and Matthew rode atop his father's shoulders. Annabelle held tightly to her mother's free hand, the hand that didn't grasp the carved cane that Kira had always needed for walking. Ahead, beyond the curve of the path, they could already hear music—flutes and fiddles—from the gathering place where celebrations were held.

* * *

It was a very small village that had had its beginnings years before in a gathering of outcasts. Fleeing battles or chaos of all kinds, often wounded or driven out by their own clans or villages, each of the original settlers had made his way to this place. They had found strength in one another, had formed a community. They had welcomed others.

From time to time, as the years had passed, people muttered that they shouldn't let newcomers in; the village was becoming crowded, and it was hard, sometimes, for the newcomers to learn the customs and rules. There were arguments and petitions and debates.

What if my daughter wants to marry one of them?

They talk with a funny accent.

What if there aren't enough jobs?

Why should we have to support them while they're learning our ways?

It had been Jonas, during his time as Leader, who had gently but firmly reminded the villagers that they had all been outsiders once. They had all come here for a new life. Eventually they had voted to remain what they had become: a sanctuary, a place of welcome.

As a child, Gabe had yawned and fidgeted when his class was taken, as each school class was, to visit the village museum and learn the history. History was boring, he thought. He was embarrassed when the museum curator, pointing to various artifacts in the "Vehicles of Arrival" exhibit, had gestured to the battered red sled and explained that a brave boy named Jonas had battled a blizzard and fought his way here carrying a dying baby.

"And today we all know that Jonas has become our village Leader, and the baby he rescued and brought here is a healthy boy," the curator had said dramatically, "named Gabriel." His classmates grinned at him. They poked each other and giggled. Gabe pretended to be bored. He averted his eyes and leaned down to scratch an imaginary bug bite on his leg.

Most of the earliest settlers, those with their histories recorded in the museum, had grown old and were gone now. Kira's father, Christopher, was buried in the village cemetery beside the pine grove. Left for dead by his enemies in a distant community, he had stumbled, sightless, to this village and been saved; with his new name of Seer, he had lived a long life here of dignity and wisdom. Kira tended his grave now, taking the babies with her while she weeded and watered the soft blanket of fragrant purple thyme she had planted there.

He was buried beside his adopted son, Matty. The villagers remembered Matty as a fun-loving young man who had been destroyed when he fought the evil, unknowable forces that had menaced the village in those harsher times, seven years earlier.

Thinking of those times as he passed the cemetery on his way to the evening's festivities, Gabe recalled the day Matty's body had been found and carried home. Gabe had been young then, only eight, a rambunctious resident of the Children's House, happiest with solitary adventures and disinterested in schoolwork. But he had always admired Matty, who had tended and helped Seer with such devotion and undertaken village tasks with energy and good humor. It had been Matty who had taught Gabe to bait a hook and cast his line from the fishing rock, Matty who had shown him how to make a kite and catch the wind with it. The day of his death, Gabe had huddled, heartbroken, in the shadow of a thick stand of trees and watched as the villagers lined the path and bowed their heads in respect to watch the litter carrying the ravaged body move slowly through. Frightened by his own feelings, he had listened mutely to the wails of grief that permeated the community.

That day had changed him. It had changed the entire village. Shaken by the death of a boy they had loved, each person had found ways to be more worthy of the sacrifice he had made. They had become kinder, more careful, more attentive to one another. They had worked hard to eradicate customs that had begun to corrupt their society, banning even seemingly benign diversions such as a gaming machine, a simple gambling device that spit out candy to its winners.

For years a mysterious, sinister man known as Trademaster had appeared now and then in the village, bringing tawdry thrills and temptations but leaving chaos and discontentment behind. It had been Jonas, as Leader, who saw through him, who sensed the deep evil in the man and insisted on his banishment.

Freed of the menacing greed and self-indulgence that had almost overwhelmed them during that time, the villagers had learned to celebrate themselves, as they were doing this evening.

Gabe stood still in the path for a moment. He noticed a small bouquet of fresh flowers beside the stone into which Matty's name had been carved. The village people honored Matty's memory with such tokens because he had made them into better people. Gabe did so more privately. He did so by reminding himself of a conversation he had once had with the older boy he had so admired.

"You must pay more attention in school, Gabe," Matty had told him. Gabe had been required to stay late after classes that day, for extra help. Now they were sitting together on the outcropping of rock at the edge of the river.

"I don't like school," Gabe had replied, feeling the fishing line between his fingers.

"I didn't either. And I was willful and full of mischief, same as you. But Seer made me work at it because he cared about me so much."

Gabe shrugged. "Nobody cares about me."

"Leader does. I do."

"I guess," Gabe acknowledged.

"He's the one who brought you here. He had a hard time of it too."

Gabe rolled his eyes. "Did you hear that at the museum as part of the tour? I wish they'd stop telling that stupid story. And give me another worm, would you? Mine wiggled off the hook."

Patiently Matty had helped him to rebait his hook. "You need knowledge," he said. "That's how Jonas got to be Leader, by studying."

"I don't want to be Leader."

"Neither do I. But I want to *know* stuff. Don't you?"

Gabe sighed. "Some stuff, maybe. Not math. Not grammar."

Matty had laughed. Then he had turned serious again for a moment. "And Gabe?"

"What?"

"You're going to find that you have a gift of some kind. Some of us do, and you're going to be one. I can tell."

Gabe busied himself with the worm and the hook. For some reason the conversation had begun to make him self-conscious.

"I know," Matty said, "it's hard to talk about it because it's hard to understand. But it's another reason why you must study. You must make yourself ready. Someday you'll be called upon for something special. Maybe something dangerous. So you have to prepare yourself, Gabe. You'll need knowledge."

"Look," Gabe said loudly, changing the subject, and pointed. "There's a big trout over there where the rock makes a shadow. He's hiding. But he sees us. Look at his eyes."

Matty sighed affectionately and turned his attention to the large fish suspended in the dark water by the rock. It withdrew further, as if it felt their sudden interest, and its shiny eyes darted back and forth. Matty watched. "He thinks he can escape us by lurking there in the dark. But not us, Gabe! We're too clever for him. Let's do it. Let's try to get him."

Thinking of it now, Gabe remembered it all: the laughter, the puzzling conversation, the sunshine that day, the sound of the slow-moving river, and then their stealthy maneuvers as they stalked the huge, silvery fish, finally caught him, and then threw him back. It had all been years ago, and they had never had another chance to talk in that way.

Matty had been correct, though, about needing to learn stuff. Gabe had tried hard to settle into his studies, and it served him well now, the math he had hated, as he measured and fitted together the pieces of his boat.

But he found himself wishing now that he had not felt so awkward, that he had confided in Matty that day. He had just discovered it then, the power that he had, the power to veer, and was still confused by it.

It had been at a feast, one of the usual celebrations. Probably Midsummer, he thought now, remembering it. With the other boys his age, eight and nine, he had joined the crowd watching a contest. Two of the village men were wrestling. Their bodies were smeared with oil so that their hands slid as they tried to grasp at each other. The crowd shouted encouragement and the men repositioned themselves, shifting on their feet, each waiting for the right instant, the right move, to topple the other and emerge as the winner. Gabe, watching intently, found his own bare feet shifting in the dirt; he panted, imitating the wrestlers. He focused on his own favorite, the man called Miller, who was in charge of grain production each fall. Miller was a large man and a likable one who sometimes on slow workdays organized the boys into teams and taught them intricate games on the playing field. Even in the midst of this intense match, Miller was laughing as he caught his opponent in a hold and struggled to down him.

Gabe, moving his own skinny body in imitation of the wrestlers, found himself wondering how it felt to be Miller: to be so strong, so in command of his muscles and limbs. Suddenly an odd silence enveloped him. He stopped hearing the grunts of the wrestlers, the shouts of the crowd, the barking of dogs, the music from the fiddlers preparing nearby. And he felt himself move, in the silence. He *veered*—though the word had not yet come to him then—and entered Miller. *Became* Miller. Experienced Miller. *Was* Miller for that instant. He knew, briefly, how it felt to be strong, to be in command, to be winning, to be loving the battle and the coming win.

Then sound returned. Gabe returned. The crowd roared in approval and Miller stood with his arms raised, victorious, then leaned forward and helped his laughing opponent up. Gabe slid to the ground and huddled there in the cheering crowd, breathing hard, exhausted, confused, and exhilarated.

After that day it had happened again, several times, until he could feel it coming, and then—later—found that he could command and control the veer. Once, he remembered guiltily, he tried to use it to cheat in school. Seated at his desk, floundering over a math test—fractions, which he had not studied the way he should have—he glanced up at Mentor, the schoolmaster. Mentor was standing near the window, looking at the board on which the test questions had been written.

If I could veer into Mentor right now, *enter* Mentor, Gabe thought, I could grab all of the answers to these test problems. He concentrated. He closed his eyes and thought about Mentor, about his knowledge, about what it would feel like to *be* Mentor. Sure enough, the silence came. He felt his consciousness shift and move toward the schoolmaster. Within seconds he was there, within the man, experiencing being Mentor.

The veer worked. But not in the way Gabe had planned. He found no math answers there. Instead he had an overwhelming feeling of a kind of passion: for knowledge, for learning of all sorts—and for the children who sat that day at the small desks, as Gabe did. He felt Mentor's love for his students and his hopes for them and what they would learn from him.

The veer ended suddenly, as it always did, and Gabe put his head into his hands. The sounds of the classroom returned, and the schoolmaster appeared beside him.

"Are you all right, Gabriel?"

Gabe found himself shaking. He had tears in his eyes. "I don't feel well," he whispered.

Mentor excused him for the rest of the day and Gabe walked slowly away from the schoolhouse, promising himself that he would study, that he would not disappoint his teacher again as he had so often in the past.

He never told anyone. Veering seemed a private act, something to both savor and sometimes dread alone.

Now, though, he found himself wishing he had confided in Matty when he'd had the opportunity. Not only about the veer. He wished he had told Matty about how desperately he yearned to know about his mother. He couldn't tell his lodge-mates; they would laugh. But Matty would have understood. And it was lonely, to yearn so, all alone.

He reached down into the path, picked up a small pebble, and tossed it toward Matty's gravestone. It tapped lightly against the rock and fell to the ground where other pebbles lay near the flowers. He had thrown each of them. "Hi," Gabe whispered.

Ahead, from the Pavilion where gatherings were held, he

heard music and the happy shouts of children. He thought of his friends, of the games they were already playing, and of the contests and dancing later. He thought of pretty Deirdre with the sprinkling of freckles across her nose. He saw smoke and could smell the pigs that had been roasting on a spit most of the day. He knew Kira would have made a pie, and there would be thick cream swirled with honey to mound on top of it. Gabe left the cemetery and his somber thoughts behind him and began to run toward the party.

FIVE

———

ER BACK ACHED badly. It had ached for a long time now, for several years, but it was getting worse, and Claire had difficulty straightening herself. She walked bent.

She had gone to see Herbalist, the man who dispensed medicines to villagers. But it was clear that his remedies were the same that she had learned in her years with Alys. The drinking of birch and willow tea would ease the pain a bit but could not take it away.

Herbalist had asked her the obvious question: "What is your age?"

"I don't know," she replied to him. That was true. She had been a young girl when she was washed from the sea to the place where she had lived for years. She had grown up there and become a young woman. She had left there and become, overnight, old. It was not a question of years.

Herbalist was not surprised by her answer. Many people who had found their way to the village had little memory of their own past. He prescribed the bark infusions for her aches but said to her, "Such pain comes for us all, in great age."

"I know," Claire said. She had no wish to explain what had befallen her.

Herbalist lifted her arm gently and felt the thin, sagging skin. Carefully he examined the dark spots on the backs of her hands. "Do you still have teeth?" he asked.

"Some," she said, and showed him.

"And your eyes? Ears?"

She could still see and hear.

"So," Herbalist said with a smile, "you can't dance or chew meat. But if you can hear the birds sing and watch the wind in the leaves, then you still have much pleasure left.

"Your time is limited now, though," he told her, "so you should enjoy everything you can. That's what I do. I think I must be as old as you. I have the same aches." He wrapped the dried barks for her, and she placed them in her carrying basket.

"I'll see you at the feast," he said as she turned to go. "We can watch the dancing and remember our young years. There is pleasure in that."

Claire thanked him, leaned on her cane, and continued down the path to her small cottage. In the distance she could hear some young boys shouting as they played some sort of game with a ball. Perhaps one was Gabe. She rarely found him at games, lately, though; most often he was alone in the clearing near the river, hammering away on the misshapen vessel that he called his boat. Claire often stood hidden in the trees and watched him at work. In a way she admired his dedication to the odd project. But it saddened and puzzled her, his wish to be gone.

When she had entered the village for the first time, like so many others, she had been welcomed, years before. The fragility of old age was new to her then, and it had still startled her when she rose in the morning with her bones aching and stiff. The memory of running, climbing, even dancing, was alive and throbbing within her, but frailty made her hobble and limp.

She had seen her son for the first time, in this place, when he was a child of eight or nine. She remembered that day. He ran along the path near the cottage to which she had been assigned, calling to his friends, laughing, his unkempt hair bright in the sunlight. "Gabe!" she heard a boy call; but she would have known him without hearing it. It was the same smile she remembered, the same silvery laugh.

She had moved forward in that moment, intending to rush to him, to greet and embrace him. Perhaps she would make the silly face, the one with which they had once mimicked each other. But when she started eagerly toward him, she forgot her own weakness; her dragging foot caught on a stone and she stumbled clumsily. Quickly she righted herself, but in that moment she saw him glance toward her, then look away in disinterest. As if looking through his eyes, she perceived her own withered skin, her sparse gray hair, the awkward gait with which she moved. She stayed silent, and turned away, thinking.

Did he need to know, after all? He appeared to be a happy child. If she were to make herself known, to tell her unbelievable story, he would be stunned, uncomprehending. His friends might taunt him. Perhaps he would reject her. Or worse—perhaps he would feel obligated to tend her in her remaining days. His carefree life would be interrupted. She would be a burden, an embarrassment.

In the end she decided that it was enough that she had found him. She would let him be. But she realized then the magnitude of the cruel exchange Trademaster had offered her.

Through the years she had watched Gabe grow from a mischievous boy into this quiet young man who now seemed to have a mission she didn't understand. Why a boat? The river was a dangerous thing. The village children could swim and play in the one protected section where the water was shallow and slow. But farther out, and farther along, the water rushed furiously over sharp rocks. She had heard that there was a steep waterfall someplace, and fallen trees here and there that could easily smash the thin boards he was so carefully tying together with strips of bamboo.

Claire was very frightened of swift-moving water. She had reason to be. She had once lived beside a river, once beside a sea. Both had brought her heartbreak and loss.

She did not want her son to be lost to water.

* * *

The crisp-skinned pork, sliced from the roasted pig on the spit, smelled delicious, but she knew it was not for her, not with her remaining teeth loose and her gums sore. Claire filled her plate from a large bowl of soft beans that had been baking all day in a sauce of tomatoes and herbs, and added a piece of soft bread. She would leave room, though, she thought, for a slice of blackberry pie.

She set her plate on a table and eased herself onto a bench next to several others. A pregnant woman smiled at her and moved slightly, making room; Claire recognized her as Jean, the wife of one of the fiddlers who were tuning their instruments and preparing to play for the dancing. Kira was there too, keeping an eye on her toddlers as they played near the table. From time to time she spooned food into their mouths, as if they were baby birds.

Eating slowly, watching the young women at her table, Claire realized that she might have been one of them. She looked down at her own gnarled hand holding a fork. An old woman's hand. Herbalist had told her she was nearing her last days, and she sensed that it was true. But inside herself? She was a young woman still. If she had not made the trade that had brought her here (*Youth!* In her memory Claire could hear still how Trademaster had breathed the word into her ear, had spat against her cheek with it, how she had nodded in assent and whispered to him: *Trade*) she would perhaps be back with Einar now, helping him tend his lambs, cooking a stew they would share in their hillside hut, talking together by the fire in the evenings.

But she would not have found her son. She would never have seen Gabe again, would not have watched him grow into the lively young man he had become. She knew it was a trade she would make again, given the chance.

She rose to return her emptied plate, to get herself a piece of pie, and looked over to the table where the boisterous young boys were sitting together. He was there. She saw him glance sideways at her as she passed; then his attention returned to his plate, heaped as it was with food, and to a lengthy joke one of his friends was telling. In adolescence Gabe was gangly and tall, and as she watched, his elbow knocked over the mug holding his drink; the other boys chortled as he sheepishly mopped up the mess with his napkin.

His hair was curly, as hers — now a sparse bun at the back of her head — had once been. His blue eyes were surprisingly pale. Jonas had the same eyes. So did his wife, Kira. Claire remembered now that she had noticed the unusual eyes when Gabe was an infant. Those early days had come back to her very slowly, and with pain attached to each memory.

The feel of the mask clamped over her face during his birth. She had shuddered when that memory returned.

How, later, she had held him for the first time, and had noticed the startling pale eyes. When she recalled it, she was suffused with a feeling of loss.

Then she remembered a dream she had had, of a hidden light-eyed baby. How, in the dream, she had kept him concealed in a drawer. Thinking of it after all this time, she almost wept at the sadness of all it implied.

She did weep when the next memory came back: of how

he had grinned and wiggled his chubby fingers at her. He had learned by then to say her name. *Claire,* he had said in his high voice. And: *Bye-bye.*

* * *

She did not regret the trade she had made in order to find him. But she was desperately sad to realize that her time was short now. Instead of the strong and vibrant young woman she should be, the mother Gabe deserved, she was now an ancient hag waiting for death. It was a hideous joke that Trademaster had played on them both seven years before.

The sky darkened as night fell and the music began in earnest. Soon it would be the time for the young people, the time for dancing and flirtation. Claire saw Gabe rise from his seat and make his way over to the pretty freckle-faced girl named Deirdre. He stood self-consciously talking to her as she helped to clean the tables. She could see that Deirdre was self-conscious too, but that she purposely walked in a way that made her striped skirt twirl and flutter.

Women gathered their dishes and babies in order to take them home. Claire watched Kira with the children. Annabelle was half asleep in her arms, but Matthew was dashing about wildly. Finally Jonas scooped him up and laughed as the over-tired two-year-old kicked and cried. Together they gathered their things and called good night, then started down the path from the Pavilion toward their home. Jonas had set Matthew on his shoulders and the couple became silhouettes against the sky as the moon rose and Claire watched.

Although Jonas had no awareness of who she had once been, that once she and he had been contemporaries in the same community, Claire remembered Jonas as a boy. He was too young for fatherhood then; nonetheless, it had been he who had saved a baby sentenced to die because the little one was eager, and curious, and lively. Because he didn't sleep. He was—what was the word?—disruptive. Didn't fit in. Jonas had risked his own life, sacrificed his future, to bring him here. She wondered if he worried about Gabe now, about the frailty of the little boat he was striving to build and the dangers he would face if somehow he launched it into the river.

When she rose from her seat in order to start down the path to her own cottage, her hip had stiffened and she stood for a moment massaging it with her hand before she was able to walk. Finally she started down the gentle hill, carefully feeling her way in the moonlight. How soon she would be gone, Claire thought, and sighed. How little Gabe would ever know about his own past.

Then she stopped, suddenly, and stood still. *Of course*, she thought. She knew what she would do.

She decided she would tell her story, her own history that she had kept so secret until now, to Jonas. Someday, after she was gone, if the time was ever right, when the boy was old enough and ready, he could pass it on to her son.

SIX

"T RADEMASTER?"

Jonas looked astonished.

He had listened now for a long time. He was sitting with Claire on a bench in a secluded area behind the library. She had thought about how much to tell him, *how* to tell him, and finally, ten days after the feast, she had approached Jonas and asked if she could talk to him alone. He had brought her here late on a damp morning, carefully wiping the moisture from the bench and helping her to sit comfortably.

She hadn't known exactly how to begin. Finally she said, "I knew you when you were a boy."

Jonas smiled. "I didn't realize you were here then. I thought you came to the village more recently. I would have guessed, oh, five or six years ago. But we lose track of time, don't we?"

"No," Claire said. "You're right. I arrived here close to seven years ago. But I had known you long before then. Back in the community where you had grown up."

He looked more closely at her. "I'm sorry not to recognize you," he said. "I was a child there, of course. I left there after I turned twelve. But I did many of my volunteer hours in the House of the Old. Were you there then? I remember a woman named . . . What was it? Larissa? That was it. Did you know her?"

Claire shook her head. "No," she murmured. This was so hard. How could she describe to him something that would be almost impossible to believe?

She sighed, and kneaded her hands, which ached. It was midmorning. Often her joints ached in the morning. She cleared her throat. Her voice, she knew, was an old person's voice now, too soft sometimes, too tentative. But she took a deep breath and tried to speak firmly, to make him listen, to make him understand the incomprehensible.

"My ceremony was three years before yours."

"Your ceremony?"

"The Ceremony of Twelve."

"But—"

She held up her hand. "Shhh. Just listen."

Jonas, looking confused, fell silent.

"I received my Assignment when I turned twelve. I was assigned Birthmother." She paused. "That was a disappointment, of course. But I had not been a good student."

She could see that he was still puzzling over her words. There was nothing to do but go on. "After a while, when I was deemed ready, I moved into the birthing unit."

Around them, the pace of the village continued. Some women were gossiping as they weeded in the community garden. Nearby, small children played with some puppies. From Boys' Lodge, the usual group emerged and ran down the path, calling laughing insults to one another. Gabe was not among them. He had gone to his place by the river much earlier and was alone there, fitting the last parts of his odd little boat into place.

All of this fell away from their awareness as Jonas and Claire sat together. She talked. He listened attentively. Now and then he interrupted her softly to ask a question. The pills. When did she stop taking the pills?

"I did too. I just threw them away," he told her. "Did you feel the change?"

"I felt different from the others. But I was already different in so many ways."

He nodded. She could tell that he was slowly accepting the story she was telling him. But she saw him look carefully at her, at her thin gray hair, her stooped shoulders and gnarled hands, and knew that he could not comprehend yet how she had become what she now was.

She told him of her work at the fish hatchery, after her discharge from the Birthing Center. Of her search for Gabe, and her visits to him.

She described how the infant had begun to say her name. How he laughed at the funny face she made, and tried to imitate it. Claire thrust her tongue into her cheek and made the face for Jonas.

He looked startled. "I remember it!" he told her. "When he and I were together — you know he stayed in my dwelling at night?"

"I know."

"Sometimes he made that funny face for me. But of course I didn't know — " He paused, still trying to comprehend.

She continued her story.

The midday bell rang. Villagers began to gather for lunch. Jonas and Claire ignored it.

"Will Kira be wondering where you are?"

He shook his head. "No. She was taking the children on

a picnic with some friends. Please — go on. Unless you're hungry. Would you like to stop for lunch?"

Claire said no. "I don't have much of an appetite anymore."

"You're too thin."

"I eat very little. Herbalist says it's not unusual for someone my age. It's part of the natural process."

"Your age?" Jonas asked. "But you were three years older
than I was! What happened?"

"We'll get to that. Then you'll understand."

She went on with the telling. It would take a long time.
She felt that in order to understand, he must know every detail.

* * *

The day cleared and a pale sun dried the moisture. By late
afternoon, the shadows had lengthened and they were sitting
in deep shade. The air had turned cool. Jonas had placed his
jacket across Claire's shoulders. She was very tired by now, but
felt oddly invigorated by relating the story to someone at last.
It had been her secret, her private burden, for years. She told it
slowly, and he didn't hurry her. Now and then she had paused
to rest. He had brought her water, and a biscuit. The entire day
had belonged to them and to her story.

She described the torturous climb up the cliff at length, feeling the need to relive it inch by inch as Einar had told her he had, remembering each handhold, each precipice and narrow ledge. Talking slowly, she felt the muscles in her arms and legs respond to the memory. Jonas noticed it, how she shifted her body as in her mind she made the climb again. He winced when she told of the attack by the bird. She showed him the scar on her neck.

Finally, as exhausted almost by the telling as she had been when she reached the top of the cliff that long-ago dawn, she described the terrible trade she had made.

✳ ✳ ✳

Jonas leaned forward, his elbows on his knees, and put his face into his hands. "Trademaster," he said. "I thought he was gone. We banished him from the village a long time ago. I was Leader then."

"Who is he?" Claire asked.

He didn't respond. He stayed silent, looking now into a distant place, a place that Claire couldn't see.

"I should have known," he said, after a moment. "I felt something out there, something related to Gabe, but I didn't realize what it was. I think I was feeling your presence," he mused, "and that was puzzling, but benign. But there is something else. Something malignant. It must be *him*."

"Who *is* he?" Claire asked again.

"He is Evil. I don't know how else to describe it. He is Evil, and like all evil, he has enormous power. He tempts. He taunts. And he takes."

"Gabe has your same eyes," Claire said suddenly. "You and Gabe have the same pale eyes."

"My eyes?" he said, answering her. "They see beyond the places most people can see. I'm told it's my gift, that there are others with different gifts. And yes, Gabe has the same eyes. Sometimes I wonder—"

From the top of a pine tree near the river, a large bird suddenly lifted itself and swooped past them in the late golden light.

"Were you scared of birds at first?" Claire asked him suddenly.

"What?"

"When you ran away from the community. When you first saw birds. Were you scared?"

Jonas nodded. "Just at first. And other things too. I remember the first time I saw a fox. Gabe was so little; he wasn't afraid of anything. It was all new and exciting to him."

Claire realized suddenly that he was talking to her in a different way. He had known her since she had arrived in the community and he had always spoken to her in a kindly fashion. He had been helpful and patient: a young man to an old woman. But they had never been more than acquaintances. Now they were reminiscing together as old friends who had just reunited.

"I thought of taking him," she confessed. "But I didn't know how to hide him, or where I could go. And then your father showed me that he wore a special bracelet on his ankle, so I realized that I'd be caught if I tried to take him."

"Yes. An electronic bracelet."

Claire frowned. "I don't remember what that means. What it was."

"There was so much in the community that isn't part of our lives anymore. But that's what our memories consist of: small things," Jonas said.

"My bicycle. I haven't seen a bicycle since then. Except the one in the museum. That was—"

"My father's bike. I stole it. It had a seat for Gabe."

Claire nodded. "Yes. In my memory I can see him riding in it. He held a toy."

Jonas laughed. "His hippo."

"He called it Po, didn't he? It's coming back now."

"Yes. Po."

Now she could almost hear and see it: the dimpled hands clutching the stuffed toy; the high, happy voice. "Did you take the hippo with you when you escaped?"

Jonas shook his head. "I couldn't. It all happened so fast. I discovered they were going to release . . . No. Not *release*. They were going to kill Gabe. I took him and fled. And I had to take food. There was no room for anything else."

"I would have gone with you, if I'd known. Things would be different now if I had." She shifted on the bench and rubbed her sore hip. "I wish — " But then she fell silent.

Jonas was quiet. He didn't reply.

"I was so frightened of birds," she said suddenly. "Of their feathers and beaks. Then Einar brought me one, in a cage, as a pet. I named it Yellow-wing."

"Einar? He was the one who — "

"Yes, the one who prepared me for the climb out." Her eyes went to her feet, thick and bunioned in primitive sandals. She pulled them back beneath the bench to hide them. He knew she was remembering how limber she had been then, how balanced and sure.

"I loved Einar," she told him.

"Do you wish you had stayed?" Jonas asked her after a moment.

"No," she said firmly. "But I wish it had not been Evil that brought me here."

✳ ✳ ✳

Jonas helped her up from the bench, his hand under her arm. They had been sitting together for a long time, and Claire was stiff. She stretched slowly and took a deep breath.

"Are you all right?" he asked, looking at her with concern.

She nodded. "I'll be all right in a minute. My heart's fluttery sometimes. And I'm just a little slow to get moving."

Jonas continued looking at her. "I remember you," he said, after a moment.

"We never spoke to each other," Claire pointed out.

They began to walk slowly. He was seeing her home.

"No. But I saw you. My father mentioned you—the girl who came now and then to the nurturing center, and played with Gabe. He pointed you out to me one time. I think you rode past on your bike, and he said, 'That's the one.'"

"It seems so strange, to realize who you are. He pointed you out to me: 'That's my son,' he said. He told me your name. It brings it all back, those days in the community."

"I don't think about it anymore. I've made a life here, where it's so different."

"So has Gabe."

Jonas nodded. "He doesn't remember the community."

"It's just as well."

"I'm not certain. It frustrates him, not having a past, or a family."

"So he's wondered?"

"More than wondered," Jonas told her. "He has a passionate need to figure out his past. I try to tell him what he wants to know, but it's never been enough. That's why he's building the boat. I told him we had lived by a river, perhaps this same river. He's determined to find his way back."

They both fell silent.

"Then we must—"

"Maybe together we—"

They had both spoken at the same time, and they were both saying the same thing: *We must try to tell all of this to Gabe. Together we can help him understand.* But there was not time to discuss it. They were interrupted by the shouts of boys, excited, perhaps alarmed. The noise was coming from the riverside, the place where Gabe had been working for weeks on the little boat.

———

SEVEN

GABE HADN'T WANTED an audience for the launch. He wasn't certain the boat was completely ready, and he didn't want to be humiliated if anything went wrong. His plan was to sneak away alone. Yesterday he had moved the boat closer to the water, shoving it across some underbrush. Now it was lying on a low, muddy section of the bank. The paddle was resting diagonally inside.

The picture in his book, the book he had borrowed from Jonas, showed the lone man in the ocean, lying doomed in his small boat. His arms were taut and muscled, but useless; it was clear that the huge waves were going to be the ruin of him. He had no paddle, Gabe had thought, looking intently at the painting. Maybe he lost it. Or maybe he forgot to bring one?

There was no way the man could save himself in that over-whelming sea. He needed a paddle.

For a foolish moment Gabe focused intensely and tried to veer into the picture of the painted man, to know how it felt to be afloat, to be about to die in the sea—and to know it while safe himself, able to end the veer when he chose. Just to feel the fear briefly, and the movement of the churning waves.

But it didn't work. The man was not real. He was the painter's idea of a man, simply daubs of paint, nothing more. A painted man who needed a paddle.

Gabe was proud of the paddle he had made. He was proud of the entire boat, but he realized it was a rough, primitive construction. The paddle was different. He had felt very fortunate to have found a slender young cedar that broadened at its base: just the right potential for his plan. Carefully he had cut the tree down and then shaped the paddle from its trunk. It seemed to take forever. But he carried it back and forth to Boys' Lodge and was able to work on it there in the evenings: carving carefully, smoothing, shaping. His friends, even those who ridiculed his boat, were impressed with the paddle, with its sweet, cedary smell, its graceful curved edges, and the sheen of its wood now that he had rubbed it with oil.

"Can I carve my name on it? Just small, but so you can

remember me?" Nathaniel had asked. Gabe had agreed, and watched while his friend carved his name meticulously.

Then Simon asked, and Tarik, and others. Even those boys who had made fun of his project now took pains to add their signature.

Watching them, Gabe found that he could make tiny veers into each of the boys as they bent over the paddle, carving carefully. He could feel their feelings.

I don't think he'll make it, he felt Nathaniel worrying. *He might die in the river.*

I hope he finds his mother, he felt from Tarik. *He wants it so badly.*

He's something of a fool. But he's courageous, I'll say that for him. I wish I had his courage. Gabe was surprised to feel that from Simon, who had been scornful of the whole project.

At the last, he had shyly asked Jonas to carve his name as well. He felt Jonas's fear for him, but Jonas gave no sign. His face was calm, and he smiled when he handed the paddle back with his name inscribed.

He had left a rounded knob at one end for a handhold. The other end fanned out into a broad triangle. He had stood on the bank by the water and dipped it in, pulling it through to feel the river's resistance. It required strength. But Gabe was strong. In recent months he had begun to fill out; his muscles were firm and his energy boundless.

He had been delayed after lunch by some chores he had left undone. Grumpily he folded his laundry, put it away, and straightened his room. Now, heading back to the river, he assessed the weather. The misty morning had cleared and through the clouds a bit of sun made a narrow glint of light. The river would be smooth, Gabe thought. Sometimes after a storm it became turbulent and dangerous. He wasn't worried. His boat could manage, he was certain. But for this first test, he was glad of the calm weather; he would take it slow. He needed to learn how exactly to wield the paddle, how to steer. He flexed one arm, admired his own bicep, and wondered if Deirdre would ever notice. Then he blushed, embarrassed that he had even thought such a foolish thing.

"Gabe!"

"Hey, Gabe!"

He recognized Tarik's voice. Then Simon's, and Nathaniel's. They had spotted him on the path. Annoyed, Gabe stopped and waited. They had guessed what he was doing. His whole group from Boys' Lodge caught up with him, just Simon and Tarik at first; then they were joined by the others, who came running. "You going to do it, Gabe? Put it in the water? Can we watch?"

"We'll be your rescuers!" Tarik suggested.

He had wanted to be alone for this. Too late now. Well,

let them watch. When the time came, the *real* time, the time when he would leave for good—he would do it alone. Maybe at night. He'd leave a note at Boys' Lodge. A separate note for Jonas, he thought, with a thank-you; Jonas had done his best for Gabe. Deirdre? No, that would be foolish. No note for Deirdre. Let her wonder about him always.

For now, though, no notes. This was just a practice. What was it they called it, in that book about boats? A sea trial. That's what it would be.

"Hey, Gabe?" Simon saw the coiled rope beside his little shed. Gabe had tied stacks of boards together in order to drag them into place. He planned to return the rope soon.

"What?"

"How about if you tie one end of this rope to the boat, and we'll hold the other end when you push off? Then if you have any kind of trouble, we can haul you back in!"

Gabe scowled at Simon. "Like a baby with a toy boat in the pond?"

"No, I meant—"

"Forget it, Simon. Leave the rope where it is. I borrowed it from Jonas. He wants it back.

"Anybody who wants to help? Give me a hand pushing it into the water." Several of the boys came eagerly to the bank where the boat was wedged in the slick mud.

"But listen, Gabe!" Nathaniel sounded worried. "Maybe you should at least take the rope with you in the boat. Because when you want to come ashore, you'll need to grab something. Maybe you could make a noose in the rope and throw it over a tree stump or a bush."

"Yeah, he's right, Gabe!" someone else said.

Gabe stood beside his boat, furious. They were ruining everything, crowding around, criticizing, predicting disaster.

"Look there, where these two boards don't quite come together," a boy named Stefan said suddenly. "Won't water come in through that crack?" He pointed.

Gabe glanced to where Stefan was pointing. He had meant to fill that wide crack with thick mud and let it dry and harden. "When the boards get wet," he said, "they'll expand and come together there."

Stefan looked skeptical. "But what if —"

"Look," Gabe said impatiently. "If you're going to be all worried about it, I'll stuff something in the gap. Hand me that rag." He gestured toward the piece of cloth he had used to oil the paddle. It was lying near the shed. Stefan tossed it to him, and Gabe ripped it into strips. Then he stuffed one wadded strip of cloth into the space between the boards. "There," he said. "Happy?"

Stefan glanced nervously at the others standing on the

bank. Simon shrugged. Nathaniel looked very worried. Tarik grinned. "Sure," he said. "Happy."

"Happy to see you sink," muttered one boy, and several others laughed.

Gabe ignored them now. He was concentrating on moving the boat into the water from its muddy resting place. His hands were slippery on the rounded wood. He leaned his shoulder against it and pushed. Several of the boys were pushing as well, and with a sudden lurch the bottom of the boat lifted from the mud and moved forward into the water. Gabe leapt in, tumbling onto his backside, and grabbed the paddle.

The river water was very still here at the shallow edge. Gabe raised himself first to his knees; then he stood upright, holding the paddle against the wooden floor of the boat for balance. He hadn't anticipated that it would rock and tip the way it was, but he spread his bare feet for balance. He was still quite near the shore, and he forgot his anger and impatience in the triumph of the moment when he was finally standing upright without faltering. In a moment he would kneel and begin to steer with the paddle. But for now, it seemed appropriate to stand tall, to raise one hand from the paddle and salute his friends, who were watching apprehensively. They grinned.

Then, to his surprise, the boat began to rotate. Now he was no longer facing the shore and his friends; he was looking out toward the center of the river and across to the trees on the opposite bank.

Well, of course, he thought, realizing that he wasn't steering it yet. He knelt. Balancing awkwardly, he raised the paddle and dipped it into the water. He had practiced this, pulling the water with the broadened end, and he knew how it felt, so the resistance didn't surprise him. Leaning forward, he pulled the paddle against the current, and the boat responded slightly, revolving a bit, so that again he saw the boys, but they were farther from him now. The river was drawing him outward, away from the bank.

He had planned this. This was his time to practice controlling the boat, propelling and steering it. With the paddle, he moved it slightly toward the bank he had just left. But the river pulled him farther out again. *All right,* he thought. *I need to steer faster.* He took several long pulls with the paddle and brought himself, again, closer to shore, but he was moving with the current down the river, and a group of young alders were hiding the boys from him now.

He realized it would be hard to get back to them. The current was pulling him away from where they stood.

"Are you all right?" He recognized Nathaniel's voice.

"Yes," he called back. "I'm just figuring out how the paddle works!"

The boat spun slightly and tilted. It was hard for him to regain his balance. He planted his knees and feet. He realized suddenly that they were wet — not from the damp mud of the riverbank, but from water that was streaming in through cracks between the boards. He tried to aim for shore, pulling through the water with his paddle, but the boat felt heavier now, with water in it.

He could hear the boys' voices, shouting, getting closer to him. He realized that his friends were running along the riverbank, following him as he moved, the boat twirling clumsily out of control. The water had risen and covered his lower legs. The paddle seemed more and more useless as a steering device. Finally, angrily, he plunged it straight downward through the water and felt it scrape the bottom. It slowed the boat. Through the bushes the boys appeared, calling to him.

"Here!" Tarik shouted. "I brought the rope! If I throw it to you, we can pull you to shore!"

Gabe knew what he wanted to call back. He wanted to call: *Don't bother! I can paddle myself to shore!* But it wasn't true. The paddle was stuck in the muddy bottom of the river and it was, at the moment, precariously holding the boat still. But the swirling water was rising.

"All right, throw it!"

At least he caught the rope on the first throw so he wasn't

additionally humiliated. He wrapped it around his wrist and waited until Tarik had found a firm footing on the riverbank. Two other boys reached for the rope as well, and when Gabe called, "Now!" they pulled as he lifted the paddle that had held him still. The boat swayed and the water sloshed around his lower body. Gradually it moved to shore.

When he looked up as the bottom of the boat scraped against the rocks at the shallow edge, he saw Jonas there as well, looking concerned.

"It needs work," he muttered as he climbed out. He tied one end of the rope to the boat, threading it through a gap between some boards near the top. He took the other end from Tarik and looked around for a tree trunk to tie it to.

"Boys," he heard Jonas say, "it's time to start getting ready for supper. You go on. I'll stay here with Gabe. Thanks for your help."

Gabe knotted the rope around the slender trunk of a nearby sapling and glanced back at the small, leaky failure of a boat that he had been so proud of a short time before. It was smeared with mud and the torn rag was dangling from the gap he had stuffed it into.

Jonas was waiting for him, standing silently, his expression sympathetic.

"I don't know why I'm tying it up. I should just let it float out there and sink." Gabe's voice was shaking with tears very near the surface. He wiped his wet, dirt-smeared hands on his dripping shorts and climbed the bank to face the man who was the closest thing he had to a father.

"I'm sorry," Jonas said.

"It's not even a real boat. It's just a bunch of boards tied together. That's all it is." He wiped his face with one dirty hand and looked angrily at Jonas, defying him to disagree.

"It floated, though," he added.

"Yes. It did float."

"And my paddle really worked well."

All that work. The weeks and weeks of planning, of building, of hoping. And all he could say now was that the paddle worked well. Gabe felt it all slipping away: his dream of returning, of finding his mother, of becoming part of something he had yearned for all his life. He had envisioned a triumphant return to the place where his life had begun. He had daydreamed about being recognized and greeted: *"Look! It's Gabriel!"* In his imagination he had seen his mother running, her arms outstretched to enfold him as he stepped smiling from his sturdy little vessel.

The river still surged past. It moved and churned, foaming and dark, carrying leaves and sand and twigs from one place to the next. What a fool he had been, to think that it could have carried him as well.

Angrily he kicked at the boat, then turned away.

"Come with me, Gabe. You can come back to my house and get cleaned up there. Kira will give us some supper and we can talk. There's something important I need to tell you."

Gabe scowled at his ruined boat one more time. Then, grudgingly, he climbed the slippery bank. Carrying his paddle, he followed Jonas to the path that led back to the village.

EIGHT

DO YOU REMEMBER Trade Mart, Gabe?"

"Yes, sort of. Though they didn't let children go. You had to be older than twelve."

"Thank goodness for that," Jonas said.

Gabe reached toward the plate and took another cookie. Kira was a wonderful cook. The cookies she had served for dessert were crisp and studded with dried fruits and nuts. He hadn't been counting really, but he thought this was his sixth.

Gabe and Jonas were seated together on the pillow-strewn couch. Gabe had had a bath and Jonas had provided him with clean clothes. He was glad he hadn't had to go back to Boys' Lodge after the boat disaster. The other boys would have made jokes about it. They probably would for weeks to come. But at least for now, this first evening, he wouldn't have to listen and try to smile.

Kira was tucking the children into bed. Gabe had watched her with them earlier, as she fed them their supper and wiped their smeared, sleepy faces, talking softly to them about the nice day they had had, about a picnic, and the flowers they had picked. In a small earthen pot on the table, the bouquet of yellow loosestrife, purple coneflowers, and lacy ferns cast a shadow against the wall in the dimming light.

Gabe had little interest in babies. He would rather talk to Frolic, the old, overweight dog asleep on the floor, than to Matthew and Annabelle, with their grabby hands and screechy giggles. He was relieved when Kira finally took them off to bed. It amused him that Jonas kissed their sweaty little necks and called night-night affectionately as they toddled off with their mother.

But still. *Still.* He felt an enormous sadness that he didn't entirely understand, when he watched Kira with her children. He felt a loss, a hole in his own life. Had anyone—all right: any *woman*—ever murmured to him that way, or brushed crumbs gently from his cheek? Had anyone ever *mothered* him? Jonas had told him no. "A manufactured product," Jonas had said, describing his origins sadly.

But he thought he remembered something else. A dim

blur, that's all; but it was there. Someone had held him, had whispered to him. Someone had loved him once. He was sure of it. He was sure he could find it. Could find *her*. If only the stupid boat . . .

"Try to stay awake, Gabe. I know it's been a long day. But I want to talk to you."

He had been drifting off. Gabe shook himself fully awake and took another sip from his cup of tea. "About Trade Mart?" he asked. "I barely remember it. Just listening to people talk about it. It was creepy in some way. But kind of exciting. We always wanted to sneak in, me and the other boys."

"It had been going on for years," Jonas described. "I never paid much attention to it until I became Leader. Then I began to see that . . ." He paused when Kira came into the room, carrying a cup of tea. She sat down in a nearby chair.

"I'm telling Gabe about Trade Mart."

Kira nodded. "I wasn't here then," she told Gabe, "but Jonas has described it to me." She made a face and shivered slightly. "Scary."

Gabe didn't say anything. He wondered why they were talking about an event that had ended years before.

"It had always seemed to me like a simple entertainment," Jonas said. "Everyone got dressed up. There was a lot of merriment to their preparations. But as I got older I began to sense that there was always a nervousness to it, an uneasiness. So when I became Leader I began going, to watch."

Gabe yawned. "So what happened, exactly?" he asked politely.

"It was a kind of ritualized thing. Every now and then this man appeared in the village—he always wore strange clothes, and talked in an odd, convoluted way. He was called Trademaster. He got up on the stage and called people forward one by one. Then he invited them to make trades."

"Trades?" Gabe asked. "Meaning what?"

"Well, people would tell him what they most wanted. They'd say it loudly. Everyone could hear. And then they told him what they were willing to trade for it. But they whispered that part."

Gabe looked puzzled. "Give me an example," he said.

"Suppose it was your turn. You would go to the stage, and tell Trademaster what you wanted most. What might you ask for?"

Gabe hesitated. He couldn't put into words, really, the thing he truly wanted. Finally he shrugged. "A good boat, I guess."

"And then you would whisper to him what you were willing to trade away in order to get it."

Gabe made a face. "I don't *have* anything."

"Most people think that. And they thought that, then. But they found otherwise. He suggested to them that they trade *parts of themselves*."

Gabe sat up straighter, more awake, intrigued now. "Like a finger or something? Or an ear? There's a woman here in the village who only has one ear. The other got chopped off before she came here. As punishment for something, I think. There are places that do those kinds of horrible punishments."

"I know. And I know the woman you mean. You're right. She escaped from a place with a cruel government.

"But Trademaster was asking for something different. You had to trade — let me think how to describe it — part of your basic character."

"Like what?"

"Well, if you wanted a boat, he'd be able to provide that. But let's think about your character, Gabe. You're — what? Energetic, I'd say."

"And smart. I do pretty well in school."

"Honest. Likable."

"Well, I'm honest. That's true. I'm not always likable. I'm pretty mean to Simon sometimes."

Jonas chuckled. "Well, you're energetic. Agreed?"

"Yes. I'm energetic."

"Let's use that, just for the example. Suppose Trademaster could give you a really fine boat, Gabe. You'd have to trade for it, though. You'd have to trade your energy. You'd be on the stage. He'd whisper to you what the trade would consist of. No one would be able to hear. Just you. But then he'd say loudly: '*Trade?*' And you'd have to reply."

"Easy. A fine boat? I'd say, 'Trade!'"

"He'd write it down."

"And I'd get my boat."

"You would. I never knew of anyone asking for a boat, so I don't know how it would appear. But he had amazing powers. Probably a fine boat would be waiting for you the next day, at the river."

"*Yes!*" Gabe was wide awake now, fascinated by the thought of how easily he might have obtained a boat.

"But don't forget: you would have made a trade for it. And your energy would have been taken from you. You might wake up the next morning and be unable to get out of bed."

"So I'd rest for a day till I felt energetic."

"Gabe, Trademaster has enormous power. He could take your energy permanently."

"So I'd be in a wheeled chair or something for the rest of my life?"

"Could be."

"All right, that wouldn't work. I wouldn't trade my energy."

"But what would your other choices be?"

Gabe thought. "Honesty. Smartness. I could maybe trade one of those."

"Think about it."

"Well, I could trade my honesty. Then I'd be a dishonest person, but I'd have a really good boat." He shrugged. "That might work."

Jonas laughed. "Anyway," he said, "that's what Trade Mart was all about. It began to corrupt the people of the village. They traded away the best parts of themselves, the way you would have, in order get the foolish things they thought they wanted, or needed."

"A boat isn't foolish," Gabe argued. He yawned.

Jonas got up and went to where the teakettle was simmering. He made himself another cup of tea. "Kira? Tea?" he asked, but she shook her head.

"Take my word for it, Gabe," he said when he sat back down. "Trademaster was taking control of this village. And he was pure evil. It became clear when Matty died. That was the end of Trade Mart."

Gabe saw that Kira had put her hands to her face. She had been very close to Matty.

They all were silent for a moment. Outside, it had begun to rain. They could hear it against the roof. Then Jonas said, "I want to talk to you, Gabe, about powers."

"Powers?" Gabe suddenly felt uneasy. They were entering a realm that they had approached before.

"Maybe a better word is 'gifts.' I have a certain power, or gift. It became apparent when I was young, twelve or so. I was able to focus on something and will myself to see . . ."

He sighed, and looked at Kira. "I don't know how to describe this to him," he said.

Kira tried. "Jonas can see *beyond*, Gabe. He can see to another place. But he has to work very hard at it. It depletes him."

"And the power is ebbing," Jonas added. "I can feel that it's leaving me. Kira is experiencing the same thing."

"You mean she has a gift too?"

"Mine's different. Mine has always been through my hands," Kira explained. "I realized it the way Jonas did, when I was young. My hands began to be able to do things—to *make* things—that an ordinary pair of hands can't. But now . . ."

She smiled. "It's leaving me, as well. And that's all right. I think Jonas and I don't need these gifts anymore. We've used them to create our life here. We've helped others. And our time of such powers is passing now. But we've talked about you, Gabe. We feel certain that you have some kind of gift."

"I felt it when you were very young, Gabe," Jonas said. "When I took you and escaped the place where we were. I've been waiting for it to make itself known to you." He looked at Gabe as if something might become apparent at that moment. Gabe shifted uncomfortably on the couch.

"Well," he said finally, "it's not a gift for boatbuilding, is it?"

Jonas chuckled. "No," he said. "But you're very determined. That serves you well. And I think you're going to need that determination, and your energy—in fact, *all* your attributes—plus whatever special gift you haven't discovered yet—"

I have discovered it, Gabe thought. *I can veer.* But he stayed silent. He simply didn't feel ready to tell them.

"—because you have a hard job ahead of you," Jonas continued.

"What do you mean?"

"I'm going to use the last of my own power," Jonas said. "I'm going to see beyond one final time."

"Why?" asked Kira, startled.

Gabe echoed her. "Why?"

"I have to find out where Trademaster is," Jonas told them both. "He's still out there somewhere. He's quite near. And he's terribly dangerous."

The rain had become louder, drenching, and a wind had risen. Tree branches whipped against the side of the house. Kira rose suddenly from her chair and pulled a window closed. Jonas paid no attention. "And Gabe?" he said. "When I find him . . ."

Gabe waited. He was wide awake now.

"It's going to be up to you, then. You must destroy him."

"*Me?* Why me? He's nothing to do with me!"

Jonas took a deep breath. "It's everything to do with you, Gabe. But it's a very long story. I was going to tell it to you tonight, but I can see how tired you are. And it's late. Let's get some sleep now. And in the morning I'll explain it to you."

NINE

T HE LEAVES DRIPPED onto the wet grass, but the rain had stopped and a pale sun had risen. It was late morning now and Gabe was just waking. He had slept fitfully on the couch until finally, nudged awake by the houshold noises, he yawned and opened his eyes. He watched Kira tending the children. In her soft voice she spoke firmly to Matthew, who was trying to grab a toy from his sister. Annabelle held it tightly in her fist and looked defiantly at her brother. "No!" she said.

Kira laughed. When she saw that Gabe was awake, she turned away from the little ones.

"How are you feeling?" she asked. "You slept a long time."

Gabe nodded. He looked around the room. "I'm all right. I had strange dreams. I'm sorry I slept so late. You should have woken me. Is Jonas here?"

"No. He had to leave."

"But he promised to explain—"

"I know. And he will. But he got an urgent message early this morning. Someone in the village is quite sick."

"Why did they call for him? He's not a healer. They usually call Herbalist."

Kira shrugged. "I'm not sure. Apparently she asked for him. Are you hungry? The children just had some bread and jam. Would you like some?"

Gabe went to the table. She poured milk into a thick cup for him. He drank some and spread raspberry jam on the crusty, freshly baked bread. He watched when she turned her attention again to the toddlers.

"Do you think they'll remember this moment when they're older?" he asked suddenly.

"Fighting over a toy? Eating bread and jam? Probably not. They're too little for specific memories like that. But I think they'll remember the general feeling of being taken care of, of being scolded now and then, maybe of being held and hugged." She poured more milk into his empty cup. "Why?"

"I don't know. I just wondered."

"I think I remember being very small and sleeping beside my mother. When I think of it, I feel her warmth. And I think maybe she sang to me. I suppose I was just about the age of

Annabelle." Kira smiled. "I didn't walk when I was her age. It took me a long time to walk because of my leg."

One of her legs was twisted. It was why she leaned on a stick when she walked. He glanced at her, at the stick, when she spoke of it. But his mind was not on that.

"I don't have a single memory like that."

"What *do* you remember, Gabe?" Kira asked him.

"I rode in a seat on the back of a bike. You know that bicycle in the museum?"

"Of course."

"I remember that, a little. But it was Jonas who brought me here on that bike. He wasn't my parent. I don't remember a mother, the way you do, the way Annabelle and Matthew will. Except . . ."

He paused.

"Except what?"

Gabe squirmed on his chair. "There was a woman. I *know* there was. And she loved me."

Kira smiled. "Of course she did."

"Kira, I mean I *really* know. Last night, when you and Jonas were talking about your gifts . . ."

She looked at him. "Yes?"

"I didn't want to tell you. I don't know why. Maybe I just needed to test it one more time."

"Test what?" Kira glanced toward the children, who were now playing quietly. She came to the table and sat down in the chair next to Gabe.

"My gift. I do have one. I call it *veering.*"

"Go on."

"At first it just happened. It always surprised me. But then I found I could choose the time. I could direct it. I could cause it to happen. Was it that way for you?"

Kira nodded. "Yes. It was."

"And this morning, just a few minutes ago, you were over there, with the children—" Gabe nodded toward the corner of the room where the two little ones were industriously piling blocks into towers. "I was lying on the couch, half awake, watching, and I decided to veer into Matthew."

"Into Matthew?" Kira looked puzzled.

"Yes, because he's the boy. I suppose it's not that different with a girl, but I needed to know how it felt to be a small boy looking at his mother."

They both glanced over at Matthew. His tongue was wedged between his lips and he was frowning with concentration as he balanced a blue wooden triangle on top of a pile of square red blocks.

"So I concentrated really hard. The first thing that happens is a silence. You were talking to the children, showing them how the blocks fit together, and just as you said, 'See the shapes?' You were holding up a yellow one, and—"

"Yes. Annabelle took it from me," Kira said.

"Maybe. I don't remember that, because the silence happened. I never notice what's happening when the silence comes. But then I, ah, well, I veered into Matthew. I entered Matthew."

"You never moved from the couch."

"No, my body doesn't move. But my awareness shifts."

Kira nodded.

"And then," Gabe went on, "I became part of Matthew's feelings at that moment. I *felt* them. I *understood* them."

"So your gift is understanding how someone feels?"

"More than understanding it. *Feeling* it. And this morning, when I did that, I felt my own little self, my baby self, experiencing what Matthew was experiencing at that moment. He was receiving so much love from his mother."

Kira, beginning to understand, nodded. "For Matthew, that was coming from me. But for you, Gabe, you were remembering . . ."

"Yes. I don't know her name or where she is now. But I know for certain who she was."

The two of them sat silently, watching the children play.

* * *

Later, after he had helped her clean up the lunch dishes, Kira said, "I'm going to take the children for a walk. Want to come?" She lifted two small jackets from a hook on the wall.

"When's Jonas coming back?"

"I don't know. I'm surprised that he's been gone so long."

"Is it all right if I wait here for him?"

"Of course. You and he have a lot to talk about."

Gabe looked through the window, down at the winding paths that crisscrossed the village. People hurried along, busy with midday tasks. Beyond the orchard, he could see the library; it appeared closed. Nearby, in the playing field, children were running around with a ball that they passed back and forth; he could hear their shouts. It was an ordinary day in the quiet, well-ordered place. Yet someplace in the village, someone was very ill, and Jonas was there.

"I think I'll go look for him," Gabe said suddenly. "Do you know where he went? Who is it who is so sick?"

Kira reached into a small sleeve and guided Annabelle's chubby arm through. "Other side now," she said to the little girl, and held open the other sleeve. "Can you do yours by yourself?" she asked Matthew, whose jacket was on the floor in front of him. He grinned and shook his head no.

"A woman named Claire," she said to Gabe, in answer to

his question. "I'm sure you've seen her in the village. She's very, very old."

"Oh, *her!* Yes, I've seen her often."

"Well, I fear you won't be seeing her much longer. It sounds as if her time is running out." With both children now buttoned into their jackets, Kira headed to the door with Annabelle in her arms and Matthew by one hand. "Can you open the door for me?"

"Is it all right if I leave my paddle here?" He looked toward the corner where it was propped against the wall. The sunlight made it gleam golden.

"Of course. I won't let the children play with it."

Gabe helped her through the door and down the front steps. "Do you know where she lives? Or is she in the infirmary?"

"Jonas went to her house. It's over there someplace." Kira indicated, nodding her head, a place beyond the library, beyond the schoolhouse. He could see the small cottages, deep in shade, that dotted the wooded area.

Gabe thanked her quickly for the place to eat and sleep after such a bad day. Then, as Kira headed with the children to the play area nearby, he began to jog toward the place where Claire lived and where Jonas was with her now. He wanted to talk more about what Jonas had proposed last night. It had

been on his mind since he had awakened. He was to *kill* someone named Trademaster? It made no sense. Jonas was a peaceful, compassionate man. All right, maybe this Trademaster guy
was bad. Maybe even pure evil! But he wasn't bothering anyone
they knew. They would watch out for him, would fend him off
if he showed signs of trying to return to the village and do
harm.

Hah, Gabe thought with a wry smile. *Maybe they should just
put him into my stupid boat and give it a firm shove into the river.*

❋ ❋ ❋

The little cottage was deep in a thicket of trees, but he had
no trouble finding the place where Claire lived. Several aged
women stood somberly outside, murmuring to one another.

"So sudden," he overheard one woman say to another.
"Came upon her just like that. She was fine last night."

"Happens that way," a tall white-haired woman said
knowingly, and several others nodded.

Gabe excused himself politely as he passed them. "Is Jonas inside?" he asked. A woman nodded.

"She asked for him, first thing. Strange," she murmured.

"Is it all right if I go in?" Gabe asked.

No one seemed to be in charge. They all looked at him

blankly, and he took it as permission. The door stood partially open, and he entered after a quiet knock on the wood, which drew no reply. The interior was very dim. It was bright outside on this clear day after the night's rain, but the windows of the cottage were small, and woven curtains were drawn across. He smelled stale food, old age, dried herbs, and dust.

Herbalist, who ordinarily tended the sick, sat quietly in a rocking chair.

Gabe looked around. "Jonas?"

"Over here." He followed the voice and found Jonas sitting in the shadows beside the bed. Again he wondered: *Why?* Why had the old woman asked for Jonas?

And how soon could Jonas excuse himself and come away? Gabe needed to talk to him. Their conversation last night had seemed urgent. More than urgent; it had been alarming. Jonas, the most peaceful of souls, seemed to be commanding Gabe to commit a murder. He had not explained, not really. He had said they would discuss it more fully in the morning.

Now morning had passed, and Gabe wanted to know more. The old woman was dying, as old people always do. It was the natural way of things. Her friends were nearby, and Herbalist was sitting in the corner. She didn't need Jonas. Not as much as Gabe did.

"Can't you leave?" Gabe whispered, moving closer. "We need to talk. You promised to explain—"

"Shhh." Jonas held up a hand.

Now, through the dim light, he could see Jonas more clearly, and the woman in the bed as well. Her eyes were open, and it was clear that she had seen Gabe approaching. Her thin fingers moved, plucking at the blanket. Jonas was watching her very closely; now he leaned forward, as if to listen. Her thin, dry lips were moving. Gabe could not hear, at first, what she said. But Jonas did. Jonas was nodding.

Gabe stood there uncertainly. The woman's mouth began to move again, and he found himself leaning forward to listen. This time, nearer, he could hear her words.

"Tell him," she was saying to Jonas.

TEN

I'M SORRY. I just don't believe you."

Gabe's voice was both skeptical and firm.

Jonas leaned forward, his elbows on his knees. He cupped his own face with his hands. They were sitting together on the bench behind the library, the same bench where he had so recently sat with Claire.

He looked up and sighed. "I felt the same way yesterday when she told it to me. I sat here thinking: *This woman is crazy.* Is that what you're thinking now of *me*, Gabe?"

Gabe shook his head and looked away. He wanted to be someplace else. Off with his lodge-mates. Building another boat. *Sinking* another boat. He didn't care. Anywhere but here, listening to this unbelievable story being told to him by a man he loved. And last night this same man had talked of the need to destroy someone. It was scary. It was sad.

He turned to Jonas and tried to speak in a soothing voice. "You know what? You've been working awfully hard. Probably reading too much. You should take a long walk along the river. Have a nice relaxing, restful . . ."

"Gabe. Listen to me! We don't have much time. This is not a wild made-up thing. This is *real.* She remembers you. She remembers me. She—" Jonas paused and took a deep breath. "I know you were very young when we left the community, so you won't recall these things. But I do, Gabe. I remember *seeing* her there. She used to work at the fish hatchery. But in her spare time she came to the nurturing center and helped out. She did that because you were there, Gabe.

"She had given birth to you. It's the way things were done there. Young girls produced babies—they weren't called babies; they were called newchildren. The birthmothers turned them out like factory products. Then the babies were moved to the nurturing center, and eventually assigned to couples who applied for children."

"That's how your parents got you?" Gabe asked.

Jonas nodded.

"So some girl had given birth to you?"

"Yes."

"But you don't know who?"

Jonas shook his head.

"And some other girl—or maybe it was the same one?—gave birth to *me* years later—"

"*Claire* gave birth to you. You were the only child she ever had."

"But you're saying she ended up working in the fish place."

Jonas nodded. "Yes, they determined that she couldn't handle any more births. She had difficulty when you were born. So they gave her another job. But she spent all her time watching over you. She *loved* you, Gabe. But love wasn't permitted."

Gabe leaned down, slipped off one of the sandals he was wearing, and dislodged a pebble that had been rubbing against his toe. He watched a bird flutter in a nearby tree, and noticed that it had a twig in its beak. He examined a scratch on his arm. He yawned, and stretched. He unbuttoned and rebuttoned the neck of his shirt. He investigated his fingernails.

Jonas watched him.

"You know what?" Gabe said at last. "I guess I can believe all of that. You've told me before about what the community was like. So: there was a girl; she gave birth to me. I believe that. And, Jonas? I know it's true that she loved me. But—"

Jonas nodded. "I know. It's the rest of it."

"Yes, the rest of it is just crazy. That old woman? I'm supposed to believe that some man in strange-looking clothes—"

He noticed that Jonas was no longer looking at him. He was looking across the grassy area, to the path beyond. Gabe followed Jonas's gaze and saw Mentor, the elderly schoolmaster, walking slowly along the path. Nothing unusual. It was school vacation now. Mentor was a part of the village. One often saw him walking around.

To his surprise, Jonas rose from the bench and called to Mentor. "Come with me, Gabe," he said.

He followed Jonas's quick strides toward the path where Mentor had stopped and was waiting. The bearded schoolmaster was stooped, and his face was lined. But his eyes were keen and intelligent. Gabe had always liked Mentor, even when he had not liked school. "Good morning," he said. "What can I do for you gentlemen this morning?"

"Mentor," Jonas began, "I'm trying to explain to Gabe here about Trademaster. About his powers."

Mentor visibly winced. "That's of the past," he said abruptly. "It's forgotten."

"I'm afraid it isn't," Jonas told him. "We have a rather urgent situation. I'll describe it to you later. But right now I need you to help me convince Gabe that the powers exist. He finds it hard to believe."

"It *is* hard to believe," Mentor agreed, nodding. "In a peaceful village like this, it is hard to conceive of true evil."

"We don't have a lot of time, Mentor. Could you describe, to Gabe, the trade you made?"

Mentor sighed. "This is necessary?" he asked Jonas.

"Necessary and very important."

Mentor nodded. "I see. Very well, then. It was years ago, Gabe. You were a little boy. I remember how mischievous you were in school. Sometimes inattentive."

"I know," Gabe acknowledged in embarrassment.

"You were too young to go to Trade Mart. But surely you knew of it?"

Gabe shrugged. "I guess. It seemed kind of mysterious."

"Some of us adults went every time. There was a kind of entertainment to it, watching other villagers make fools of themselves. But you didn't usually attend, did you, Jonas?"

Jonas shook his head. "It didn't ever interest me until it got out of hand, and by then I was Leader and had to take action."

"Well, I was a fool. Many of us were. I was an old man—widowed, lonely. I lived with my daughter, but I knew she would marry someday and I'd be alone. I felt sorry for myself. I had this birthmark. The schoolchildren used to called me Rosie because of it; remember, Gabe?"

Gabe looked at the deep red stain on Mentor's cheek. He nodded. "We didn't mean any harm."

"Of course you didn't." Mentor smiled. "But I was self-pitying and foolish. And there was a woman, a widow, I was attracted to. You understand about that, don't you? Boys your age would understand."

Gabe's instinct was to pretend ignorance. The question embarrassed him. But with both Mentor and Jonas watching him intently, it seemed a time for honesty. "Yes," he said. "I understand."

"So," Mentor said with a deep sigh, "I went to Trade Mart and for the first time, I asked to make a trade."

"What did you ask for?"

Mentor laughed, but it was a sardonic laugh. "I told Trademaster that I wanted to be younger, and handsome. I wanted Stocktender's widow to fall in love with me."

Gabe looked at the ground. He was embarrassed for Mentor, that he must make such a confession of his own idiocy. "He couldn't do that kind of transformation, could he? You should have asked for, oh, I don't know, maybe a set of new desks for the schoolhouse!"

"Evil can do anything, Gabe," Mentor said, "for a price."

Gabe stared at him. "What was the price?" he asked, after a moment.

"His terms were vague. Vague enough that they sounded unimportant. He's very clever, Trademaster is. He sets his terms but we don't really understand them when we agree to the trade. He told me I would have to trade away my honor."

"So you said no."

Mentor shook his head. "I grabbed at it. *Eagerly.* I told you I was a fool."

"But, Mentor! You are an honorable man! Everyone knows that. And—I don't mean to be rude, but you're not young and handsome. So the trade didn't work! No one has that kind of power, not even someone evil."

"Oh, it worked. It worked for many of us here in the village. Me—I grew taller, and my bald spot disappeared. Thick hair where once there had been just this shiny dome! Birthmark? Faded, faded, then poof! Gone! You may not have noticed, Gabe; you were a child then, and it was summer so you weren't in school. But briefly I was a younger, handsome man. I began courting the pretty widow.

"But you know what, Gabe?"

"What?" Gabe was stunned. So Trademaster, whoever he was, *did* have incredible powers. He could have made a trade with the woman—what was her name, Claire? He tried to pay attention to what Mentor was saying, but his thoughts now were on what this all meant—what it meant to him, Gabe, and to the woman, Claire, who may have made a terrible trade in order to find her . . . her . . .

"I am her son," he whispered aloud.

Mentor hadn't heard him. He continued talking. "I had traded away the most important part of myself. I turned selfish. Cruel. The pretty widow didn't want a man like that! So I had made a meaningless trade, and I had turned into a person I hated—but a handsome one! And young!"

Gabe forced himself to pay attention to the schoolmaster. "What changed you back? You're a man of honor now, Mentor."

"Jonas stepped in. Trade Mart had corrupted the whole village. Many people had traded away their best selves. We turned on each other. There was greed, and jealousy, and . . . Well, it had to end. There was a set of horrible events—we lost one of our best young people—"

"Matty?"

"Yes, Matty died, battling the evil. But because of him the rest of us survived and were restored. I got my bald head and my birthmark back!" He laughed. "And I lost my silly romance. Still a bachelor today."

"And we banished Trademaster," Jonas reminded them.

"We did. Forever." Mentor said it with a kind of relief

and satisfaction. He turned to leave. Then he said slowly, with a questioning look, "Something's wrong?"

Jonas nodded. "He's returned," he said.

Mentor looked stunned. "So this battle must be waged again?"

Jonas nodded. "This time we must be sure it's final."

"Whom do we send this time, to die?" Mentor's voice was bitter and sad. Like everyone, he had loved Matty.

"I'm going," Gabe told him.

Mentor was silent. Then, without speaking, he turned away from them.

Gabe and Jonas stood watching the aged schoolmaster walk away. His shoulders were slumped.

"He got himself back," Gabe said, after a moment.

Jonas nodded. "He did."

"That means a trade can be reversed," Gabe said.

Jonas nodded.

"I'm scared."

"I am too," Jonas replied. "For you, for all of us."

She is my mother. She is my mother. Gabe took a deep breath. "How much time do we have?" he asked.

———

ELEVEN

THEY HURRIED BACK to the cottage where Claire was dying. The sun was setting now. Someone had lit an oil lamp on the table. This time, in the flickering golden light, Gabe approached the bed without hesitation. He knew, he thought, what he wanted to say: that he'd been waiting all his life for her to find him. That he understood the sacrifice she had made for him. That it didn't matter that she was old. What mattered was being together.

But when he knelt beside her, he thought he'd come too late. Her eyes were half open and glazed. Her mouth fell slack. Her hand on the coverlet, when he took it in his, was limp and cold.

Crying unashamedly, Gabe turned to Jonas, who stood

behind him. "I wanted to tell her I knew! I wanted to tell her I remember her! But I'm too late," he wept. "She's gone."

Jonas gently moved Gabe aside. He leaned down and touched Claire's thin, veined neck. Then he rested his head against her chest, listening carefully.

"Her heart is beating still," he told Gabe. "She's very close to death. But she is still alive. We have very little time, and I have very little left of the gift I once possessed. But I am going to use it. I am going to look beyond and try to see where he is. After that, it will be up to you. Your gift is still young."

"Do you need to go to some special place?" Gabe asked, wiping his eyes on the sleeve of his shirt.

"No. I just need to gather my strength. And I need quiet, for concentration.

"Claire? Can you hear me?" Jonas said toward the old woman. She didn't respond. She took a slow, deep breath.

"Gabe will sit here beside you. Gabe, hold her hand so that she knows you're there."

Gabe took the gnarled hand in his own.

"I'm going to close the door to the cottage so that no one comes in, so that it will be quiet. I'll be here, by the window." He was speaking to them both. "I'm told that this is difficult to watch, Gabe. But don't be afraid. It's not painful for me, just very draining. It shouldn't take long."

Jonas went to the front of the cottage, spoke briefly to the people gathered outside, then closed and latched the door. Gabe, watching him, could see that already he was changing in some way; he was becoming something different from the ordinary and pleasant man he had been. He went to the window and stood looking through it into the night, though his eyes were half closed. He was breathing deeply, in and out, very slowly. Suddenly he gasped, as if he were pierced by pain. He moaned slightly. Gabe found himself squeezing the old woman's hand. He continued to watch Jonas.

On the bed, Claire breathed occasionally, with a tortured sound.

Jonas began to shimmer. His body vibrated and was suffused with a silvery light.

"He is beyond now," Gabe said to Claire, hoping that somehow she could hear and know how desperately they were trying to save her.

Jonas gasped loudly again.

"I think he is seeing Trademaster," Gabe whispered, and felt Claire shudder.

Then he fell silent and waited.

✳ ✳ ✳

Afterward, Gabe had to help Jonas to the nearby rocking chair. He collapsed into it, panting and trembling. "What did you see?" Gabe asked. "Could you find him?" But Jonas was unable to speak. He closed his eyes and held up one hand, asking Gabe to wait. Finally, after resting for several minutes, Jonas opened his eyes.

"I don't think I'll be able to do that again," he said hoarsely to Gabe. "It was the last time. It has become too hard."

He turned slightly and looked toward the bed. "How is she?"

Gabe went to Claire and took her hand. There was no answering squeeze from her. Her hand and arm were limp. But he heard a long, slow breath.

"Alive," Gabe told Jonas, returning to the chair where he was slumped.

"There's not much time." Jonas sat up a little straighter, still breathing hard. "But I saw him; he's close by. It's up to you now, Gabe. I'll stay here with her."

Close by? What did that mean? Gabe found himself looking around the room, and toward the window. *Was someone standing out there in the trees?* A closet door was open in the corner, the interior dark. *Was someone in the closet?* A board creaked, and Gabe jumped nervously. But it was just Jonas's chair, its curved rockers moving against the wooden floor.

He found a pitcher of water and brought Jonas a cup. Jonas drank, and sat up straighter.

"I forgot to tell you something else that she and I both remembered. When you were a baby—a newchild—you had a stuffed toy." He smiled. "It went everywhere with you. Your hippo."

A blurred image appeared to Gabe. A soft, comforting object. With ears. He had chewed on the ears.

"*Po*," he said.

"A fine water beast," Jonas said. "You've always been attracted to water, Gabe. And now you must become like Po. Trademaster is on the other side of the river."

* * *

It was dark when Gabe stood at the water's edge, alone. He had begged Jonas to come with him. But Jonas had said no.

"Years ago, Gabe, when I took you and ran away, there was a man I loved and left behind. I wanted him to come with me but he said no.

"He was right to refuse. It was my journey and I had to do it without help. I had to find my own strengths, face my own fears. And now you must."

Gabe had leaned down and kissed the papery cheek of the silent woman in the bed. There were long pauses between her breaths now, and occasionally a gurgle deep in her throat. Jonas moved his chair so that he could sit close to her. Then he told Gabe where he would find Trademaster—in a grove of birch trees on the far side of the river—and he grasped Gabe's hand. "Go," he said. "This is your journey, your battle. Be brave. Find your gift. Use it to save what you love."

* * *

Now, standing barefoot in the pebbly sand, Gabe didn't feel brave. It was very dark. Clouds covered the moon. There were no sounds but the rushing water, and though the river had always lured him, fascinated him, he had never been here before at night. Suddenly, in the dark, it seemed dangerous and forbidding.

Gabe was a good swimmer. But the place where he and his friends swam was farther down the river, a bend where the water, protected by encircling rocks, was calm, separated from the fast-moving water farther out. It was safer there, less treacherous. But Jonas had told him to cross the river here. The current would move him downriver and he would emerge at the other side very near to the wooded grove where Trademaster, gloating, was waiting for Claire to die.

"Why is he there?" Gabe had asked.

"I think he must feel a certain satisfaction at knowing how things end. He sets them in motion and then watches from a distance. He has probably been aware of Claire for all these years, since she made the trade."

"Is it just Claire he's been watching?"

"Oh, no, he must have many, many tragedies to keep track of. I suppose they nourish him in some terrible way."

Gabe moved forward and felt the pull of the current against his ankles. He knew, from the disaster with his little boat two days before, how strong the swirling motion of the water was. But he was strong too, and he felt certain he could fight his way across the river. He was holding his cedar paddle. The mud-smeared boat, leaky and useless, was still tied to a tree. But he had run back to Jonas's house and retrieved the paddle for the night swim. He thought he could use it to push himself away from rocks, and perhaps, when he reached the other side, he would need it as a weapon.

He wished he had the power that Jonas had used: the gift of seeing beyond. He would like to know what Trademaster was doing at this moment. Did such a man sleep? Eat?

He had no idea how he was to destroy this evil. Gabe knew—all village children had been taught—which berries, which plants, were lethal. Perhaps he should have crushed some leaves of oleander, or chopped up nightshade root, and somehow found a way to sneak the poison into Trademaster's food. Of course there had been no time for plans like that.

If he were to find Trademaster asleep, then a heavy rock brought down on his head would do it, Gabe thought. Awake? He could use the paddle as if it were a spear or a bludgeon.

The thought made him feel sick.

He was now in the water to his knees, and he realized that instead of plotting how to do away with the enemy — and sickening himself at the thought of it — he must first concentrate on the dangerous swim he was about to undertake. The current pulled at him, and he waded deeper. Soon his feet would be lifted from the bottom and he would be fighting his way across. He held the buoyant paddle in both hands, crosswise in front of him. His feet lifted and he began to kick and move forward.

The speed with which the current caught him was frightening. He felt himself propelled downriver instead of across. The water rushed over his head and he forced himself up through it to catch his breath. In the darkness he could not see how far out into the river he had been swept, but he could feel the current; he continued kicking his way across it, even as it pushed him sideways against his will. Suddenly his paddle caught against two large rocks and he was held there, able to rest and breathe. The water parted and foamed around him and he waited, gathering his strength. He knew he would have to leave this wedged protection and enter the river's surge again. But for this moment he rested. Then, as he pondered the mission that lay ahead for him, he realized, suddenly, he could not fulfill it.

I cannot kill someone, he thought.

As he had the realization, a cloud slid beyond the moon and pale light illuminated the river. He could see where he was, nearing the halfway point, and where he must aim for. The water between him and the other side was very turbulent, but in the gleaming moonlight, the grove of birches, his destination, was visible. Trademaster would be lurking there. He must pull the paddle free from the rocks now and force himself into that maelstrom. He would fight his way across, and—

I cannot kill someone. The unbidden thought was so strong the second time that he may have said it aloud, into the night, into the roaring sound of the turbulence.

Oddly, as if affected by his thought, the motion of the river subsided slightly. As he waited there, suspended from his paddle between the rocks, his legs could sense the change in the current. For a moment the water around him was still. The water ahead of him was calm. Then it began to move again, to swirl and suck at him.

What had changed?

Nothing, except that into the night breeze, into the noise of the river, he had whispered a phrase. He began to say the words again.

I cannot kill—

Three words was all it took. The three words that he had spoken soothed the sky, the river, the world.

He repeated them, like a chant. He loosened the paddle from where it was wedged. With his fingers he could feel the carved names in the smooth wet wood: *Tarik. Simon. Nathaniel. Stefan. Jonas.* Though she had not carved her name, he added Kira in his mind. Then little Matthew, and Annabelle. Finally he said his mother's name—*Claire*—aloud, adding it to the list of those who cared about him. He shouted it—"Claire!"—into the night, begging her to live. Holding tightly to the paddle, he began to kick his way easily across the gently flowing water in the moonlight. While he propelled himself, he said the words in rhythm with the movement of his fluttering kick—*I cannot kill, I cannot kill*—murmuring them until he reached the opposite bank easily and pulled himself, dripping, ashore.

When he fell silent, he heard the river resume its relentless churn and pull. A brisk wind blew. Above him, the moon receded and disappeared again behind clouds. Around him the shadows darkened and enveloped the swaying shrubbery and trees. At the edge of the bushes stood a tall man wrapped in a dark cloak.

TWELVE

GABE SHUDDERED. SUDDENLY he was very cold. The wind that was rustling the bushes and making the trees sway was also causing his wet garments to feel icy against his skin.

But his shudder was more fear than chill. He could see the man standing in the shadows.

Somehow Gabe had anticipated that he would arrive on the river's far side, catch his breath, get his bearings — he had never crossed the river before — and then begin to search. He had assumed his enemy would be hiding. He had planned to make his way with stealth to the place where they would encounter each other. He thought he would have time to prepare, though he had not known how.

Instead, the man was not hiding at all. He stood, wrapped in a dark cloak, in full view at the edge of the trees. Even through the darkness, Gabe could see that his eyes glittered. His face was expressionless, but his eyes—they were staring directly at Gabe—were excited. Then he spoke.

"What a pleasure," the man said with an air of mocking hospitality. "Seldom do people come looking for me."

Gabe didn't reply. He didn't know how to. Nervously, he clutched the slim stalk of the paddle, the only thing in this strange place that felt familiar and comforting. Beneath his thumb he could feel the ridge of the gouged *J*, the place where Jonas had carved his name.

"Are you not going to introduce yourself?"

Gabe cleared his throat. "My name is Gabriel," he said.

There was a flurry of cloak and motion. The man, who had been standing some distance away, was suddenly so near that Gabe could smell the stench of him. Odd, as he looked very clean, Gabe thought. His clothes, visible in the parted cloak, were pressed, almost stiff with creases. His face was pale and seemed very white against the darkness. His dark hair was combed and oiled.

And he was too close. When he leaned forward and said harshly, "You fool! Did you think I didn't know your name?"

his rancid breath was hot against Gabe's face. "And you, of course, know mine.

"Don't you?" he sneered. *"Don't you?"*

"Yes," Gabe said. "I know your name, Trademaster." He stepped back, slightly, away from the smell. The foul breath was making him feel nauseated.

"And we both know why we are here." The voice had become soft, as if the man were confiding a secret.

Gabriel nodded. "Yes," he whispered back. "I do."

"You hope to destroy me, and I plan to destroy you."

In a quick flash of memory, Gabe thought of Mentor, his teacher, standing in front of a class of restless children, teaching them about language. About verbs. *Hope. Plan.* How different the meanings were. *Hope* seemed tentative, uncertain—exactly how Gabe was feeling. He took a deep breath and tried to calm his own anxiety.

"What weapons do you have? Can they match mine?" Trademaster's gloved hand reached inside his thick cloak. Gabe grasped the paddle more tightly, trying to steady himself. His knees felt weak.

"I see you have brought a crude stick. Pathetic. Is that the only weapon you have?" The voice was contemptuous.

"This isn't a weapon," Gabe confessed. "I didn't bring a weapon. I cannot kill—"

He began to repeat the phrase that had mysteriously helped him cross the river. To his surprise, Trademaster winced. The wind stopped, suddenly. The restless movement of the trees ceased. Again the moon slid from the clouds and the night brightened slightly.

* * *

Back in the cottage, Jonas had been waiting in the rocking chair beside the bed. Earlier, Kira had brought him supper. Together they had moistened Claire's dry lips with water and her tongue had moved slightly. But her eyes had remained closed and her breathing was irregular. Sometimes she gasped and her fingers plucked at the blanket. But mostly she was silent and still. He knew she would die during the night, unless —

He tried not to think of the *unless*. He had seen, when he looked beyond, that Trademaster was out there in the birch grove. He had seen too — but had not told Gabe — that Trademaster was waiting for the boy.

Gabe had always been a determined child. Even as an infant, when Jonas had brought him here after a long and torturous journey, Gabe had held out, had been strong, had stayed alive, when he, Jonas, had almost given up. It had always been clear to Jonas that Gabe had some kind of gift. And it might have been simply this: the tenacity of the boy, the stubbornness. Who else would have worked so hard at an impossible project like the doomed boat?

But now, waiting through the night, thinking of how Gabe had set out on another probably impossible mission, one that might well cost him his life, Jonas found himself hoping desperately that the stubborn energy would be accompanied by a deeper gift of some sort, something that would be able to pierce the very core of the creature he would be facing soon. Jonas shuddered. Trademaster was so inhuman, so dangerous. So evil. And Gabe was so young and vulnerable.

He would be across the river now, Jonas realized, checking the time. *He is on the other side by now.*

* * *

The shift in the atmosphere calmed Gabriel. It had happened the same way in the river: the moon had appeared and the rush of water had subsided; the world had been somehow soothed. Standing now in the moonlight, Gabe stroked the paddle, feeling the carved names, and wondered if perhaps Trademaster had felt the sudden shift.

But instead of calmed, his opponent was angered. The gloved hand emerged from the deep folds of the cloak and in the moonlight Gabe could see that it now held a gleaming knife with a long, very narrow blade and pointed tip. Frightened, he stepped back.

"*Stiletto*," Trademaster hissed. "You don't have one of these tucked away someplace? It would serve you well. Quite sharp. Quite deadly.

"Here!" he said suddenly, and tossed the stiletto to Gabe. "Take mine!"

Gabe dropped the paddle and caught the handle of the weapon awkwardly, relieved that the blade had not sliced through his hand. The knife was surprisingly heavy. He didn't want it. But he seemed to have no choice. He tightened his grip on the cold steel handle.

"*Now* you can kill," Trademaster said with a short, mirthless laugh. He reached again into the folds of his cloak. The sky darkened again and the wind resumed, whipping the tree branches back and forth. Gabe peered through the darkness, trying to see what weapon might appear. Another stiletto? Would the man lunge forward with his own narrow blade? Terrified, Gabe held his knife up, hoping to deflect the attack that was coming.

Then suddenly the stiletto was on the ground and Gabe's hands were empty and defenseless. Trademaster was inches from him and had struck the knife out of Gabe's hand with a larger weapon, something with a terrifying curved blade.

"*Guan dao,*" Trademaster whispered into Gabe's ear, naming it.

The wind howled. The man held Gabe's neck with one gloved hand, raised his weapon with the other, and touched the tender skin there with the blade. Gabe held his breath, afraid that the slightest movement would cause it to slice into his skin. He could feel the exquisite sharpness of the steel.

The two of them stood motionless in an embrace that was wrought by hatred. Gabe hoped that his death would be quick. It was the only thing that he could hope for now.

Then, to Gabe's surprise, still with the knife poised, Trademaster began to talk. Gabe could again smell his foul breath. His voice was low, and he recognized the tone, superior and arrogant, as bragging.

"You're such a small, unworthy opponent," Trademaster taunted. "I've destroyed people far more important than you."

Gabe said nothing. He barely breathed. He was motionless, still aware of the blade against his skin.

"Leaders. Whole families." The voice was excited. "I've torn them to pieces. Left them in whimpering shreds!"

Gabe felt a sharp sliver of pain, and something trickled from his neck onto his bare shoulder. Trademaster had allowed the razor-sharp blade to make a shallow cut.

"Wars," the voice went on. "I've caused wars!"

Gabe stood motionless, paralyzed, but sensed that the man wanted a reaction from him. Some kind of admiration, perhaps. He stayed silent.

"I've destroyed whole communities," the man murmured gleefully into Gabe's ear. "Do you believe me?"

"Yes," Gabe whispered. And it was true. He *did* believe that he had such power. This was not a man, Gabe realized. It was a *force* disguised as a man. It was nothing human. It was simple evil, wearing a cloak. Jonas had told him this but he had not understood, not until now. He tried desperately to remember what advice Jonas had given him. How should he fight this battle? Finally he said the only thing he could think of to say.

"If you have such power," Gabe whispered, still trying not to move, "why kill someone as unimportant as me?"

To his amazement, Trademaster withdrew. He lifted the blade from Gabe's skin and tossed it to the ground, where it fell beside the stiletto. Then he smoothed the folds of his cloak. "I have other weapons," he said. "Cutlass? Pole-ax? Machete? Cleaver? Pick one and we'll duel." He licked his lips and gave a harsh laugh.

Gabe could think of nothing to reply. He remained silent.

"No? Dueling doesn't appeal? Forget the weaponry, then.

I'll make it more fun, the way Trade Mart was," he announced. "I'm going to offer you a trade."

* * *

Through the window, quite suddenly, the moonless night brightened. A pale golden stream of light appeared across the floor, reaching almost to the bed. At the same time, Claire's hoarse, uneven breathing changed slightly. She seemed quieter, more comfortable. Jonas reached over and took her hand. He had been holding it, stroking it, off and on throughout the night. The veins had been thick and knotted under the thin, frail skin; the fingers were thickened at the joints.

Now, startlingly, the old woman's hand felt different. Smoother. More pliant. In the sudden light he leaned down to look. But at that moment the moonlight disappeared; the night was dark again. He thought of going to relight the oil lamp in the corner, to bring it closer to Claire. But why? *Let her sleep,* he thought. *She is at peace. Let her die without knowing the peril her son is in.*

Perhaps this is what death does, he thought, still touching her hand. Smooths the skin, eases the painful joints. *Yes,* he thought. *This must be death coming.*

Jonas nodded off against his will and dozed fitfully. It had been such a long, exhausting day. He didn't see the moonlight reappear, then recede, then reappear. Claire's hand slid away from his. He didn't see the skin clear, its dark spots fading, or how the thickened, discolored nails became shell-like and translucent.

✳ ✳ ✳

"A boat." The offer was abrupt and angry.

"I don't need a boat."

Trademaster looked at him slyly. "It's not a question of *need*, my stubborn, stupid lad. It all has to do with *want*. It's *always* want."

Gabe stood there silently. He was cold. He was wet, still, from the river, and now the stiff breeze had resumed. He rubbed his own arms briskly.

"Chilly?" Trademaster said with a sneer, seeing him shiver. "I could loan you my cloak." He twirled it. "You could come inside. I could *envelop* you."

Gabe didn't reply. The thought of being inside the dark cloak revolted him.

His eyes glittering, Trademaster said, "All right then, stand there and shiver. Let's revisit the boat idea, shall we? Not need, but want. Do you *want* a boat? Wait—don't answer yet.

Let's make it, oh, a fine sailboat. And part of the deal, guaranteed: billowing sails, a sunny day, a smooth lake, and a strong wind."

He leaned forward and beckoned with a thin, gloved finger. *"Want it?"*

Not long ago Gabe would have wanted it very much indeed. But things had changed for him. A boat no longer held any appeal. He no longer needed a boat. His quest for belonging, for love, had ended when he had knelt by a bed and held his dying mother's hand.

He stood silently for a moment, trying to think of how to say no without further enraging Trademaster.

"Wait! I'm going to add something!" The man leaned even closer.

Gabe didn't reply.

"On the fine teak deck of this superior sailing vessel? Seated there, her hair blowing in the wind, smiling at you, looking at you very affectionately—extremely affectionately—as you sail your craft, maybe leaning forward to offer you something . . . Let me think. An apple—she has just peeled a fine round apple and she will offer you a bite, she being, of course, someone you care about deeply, maybe that freckle-faced girl named . . . Deirdre?

"Want it?" Trademaster put his mouth to Gabe's ear and breathed the question hoarsely.

"No," Gabe said. "I don't."

Trademaster laughed cruelly. "Of course you don't," he rasped. "You're waiting for something more? Let's do it, then! Still the boat. You can have the boat and the lake and the sunshine. And she'll still be there, leaning forward, offering you food and sustenance and affection—but it's not silly little Deirdre at all. Know who it is?

"Got a guess?" he hissed.

Gabe did. But he refused to say it. He tightened his hands on the smooth wood of the paddle. When he did, he felt the curved indentations, the places carved here and there with names: *Tarik. Nathaniel. Simon. Stefan.*

"It's Claire," Trademaster murmured to him. "Sweet, young Claire with the long, curly hair. She could be there with you. You know who Claire is, don't you?

"Want it? Want her?"

Gabe felt the place where the name *Jonas* had been carved. The sweet cedar of the paddle was infused with all of them: the ones who cared about him, the ones who at this moment were sending strength to him. As his hand lingered on the wood, he suddenly felt something unfamiliar beneath his fingers. The paddle had been smooth in this spot. Now, to his surprise, it had been carved. He felt the rounded curve of a *C*. An *L*. And then the four letters that followed.

"Don't you dare to speak my mother's name," he said fiercely. "I don't want your trade."

Trademaster stared at him with his hostile, gleaming eyes. Gabe remembered what he knew, what Jonas had told him, of Einar, who had refused an offered trade and been mutilated so hideously. He saw that Trademaster was glancing now at the weapons near them on the ground.

Frantically he tried again to remember what Jonas had told him. *Use your gift.* That was it. *Use your gift!*

He was very frightened, but looking directly at Trademaster, he concentrated and willed himself to veer.

THIRTEEN

⸻

THE SILENCE CAME, lowering itself on him as if a curtain had been drawn. The rush of water behind him disappeared. The leaves on the surrounding trees still moved in the wind, but without sound. Gabe entered Trademaster. He found himself whirling through eons of time, destroying at random, screaming with rage and pain.

He became Trademaster. He was sick with searing hatred, and in the endless vortex through which he whirled, there was no comfort.

He *understood* Trademaster, and the deep malevolence that inhabited him. It was true, what he had earlier sensed, that Trademaster was inhuman. He was not a man but simply disguised as one. He was the force of evil, of all evil for all time.

Gabriel floated and spun within the veer, being part of evil, feeling the anguish and loneliness of it, of having been cast out again and again throughout history. Of gathering strength once more. Gaining power. Weaponry. Treachery. Cruelty. The feelings were strong enough to destroy one human boy, but he fought through them, concentrating on the knowledge of himself and his task. There must be something within the gift of the veer that would help him now when he emerged to face Trademaster for the final time.

※　※　※

Jonas was startled out of his fitful doze by a sound.

Claire was sitting up. The room was still quite dark, but he could see that she had pushed her coverlet aside. Her eyes were bright, and her shoulders, once frail and hunched, were now straight and firm.

"I'm hungry," she said.

※　※　※

Suddenly, within the simmering wrath and agony of the veer, Gabe felt *hunger*. It startled him. Such a small and unimportant feeling—one he had felt himself often as he headed home to dinner.

But this, he realized, letting himself go deeper, to feel it completely, was not a yearning for a bowl of soup or piece of bread. Trademaster was *starving.*

Gabe remembered what Jonas had told him about this kind of evil — that it is fed by its victims.

He wants to know how his tragedies play out, Jonas had said. *He likes to see how things end. He gloats. It nourishes him.*

It came to him quickly and was so simple. Those who aren't nourished will die. Those who starve will die.

Knowing exactly what he must do, Gabriel shed the veer. Sound returned. Trademaster still stood before him, sneering, in his cloak. Nothing had changed except for Gabe's understanding.

He stood up straight and said loudly, "Remember Mentor?"

Trademaster curled his lip and laughed. "Blotchy face? Old, saggy skin? That miserable fool. Of course I remember him."

"He was my teacher."

"I ruined him."

"No. You ruined him for a while. But he's himself again. He has his honor back. He's happy."

On hearing Gabe's words, Trademaster gasped slightly. He clutched his stomach as if a sharp pain had stabbed him. Or perhaps a gnawing ache? Hunger?

"Remember someone named Einar?"

Gabe had recoiled in horror when Jonas had related Einar's terrible history to him. Now he watched Trademaster's face. "He's the one who turned you down, remember? He said no to a trade!"

Trademaster spat on the ground. He laughed in contempt. "I destroyed him."

"You didn't, actually," Gabe told him calmly. "He made a good life for himself."

"The life of a cripple?" Trademaster taunted, and briefly imitated Einar's lurching walk.

"No. The life of a good man. He knows each lamb by name. He can make the sounds of every bird.

"And a beautiful girl fell in love with him," Gabe added.

Trademaster groaned. He sank onto one knee. His cloak flapped around him, too large suddenly, as if the man inside had shrunk.

"You remember her, I know. Her name was Claire," Gabe said. "She was looking for her little boy. And you know what? She found me, Trademaster.

"She was willing to give you everything she had. And you took it from her. You took her youth, and her beauty, and her energy and her health—"

For a moment, thinking of his mother, Gabe couldn't

continue speaking. He fell silent and choked back tears. Then he took a deep breath and went on, "—and it didn't matter. We found each other. None of it mattered but that.

"You won't ever know what that's like, to love someone. In a way, I pity you. But I hope you starve."

Gabe found himself looking down on his enemy, who was hunched over on the ground, whimpering.

His voice, which had earlier been low and sinuous, now gave a loud drawn-out howl, as if of grief. His eyes were closed, but he groped in the dark for the weapons that had been discarded on the ground. When he touched them, he howled again. At that moment, the moon once more emerged from dissipating clouds and the wind fell still. In the new light, Gabe could see that the weapons had changed. They were broken toys, bits of rusted tin, as if a careless child had left them out in the rain.

"Your power is gone," Gabe said.

The only response was a moan. As Gabe watched, Trademaster shrank further. Soon he had become a formless, unidentifiable heap of something that smelled of rot.

Gabe nudged with his toe at what was left. It had never been human—he knew that. Now it fell away when he touched it with his foot, and became nothing. He stared at it for a long time as the night lifted and dawn seeped into the sky. Then he found a sharp rock and dug into the earth until he had made a hole just the right size. He planted his paddle there and banked the damp earth around it so that it stood and marked the place where Evil had been vanquished.

Then he turned and looked at the river and at the pale wisps of smoke coming from chimneys in the village beyond. It was, all of it, familiar and beckoning and safe. He lowered himself into the gently flowing water and swam easily across.

✳ ✳ ✳

Sunrise woke Jonas. He had fallen asleep in the chair after feeding Claire some of the soup that Kira had brought. She had murmured a thank-you. Then he had tucked the blanket around her and waited there beside the bed while she resumed her sleep. Her breathing was stronger. He realized that tonight would not be the night of her death after all.

Was there a chance that somehow Gabe—? Jonas didn't allow himself to finish the thought. For a moment he had simply watched Claire sleep, marveling at her resilience. Then he had returned to his chair and his worry about the boy.

Now, waking, he was stiff and disoriented. He yawned, stretched, and looked around, confused, then remembered Claire and rushed to the bed. But it was empty, the covers thrown back.

The door to the cottage was open. She was standing there in her nightdress, breathing deeply of the daybreak air. She was tall and slender, with coppery hair that fell in curls around her shoulders. Hearing him, she turned to Jonas and smiled.

He thought he heard her say, "I see the sun."

Indeed, the sky was pink with dawn light. Then Jonas looked past Claire and saw Gabe approaching on the path.

THE END